A Riveting Story of Revenge, Romance and the Redemptive Power of God's Love.

REDEEMED

Sequel to *The Prodigal Daughter*

By Kathleen Steele Tolleson

Acknowledgements

❧ ☙

I'd like to first acknowledge and thank everyone who read *The Prodigal Daughter* and encouraged me to complete *Redeemed*. Your desire to know the rest of the story helped encourage me to keep writing.

I also want to thank the individuals that I have ministered to who suffer from Dissociative Identity Disorder (D.I.D.). You have given me the opportunity to receive great insight and understanding, and you have been wonderful teachers. I pray that you and others will understand that the character in *Redeemed* who suffers with D.I.D. may have alters and characteristics very different from your own, however, I did want to use this opportunity to help others understand some of the dynamics of Dissociative Identity Disorder. Also, because we may not know the complete story behind someone's behavior, *Redeemed* is a reminder of how important it is not to judge anyone. In fact, I feel it is very important that any stigma is removed from those who suffer from this complex coping mechanism.

Dissociative Identity Disorder was formerly referred to as Multiple Personality Syndrome. Many people are misinformed and believe it is a mental illness; when in fact, the children who fracture in an attempt to protect themselves mentally and emotionally from trauma, are usually highly intelligent and very creative individuals. As I wrote earlier, I have learned a great deal from those I have ministered to, and they have my utmost admiration in their ability to survive and continue forward not only as children, but as adults.

Many Christians and ministers simply think that D.I.D is wholly demonic, but it's not. Alters or parts, as the different personalities are called, can be demonized; but that does not mean the individual is possessed. There are more people than we realize suffering from this disorder, and, I believe that we as the church, must become a safe place where they can find acceptance and healing.

I also want to thank my family, the entire ministry staff, and our intercessory prayer team. There are just too many of you to mention! Thank you for your prayers, the time you have allowed me to be alone and write, and the encouragement you continue to give me along the way. Sarah Callahan has once again been invaluable in the editing process. And I thank the Lord for moving her from New York to Florida this year.

Foreword

❧ ❧

I was dying a slow death; trapped in a world no one seemed to take the time to understand. I was held prisoner inside my own mind, wracked with fear and shame. I felt for sure I must be going crazy. There was a silent scream just waiting to come out, but no one would hear it…no one seemed to care…no one, that is, until the day I met Kathy Tolleson. I figured she would be just like the previous thirteen counselors I had tried to talk to, and turn me away. So I determined to try and hide the diagnosis I had been given. We laugh at it now, like I could really hide it. Kathy saw it right away. She not only saw it, but she was not afraid of it. She understood after my first meeting with her that I had DID (Dissociative Identity Disorder) and she didn't turn me away. She didn't think I was crazy. I had come to believe that no one would ever understand what was going on inside of me and here, finally, this beautiful gift of God understood me.

Over a three year period Kathy spent hours tirelessly listening to me, loving me, and helping me put all the fractured parts of my life back together again. She never gave up on me. She saw all the ugly things that caused my mind to fracture and taught me how to allow God to heal the broken places. Slowly, with Kathy believing in my healing even when I couldn't, she taught me to turn the ugly and ungodly beliefs I had about myself into beautiful Godly beliefs.

Kathy Tolleson has an incredible gift of hearing from God and listening to His instructions. I can't begin to ever thank Kathy enough for helping me get to where I am today. She prayed earnestly for me. She cried with me and for me. She became my spiritual mother. I trust her heart…her beautiful heart…and I am eternally grateful to Kathy for opening that heart to me. Today, because of her dedication to helping and loving me, I am whole, healed, and living a joy-filled life believing all the Godly beliefs she helped me learn. I love her with all my heart!

Kathy has done an excellent job taking real-life experiences, not unlike own, and creating profound and moving novels, like *Redeemed,* which help teach and demonstrate God's redemptive power. In story form she teaches that redemption, the restoring of honor and worth, can come no matter how desperate or difficult any situation in life might be.

She truly did save my life and I know will impact yours!!!

~ Diane
One of the redeemed…

Introduction

❧ ❧

As I wrote my first novel, *The Prodigal Daughter,* the Lord showed me that there were to be two books would follow and continue the story of Deborah Noble's life. The next sequel was to be called, *Redeemed,* and the final one, *Legacy.*

The first book, *The Prodigal Daughter,* dealt with a life reconciled back to God through the integrated ministry process. In it, the reader is introduced to and comes to know Deborah Noble, her family and friends as her story is told through the ministry she receives. As she walks through personal ministry for generational sins, ungodly beliefs, spirit/soul hurts and demonic oppression, we share her struggles and her victories. *The Prodigal Daughter* was written as a teaching novel so as you continue to follow Deborah's life in *Redeemed,* you may find the writing style slightly different.

In this second book, we are able to witness how she walks out her new found healing and freedom. Who she has become in Christ and what the future God holds for her suddenly clashes with the reality of her past. The reader is able to understand how important prayer, the prophetic, and the faithfulness of the Body of Christ are in the struggle between good and evil. But most of all, it is a story of the Lord's ability to redeem lives. He truly does work all things to the good of those who love Him and are called according to His purposes.

Table of Contents

৵ ৵

Chapter 1: Free at Last……………………………………………..3
Chapter 2: The Pictures……………………………………………9
Chapter 3: Saturday Morning…………………………………15
Chapter 4: Shopping…………………………………………….23
Chapter 5: A Prayer of Protection…………………………….31
Chapter 6: Sunday………………………………………….......39
Chapter 7: The Family Secret…………………………………45
Chapter 8: The Exchange………………………………………49
Chapter 9: Monday Morning…………………………………55
Chapter 10: The Meeting………………………………………63
Chapter 11: The Ring……………………………………….....69
Chapter 12: Intervention……………………………………….75
Chapter 13: The Phone Call…………………………………..81
Chapter 14: War in the Heavenlies……………………………87
Chapter 15: The Plan………………………………………….93
Chapter 16: The Threat………………………………………...99
Chapter 17: The Discovery…………………………………....105
Chapter 18: The Notes………………………………………...111
Chapter 19: Prepared for Battle………………………………117
Chapter 20: Surprise Attack…………………………………..123
Chapter 21: The Rescue………………………………………127
Chapter 22: The Proposal……………………………………133
Chapter 23: The Evidence……………………………………137
Chapter 24: The Arrest………………………………………143
Chapter 25: The Aftermath…………………………………...147
Chapter 26: The Delay………………………………………..153

Chapter 27: Repentance…………………………………………159
Chapter 28: Sunday Lunch………………………………………...167
Chapter 29: The First Visit………………………………………...173
Chapter 30: The Next Visit………………………………………...179
Chapter 31: The Engagement Party………………………………...185
Chapter 32: The Talk………………………………………………193
Chapter 33: Preparation……………………………………………199
Chapter 34: Family Dinner………………………………………...205
Chapter 35: Forgiveness…………………………………………...211
Chapter 36: The Diagnosis………………………………………...217
Chapter 37: The Interview…………………………………………225
Chapter 38: Thanksgiving Plans…………………………………...233
Chapter 39: A Family Affair………………………………………239
Chapter 40: The Holidays…………………………………………247
Chapter 41: A Safe Place…………………………………………..253
Chapter 42: Daniel's Turn…………………………………………261
Chapter 43: Homecoming…………………………………………267
Chapter 44: Getting Ready………………………………………...273
Chapter 45: The Week before the Wedding………………………..279
Chapter 46: The Sighting…………………………………………..287
Chapter 47: The Delivery………………………………………….295
Chapter 48: The Crash……………………………………………..303
Chapter 49: The Wedding Morning……………………………….309
Chapter 50: A Radiant Bride………………………………………315
Chapter 51: A Night to Remember………………………………...321
Chapter 52: Two Years Later………………………………………325
Chapter 53: Looking Back…………………………………………329
Chapter 54: The Baby……………………………………………...335
Chapter 55: But a Vapor…………………………………………...341
Chapter 56: The Ordination………………………………………..347

The Prologue

ॐ ॐ

From the day Deborah and Daniel had reconciled their relationship at Deerfield Family Worship Center's altar, their friendship continued to deepen. As they renewed their relationship, it wasn't easy having to share the events of the past with each other.

Deborah was so thankful for the ministry she had received in Florida. Without it, she would have never been able to face Daniel with the painful details of what had happened to her since she had left home at the end of her senior year. Eighteen years was a long time, and she had lived a hard life-one full of sin and pain. But Daniel was patient and loving, and she could feel his unconditional love as they became reacquainted. She, too, had to hear about his marriage to Susan and her subsequent death. Daniel had been through his share of pain, it had just been different from hers.

The couple had submitted their relationship to Pastor Mark Harrison after the first six weeks. Just because they were comfortable with each other and had been childhood friends, did not mean the Lord had ordained their relationship. Both wanted to make sure they weren't just living in the past. Daniel still had not shared his dream with Deborah, and she had been unable to tell him of the vision she had seen as she had returned home from Palm City.

Their growing relationship was apparent to everyone,

especially Andrea Kline. Each Sunday, as she saw the relationship blossoming, Andrea became angrier and increasingly jealous; Deborah could feel her venomous glare every time she walked by her. Andrea had also stopped attending the Bible study at Anne's, Daniel's sister's, home. It had become very awkward for everyone, and Deborah and Anne were relieved when she just quit coming.

Andrea had become quite vocal about how unsuitable she believed Deborah was for Daniel and his children. She had actually told one of the other women that Aimee and David deserved much better. Andrea's comment had gotten back to Anne, and it had taken everything within her not to confront the woman.

Time and time again, Deborah used the tools of ministry that she had acquired at *Restore Your Soul Ministry* in Florida. But life was better than she had ever known it to be, and so far she had been able to face every challenge. Once and awhile, she called Lydia and Joyce for a little help. But most of the time, she was able to walk through her issues with the help of the Holy Spirit. She really was becoming a "new creation," and it felt good!

Chapter One

Free at Last

ॐ ॐ

Tommie Lee didn't just walked out of prison, he sauntered out. It was a crisp fall afternoon, and it felt great to be a free man again.

A car sent by the Renegades awaited him. Most of the guys didn't have cars, just motorcycles, and when he saw the raggedy old Chevy, he wondered if it would make the several hour trip back to New Orleans. Tommie Lee opened up the passenger's side to slide in and discovered his driver was Sanchez, a wiry Hispanic from Puerto Rico who had grown up in a gang in New York. Sanchez had been a Renegade prospect before Tommie Lee had gotten busted. He didn't know how Sanchez had gotten from New York to Louisiana orignially, but even as a prospect, he had a reputation for being both crazy and cruel. It was obvious now that Sanchez was a full patched member of the outlaw gang.

"Hey bro, I've got orders to take you back to the club. Here have a smoke," Sanchez offered as he handed him a package of cigarettes. When Tommie Lee opened the pack he discovered a half a dozen joints."

"Thanks man. I've had some pretty good stuff in jail but you can't really relax and get high in there. It's just not the same." Already breaking the terms of his probation as they drove out of the prison parking lot, Tommie Lee lit the joint and inhaled deeply.

He started in immediately, "I've got business to take care of. You remember my old lady, the one who ratted us out? Have they found anything on her?" Tommie Lee asked with his eyes closed, obviously enjoying the buzz he was already beginning to feel. With only his revenge to think about in prison, he had become obsessed with finding Debbie Lynn and getting even.

Sanchez shook his head and said, "Don't really know. I just got orders to bring you to the club. Just sit back and relax, man."

Several hours later, Tommie Lee and Sanchez pulled up to the Renegade headquarters on the east side of New Orleans. A number of the club member's came out to greet him with big, bear hugs. He felt like he had just come home. A pretty looking blonde, with only a thong, chaps and a black leather bra walked out slowly after the men. Hootch said, "Here's your welcome home present. Her name's KiKi. She'll show you to your room. We'll talk business tomorrow."

Obviously enjoying the attention she was receiving, KiKi made her way off the porch and over to Tommie Lee. The black leather bra barely contained her, and it was obvious she was well aware of her seductive power over the men. She purred in his ear saying, "I always say, the closest thing to having a virgin is a man right out of prison. It's my pleasure to meet you Mr. Tommie Lee."

Tommie Lee knew better than to protest, but more than having the blonde, he wanted to know if they had any information on Debbie. But before he knew it, Hootch tossed him the keys to the car and said, "Get in."

By this time, KiKi had slid into the passenger's seat and

Tommie Lee had no option but to take the keys and go. Two minutes later, after she had unzipped his pants, Tommie Lee could have cared less about Debbie.

———————————

KiKi satisfied every lustful dream Tommie Lee had had in prison; she also supplied him with the first cocaine he had used in months. They spent the night in a cheap motel about fifteen minutes from the Renegade's clubhouse. After getting dressed the next morning, Tommie Lee leaned over and smacked her on the butt, "Come on, wake up. I need some breakfast before I talk to the guys."

Rolling over, KiKi asked, "I'm tired, sugar, can't you go eat and just bring me back something?" He grunted and headed for the door. In the light of day and with all her make-up rubbed off, she didn't look quite like the same woman he had walked in the room with the night before.

His thoughts went back to Debbie. That was one thing about her, she always looked good. She was one woman who really didn't need any make-up. KiKi was sexy, but in a cheap sort of way. Debbie, on the other hand, was a classic beauty. He was reminded of how heads turned whenever they walked into a place. It was a shame he was going to have to kill her. Actually, he was glad to have befriended Sanchez on the way down. Tommie Lee knew he was just the man for the job. Even with all of his own stored up rage and bitterness, Tommie Lee just couldn't trust himself to do the job; but, Sanchez could—he was a cold blooded killer, who enjoyed his work.

Several of the Renegades were playing pool when Tommie Lee and KiKi returned to the clubhouse. Just to let the guys know how much he had appreciated the present they had given him the night before, he grabbed KiKi and gave her a deep kiss before sending her back out the door. The cheering and cat calls were all he needed to hear. Tommie Lee pulled up a chair and sat down at the table with Hootch and a couple of the other leaders. All business, Tommie Lee said, "Did you find her?"

A slow grin spread across Hootch's face. "Not exactly, but last week we got lucky and found out who her probation officer was. Here's the address," and he slid the piece of paper across the table.

As Tommie Lee looked at the address he said the name slowly, "Officer Brenda Stanley." If she really was Debbie's probation officer, there had to be some information in the files. All it would take would be a simple break-in and the information would be his. Tommie Lee's face lit up. He had finally hit the jackpot. Tommie Lee asked if he could use Sanchez on the job. The Renegade officers agreed. He knew the break-in would just help build the bond between them, and Tommie Lee wanted Sanchez to understand how important it was to him and the Renegades to make Deborah pay for her betrayal when she turned on them and became a witness for the state.

The two men decided to break into the probation office Friday night which would give them a head start. No one would be back into the office until Monday, and by that time they would be well on their way to finding Debbie. In the meantime Tommie Lee decided he would relax and enjoy time with Kiki and the boys. It felt good to be out and there wasn't anything he could do until then. "Bring me a beer," he called to a guy behind the bar and settled back in his chair eager to hear the latest Renegade news from Hootch and the other leaders.

———————————

When Friday night finally came, it was a piece of cake to break into the probation officer's office. Sanchez had them in the building in no time. Tommie Lee's biggest fear was relieved as soon as he saw the metal file cabinet in the corner; he was afraid that everything would be computerized and that he would have trouble finding the information. Because of Officer Stanley's mistrust of computers, she had all the information in a locked file cabinet. It couldn't have been any easier, except for one problem: Deborah's actual address wasn't in the file, but the town and terms of her probation was. "Well, it looks like we're going to be taking a trip up North," Tommie said to Sanchez. "Deerfield, Ohio, that's where the bitch is. I hope it's not a very big town."

They grabbed all the files located under "W" and headed out the door. Tommie Lee figured that, if other files were missing, maybe Officer Stanley wouldn't realize right away that this was about Debbie. But even if Debbie was warned, he relished the thought of the terror that would grip her heart when she heard the news. He wasn't concerned about finding her now. Let her just try and run.

After returning to the clubhouse, Tommie Lee went into the garage out back where some of his stuff had been stored. He found the photos he had of Debbie Lynn that would help him track her down. That same night, after receiving a go ahead and some cash from the Renegades, he and Sanchez got back in the old Chevy and began to make their way up North. It was all happening so fast. He couldn't believe that what he had planned all those months in prison was finally going to go down.

REDEEMED

Chapter Two

The Pictures

ॐ ॐ

Friday evening after work, Deborah was planning to drive out of town alone to visit her aunt. She had renewed her relationship with her Great Aunt Liberty after completing the *Restore Your Soul Ministry* in Palm City. Her aunt lived in an assisted living facility. Occasionally, Deborah would make the two hour trip south and spend the night on her aunt's pull-out sofa.

Deborah was still working at Worldwide Travel. Everyone had already left for the day and she was experiencing a bit of an eerie, apprehensive feeling as she locked the front door of the agency. Turning around, she almost expected to see someone standing behind her. Now, as she was driving, the fear seemed to get even stronger, but she couldn't figure out what could be troubling her. She picked up her cell phone to call Daniel just to make sure he and the children were okay.

The phone rang a number of times and then finally went to Daniel's voice mail. She loved the sound of his voice; it was deep, yet kind, and always reassuring to her ears. Just hearing it made her feel better. She left him a message, "Hi, Daniel, I'm on the road. I should be at Aunt Liberty's a little after seven. I hope you and the kids are having fun. I'll see you Sunday morning at church. Call me if you get a chance. I've been feeling kind of funny and just want to pray with you."

Deborah turned up the volume on the radio and began to pray in the Spirit as she listened to praise music. Before she knew it, she was pulling into the gates of Aunt Liberty's Golden Haven Assisted Living Facility. As she wove her way back towards her aunt's unit, Deborah wondered what Aunt Liberty had made for dinner. Even at eighty-seven, she was still quite active. As much as Deborah always tried to bring something for them to eat, she never won the battle. Aunt Liberty always insisted on having something ready. She would say, "Now dear, you work all day and I don't want you to have to eat some lukewarm store-bought food. Let me make you some real food." Eventually, Deborah would have to give in, but only after her aunt promised to let Deborah take her out for lunch the next day. This was only the fourth visit Deborah had made, but their dinner conversation had already become somewhat of a ritual.

Deborah grabbed her bags and headed up the walk. Even though she missed Daniel and the kids already, she knew this time with her aunt was irreplaceable. It had already helped her understand so much of the family dynamics that had always been a mystery to her. Her aunt had so much wisdom to impart, and Deborah loved to hear her talk about the Lord. Before she had a chance to ring the bell, Aunt Liberty swung the door open, catching her by surprise. "Hi dear, I thought you would never get here. I've got a surprise for you," her aunt was beaming as she pointed inside. "We're taking a trip down memory lane tonight."

As Deborah entered the living room, she saw old photo albums and boxes of loose pictures. "It looks like you've been busy Aunt Liberty. Why didn't you wait and let me help you with all this?"

"I didn't do it by myself. That nice young man who does errands around here helped me. But, I got so busy looking at pictures that I almost forgot to put on our dinner. It's going to be a few minutes. You just go on in and freshen up a bit." Deborah smiled to herself as she went in to use the bathroom. Aunt Liberty was one of a kind. She was glad the Lord had brought them back together. It was going to be fun looking at old pictures tonight and listening to her aunts narrative.

They had a simple but delicious dinner. Aunt Liberty asked how David and the children were, and Deborah filled her in on all the latest developments. She loved talking to her Aunt. She was one of those people who actually listened when you talked.

After dinner, Deborah insisted on doing the dishes. Surrounded by pictures, Aunt Liberty waited for her in the living room. Unbeknownst to Deborah, her aunt had decided that that Friday night was the night, Deborah would learn more about her father. Some stories had never been told, but tonight was a night for telling.

Daniel took off a little early from work on Friday. Deborah was out of town and he wanted to have a special evening with Aimee and David. He surprised the kids by picking them up from school himself. As soon as she saw him, seven year-old Aimee screamed, "Its Daddy," and ran to the car.

Ten year-old David, on the other hand, had to play it cool for his buddies, but Daniel could still tell he was happy to see him. "What's up, Dad?" he asked, climbing into the back seat.

"Well, I thought we would have dinner and then go to the new arcade. Would you two, like that?"

"Yeeaah!" Aimee squealed in excitement. Daniel smiled to himself; he obviously had made a good choice.

David quickly pleaded, "Can I bring a friend, Dad, please?"

"No, son, not tonight, I want some special time with you and Aimee. I have something important I want to talk to the two of you about, and we haven't spent any alone time in a while."

"That's cause you've been spending so much time with Deborah," Aimee grinned as she teased her father.

Daniel played along, "Well, I thought you liked Deborah. I guess I'll just have to tell her that I'm not allowed to see her anymore."

At that point Aimee quickly said, "I was just teasing, Dad. I like when we spend time with Deborah."

David asked, "So what do you want to talk about, what's so important?"

"I want to wait till we're at dinner so I can focus. Traffic's a little bit heavy. Why don't you two tell me about your day?" Aimee and David both began talking at the same time and didn't stop till they pulled up to the steak house.

After they had given their orders, Daniel turned his attention to Aimee and David. "Okay, I have something very important to talk to the two of you about, and I need both of you to be very honest with me." Both the children nodded and looked intently at their father. "This feels a little awkward," Daniel continued, "but I want your permission to ask Deborah to marry me. I know she's only been back in our lives for a short time, but you know that I knew Deborah years ago. I've talked it over with Pastor Mark and he's given me a green light. But this is a big step for all of us. I want you to know that if you two aren't ready, I'll wait."

The two of them looked a little surprised. Then David said, "Dad, we haven't seen you this happy in a long time, there's no way we'd want you to wait. Thanks for coming to us, but this is your decision, Dad. We trust you."

With that vote of confidence, Daniel turned to Aimee. Tears were forming in her eyes. But his concern turned to relief when she looked at him and said, "I'm going to have a mommy again." Then she looked up and said, "Thank you God for giving me a mommy."

Now tears were streaming down Daniel's face, too. "You kids are terrific. I love you so much!" He reached across the table for their hands.

The server returned with their salads to find them all praying. They looked up teary eyed, yet smiling. She left the table wondering what was going on; they seemed like a nice family. "Probably one of those divorced fathers taking their kids out for the weekend," she thought to herself as she moved to the next table.

As they made their way through the night, Tommie Lee kept pushing Sanchez to make better time. The old, green Chevy had seen better days; it groaned and shuddered at times as Sanchez hit speeds of over ninety miles an hour. As they sped down the road the two men talked about their pasts, their old ladies, the time they had done, and even about some dreams for the future. The one thing they didn't talk about was how they were going to kill Debbie. The only thing Tommie Lee had asked on the way out of town was, "Do you have a piece with you?"

Sanchez replied, "I have a machete in the trunk." Tommie Lee was just about to protest when Sanchez continued, "And that's not all," with a glint in his eye, he hit the door panel. It popped open displaying a 357 Magnum hidden inside. Then with one hand on the wheel, Sanchez opened up his jacket and showed Tommie the holster and pistol which hung under his arm. Enjoying Tommie Lee's expression, he grinned as he pulled up his right pants leg, which had a leather sheath tied to it, and drew a six inch knife out of it. Finally, he reached in his pocket and pulled out a black cord, held it in both hands, and snapped it twice. "Is this enough for you and your chiquita?" he asked with an exaggerated accent grabbing the wheel as the car veered to the right. Tommie Lee smiled, knowing he definitely had the right man for the job.

Tommie Lee and Sanchez pushed on into the night snorting crystal meth and smoking cigarettes to stay awake.

When they finally pulled over to get some gas outside of Jackson, Mississippi, Sanchez pumped gas while Tommie Lee went into the truck-stop to get coffee and a couple burgers to go. Sitting at the counter Tommie Lee pulled the pictures of Debbie out of his jacket pocket. In one of them, she was nude; the other two were sexy poses with his motorcycle. He remembered the day they were taken. She never really liked stuff like that but he had insisted. Sanchez strolled up and let out a whistle, "You sure you don't want to just take her back with us. She's one hot looking babe."

Uncomfortable, Tommie Lee tucked the nude photo behind the others and said, "Just look at her face, man. I just need you to be able to recognize her." He hated the mixed emotions he still felt when he looked at her picture.

As they got back into the car orders were issued in the spirit realm. Tommie Lee was once again filled with bitter rage towards Debbie Lynn and a spirit of murder entered into Sanchez. The Enemy didn't like to be defeated. Ever since Deborah had given her life to the Lord and then received further ministry in Florida, he and his demons had lost their grip on her. It was looking like Deborah had not only gotten free, but was going to stay free. That couldn't be allowed. They were going to have to take her out, and they were going to do it in style-inflicting as much collateral damage as possible.

Chapter Three

Saturday Morning

೫ ೬

Deborah woke up Saturday morning reflecting on what she had learned from her aunt the night before. She and her Aunt Liberty had stayed up till ten-thirty looking at pictures and talking. Daniel had finally called her after he had gotten home and put the kids to bed. It was nearly eleven by then and she had almost forgotten the fear she had been feeling earlier that evening. They had only talked briefly, but Daniel prayed for her before hanging up. Deborah had been too mentally exhausted to share any more with him that night. She needed to process everything she and her aunt had talked about that evening.

As she lay in bed, Deborah could hear her aunt puttering about in the kitchen. It reminded her of being at her one safe place in life: Grandma Ellen's house.

Things were making more sense now related to her father. Even though she had dealt with a lot of the pain and unforgiveness associated with him when she had been at *Restore Your Soul Ministry*, there still had been questions deep in her heart. "How could a father molest his daughter? How could he go to church like nothing had ever happened? Had something happened in his childhood that could turn him in to such a monster? When she considered the physical abuse her brother, Paul, had received from him, she wondered what could have possessed him to be so cruel?" Last night those questions had finally been answered. She could hardly wait to get home on Sunday and tell Daniel everything. But right now, she needed to get up and get a shower; she could already smell the breakfast Aunt Liberty had cooked up for them.

That morning Daniel let the kids sleep in late, while he enjoyed the quiet and a good cup of coffee. He slipped on a sweatshirt and made his way to the back porch. Even though the October air was chilly, it felt good to be outside. The sky was blue and the sun was still giving off a little warmth. Daniel moved one of the white painted rockers directly into the sunlight and sat down. It was good to have some time just to think and pray. Marrying again was a sobering thought and a major decision for him and the children. He was excited about their response the night before. He knew he had always loved Deborah, but both of them had gone through an awful lot since their childhood friendship. He just wanted to be careful and not do anything prematurely.

He was glad that Pastor Harrison, Anne and his parents had been there the last six months to help speak into the relationship. He thought about the surprising conversation that he had last week with Pastor Harrison. The pastor had just come right out and asked him, "So when are you going to ask Deborah to marry you?"

"I have been thinking about it, but do you think she's really ready?" Daniel had remembered asking. Over the past six months, Deborah had really started opening up to him; slowly at first, but, as he gained her trust, she began to share more and more of what she had been through since she had left Deerfield fourteen years earlier. It was hard for Daniel to fully comprehend-he had never done drugs or drank, and he had never been exposed to such a violent life style. He had only ridden a motorcycle a couple times as a teenager and had only seen outlaw bikers in movies. How she had ever got mixed up with that Tommie Lee was beyond him! She had even spent time in jail; Deborah's previous life sounded like a bad movie. He just hoped he could put a happy ending on it.

Pastor Mark, seeing the love and concern Daniel had for Deborah replied, "Actually, Daniel, I don't think she is fully ready. But, I feel the Lord is impressing on me that you and the children are part of her redemption. The three of you will actually help ready her to become a wife and mother. As you well know, Deborah's been through a lot; but sometimes, we're made ready through the relationships God puts in our lives. Scary, I know, I'm not saying it's going to be easy, but she needs you, Daniel. The children need a mother, and you, my friend, need a wife."

Breathing a sigh of relief, Daniel admitted, "That's what I've been thinking, but I thought I might be crazy. I thought you might want us to wait a lot longer until Deborah walks out more of her healing."

"You know me," the pastor said, "and I'm normally pretty conservative related to courtship and marriage. I've just seen so many couples in such terrible pain because they rushed into things or went against the counsel they had received from their parents or spiritual advisors. I don't want to see that for you and Deborah. I'd like to say, 'wait at least a year before getting engaged,' but to be honest, I don't think that's the Lord's plan in this case. I want you to also run this idea of marriage by Anne. She knows Deborah very well and I really trust her discernment. And of course, you need to talk to your parents."

Daniel agreed saying, "I know Mom and Dad love her. Until recently, mom had never told me that she had felt like the Lord had spoken to her when I was fifteen. He had given her a dream and in it, Deborah and I were being married, in this very church. When Deborah ran away from home and I met and married Susan, Mom felt like she had missed God. Now, don't get me wrong, she loved Susan and was never against our marriage; when Susan died, she was as heartbroken as I was. Susan had become like a daughter to both of them, but Mom had always wondered about the dream. Now I don't know if Mom is more excited about having Deborah back as a part of the family, or that this has brought confirmation that she hears from God. I'm sure you'd agree, it's been quite a turn of events."

As Daniel left the Pastor Harrison's office that day, he felt as if a great weight had been lifted from his shoulders. The pastor had confirmed that the nudging he'd been feeling was really from the Lord. He wasn't crazy after all! Daniel knew if he had not had that conversation with Pastor Harrison, he would have never walked into Tiara's Jewelry Store on Friday afternoon. As soon as he saw the ring he knew it was the perfect one for Deborah. It was platinum and had a very simple setting. In the center of the ring sat a stunning, yet elegant, marquis diamond. It reminded him of Deborah and it was on sale, too. He could actually afford it! He was going to ask the clerk to hold it for him until Anne could come and see it but decided against it. If this was the ring for Deborah, he would trust the Lord over it. If it was gone by Monday, it would be his answer; however, right now, it was only Saturday morning and he could hardly wait to call Anne. He took another sip of his coffee and decided that he would wait until Monday to call her. As hard as it was, he didn't want to take up any of her family time. He would just have to wait.

While Daniel was dreaming about the perfect engagement ring and just how to propose to Deborah, the Renegade's old, green Chevy continued to make its way North. Tommie Lee was driving now and his stomach was growling, "I'm going to stop and get some breakfast. You hungry, Sanchez?"

"Yeah man, breakfast sounds good," Sanchez stretched and yawned. "It'll feel good to get out of this car." He leaned over to change the radio station, which had suddenly lost reception. He found a station playing oldies and began to sing along off key. A few minutes later the two men pulled into the House of Pancakes parking lot.

While they placed their order, Sanchez who fancied himself as a ladies man, flirted with the waitress. The frivolous banter irritated Tommie Lee; and by the time their breakfast arrived, he was barely talking. He ate quickly and then impatiently glared at Sanchez who was slowly taking his time. "Hurry up!" he growled. "We don't have all day. Give me the bill and I'll pay for it." He snatched it off the table and walked up to the register.

Meanwhile the waitress came up and asked Sanchez, "Would you like a little more coffee?"

"I'd love some sweetheart, but my partner over there is in a hurry. You're such a pretty thing," he added. "Too bad I'm just passing through."

The waitress gave a nervous giggle. She didn't look a day over eighteen and wasn't quite sure how to handle Sanchez's flirting. She was rescued from responding by Tommie Lee bellowing from the front of the restaurant, "Get your rear in gear before I put my foot up it!"

Still in no hurry, Sanchez gave the waitress one last smile as he slid out of the booth. "Maybe I'll catch you on our way back. What's your name sweetheart?"

"Mindy, it's Mindy, sir. She watched shocked as Sanchez pull a hundred dollar bill out of his wallet and left it on the table for a tip. She started to say, "Mister, I can't accept…" He put a finger to her lips, "Ssshhh, sugar, you heard the man, I don't have time to argue, I gotta go." With that he walked out of the restaurant leaving Mindy wondering what had just happened. For the next several miles, Sanchez had to listen to Tommie Lee lecture him about drawing unnecessary attention to them.

———

It was one of those beautiful days in Florida; the temperature was in the low seventies and there was absolutely no humidity. Lydia rolled over in bed and nudged her husband, Stephen, with her foot. "Are you awake yet, honey?" she asked him.

"I am, now," he said rolling over and giving her a big hug. He laughed, "Why don't you just say 'wake up' instead of 'are you awake yet?'"

Lydia started to protest, "I thought you were stirring. I really didn't mean to wake you up."

"It's okay, I'm just messing with you. What do you have

on that busy mind of yours? I can tell some thing is up."

She smiled back and said, "Well, now that you're awake, I thought we might drive to Lake Moore and have a nice brunch at that little tea room Joyce and I found.

"Could there be some shopping involved in this trip?" Stephen asked with a twinkle in his eye. He knew that Lake Moore was known for its quaint restaurants and shops.

"He knew her so well," Lydia thought as she replied, "Well, I did think it might be a good time to get a head start on my Christmas shopping. I looked at my schedule yesterday and it's real busy from now until Christmas. You know how I hate crowds."

"Your wish is my command today. I am at your disposal, my love. Lead the way. I will be your bag carrying servant. After last night, it's the least I can do." he said teasingly.

Lydia blushed; he was making reference to their very passionate evening. She swatted him, "Stephen, you better stop or you could get in trouble! You know that wasn't about this. I didn't even think about going to Lake Moore until this morning."

"I know, dear. That's what made it even better," Stephen touched her face gently, getting more serious, "You are an awesome woman, do you know that?" Lydia felt herself responding to his embrace and before she knew it, they were making love again. This time it was like a gentle rain after a thunderstorm, gentle and tender, much different than the night before.

KATHLEEN STEELE TOLLESON

Chapter Four

Shopping

ॐ ॐ

Saturday after breakfast, Deborah she was still processing everything they had talked about the night before. She helped Aunt Liberty put the pictures up and then did a few chores around the apartment: she cleaned the ceiling fan, washed a couple of windows, she even repotted a plant. It felt good to bless her aunt who was obviously delighted with Deborah's help and company.

The next item on the list was to do a little shopping before they had lunch. While Aunt Liberty went to lie down and rest Deborah took another quick shower before getting ready to leave. It was almost noon before they finally left. As her aunt walked out to the car, Deborah thought about how truly beautiful and amazing her great aunt really was. Aunt Liberty hair was silvery gray, cut short, yet stylish; her dark brown eyes still had a twinkle in them; and, despite the wrinkles, her complexion was still very good. She had the same deep olive coloring Deborah had inherited from their mutual Indian ancestry. "If only I have her grace and health at eighty-seven," Deborah admired. As they got in the car, Deborah inquired, "Okay Auntie, where to first?"

"Well, dear, if it's not too much trouble I'd like to stop at the Wal-Mart pharmacy and have my prescription refilled. I do have to admit, I've been feeling better since I started taking that blood pressure medication," Liberty replied. Deborah chuckled. She knew all too well how much her aunt did not like doctors or medicine. Aunt Liberty had informed her on their first visit, in no uncertain terms, that it had been exercise, healthy eating and living for the Lord that had got her thus far. To admit to needing blood pressure medicine wasn't easy for her even at eighty-seven. "You'll need to turn at the next light. And I know what you're thinking: I guess an old lady can use a little help and if the medicine works, I don't want to be a fool! Okay, this is our turn. WalMart is only six blocks away. I hope it won't be too crowded. I need to pick up a few other things while the prescription is being filled, if that's okay?" Liberty reached over and patted Deborah's leg and continued, "You know, I always wanted a closer relationship with you, but your father wasn't going to have any of that. After last night, I hope you understand why some things were the way they were. But, the Lord's brought you back in my life right when I really need you. He really does redeem everything, doesn't He, dear?'

Deborah choked up as tears came to her eyes, "He sure does! I can't tell you what it's meant to me to get to know you. Thank you for all your prayers Aunt Liberty. I don't know where I'd be today without them. I just wished you lived a little closer."

"I'm right where I'm supposed to be, Deborah," Liberty declared. "These people at Golden Haven need me. There's some that could go any day now and they need to know Jesus. God hasn't called me to retire yet. I've got work to do here."

"I hear you, Auntie, once an evangelist, always an evangelist. I promise I won't interfere with your mission field! Now what side of the road is Wal-Mart on?"

"It's on the next block to your left. There's a turning lane. They actually redid the whole street when the super-center moved in just to accommodate the traffic. Here it is, and busy as always."

Deborah made her way into the parking lot. "I'll drop you off in front and park the car."

"Okay, I won't argue. We've still got a big day ahead of us," Liberty agreed.

They waited for a couple of cars to move and Deborah dropped her aunt at the door. As Liberty sat down on the bench out front she found herself talking to the Lord, "I don't know what's going on Lord but something's not right, and I'm not sure who or what to pray for." She was met with silence. Not knowing what else to do she prayed quietly in her prayer language. Suddenly the words came, "Protect Deborah from evil, Lord. I pray that every plan and strategy of the Enemy will be defeated. Lord, I declare that she will fulfill her destiny and possess her inheritance, and that no weapon formed against her would prosper." She finished the prayer just as Deborah walked up but decided in her heart not to say anything. No sense in troubling Deborah over something that was already in the Lord's hands. Together they walked into the busy store.

"Hello, welcome to WalMart," they were cheerfully greeted and given a shopping cart.

Sanchez was relieved when their conversation finally turned back to finding Debbie. "It shouldn't be too hard," Tommie Lee said, "Deerfield doesn't look that big. We just have to be careful because they may already know about the break-in. The one thing I'm not going to do is go back to prison so no slip-ups. I figure we should stay in a smaller town outside of Deerfield. There's one called Scranton on the map. If there's a motel there, that's where we'll be. It's just our luck that it's hunting season so an out of town plate won't attract much attention. When we get into Ohio, we're going to get ourselves some hunting gear. I'm glad my hair is still short from prison! So you and me are going to do some shopping first, and then some hunting, Sanchez. What do you think of that?"

Sanchez chuckled and said, "Whatever you say boss." He was glad to know Tommie Lee had been doing some thinking and planning. They were going to make a good team.

Meanwhile, Stephen and Lydia were heading to Lake Moore to do some shopping themselves. On the drive Lydia said, "You know who's been on my heart all morning?"

Stephen replied with a grin, "Well, I was kind of hoping it was me."

"You know what I mean, honey. I just keep getting flashes of Deborah's face. Remember the young woman Joyce and I ministered to last April?"

"I remember. Have you heard from her lately?" he asked.

"Actually, it's been well over a month. Maybe I'll give her a call tonight or tomorrow. I hope she's doing okay. Did I ever tell you that she and Daniel are now in official courtship? It's amazing how quick things happen when we get our lives back on the right track with the Lord. But right now I need to be thinking about my shopping list," Lydia said pulling paper and pen out of her bag. Stephen reached to turn up the instrumental worship music that was playing. Sounds of heaven began to fill the car and the presence of the Lord increased. Before they knew it, both of them were singing and praying in the spirit. The next thing they knew, they had arrived in Lake Moore.

Finding a parking spot could be difficult in the quaint little town; but, right as they were driving in a car was pulling out. Lydia exclaimed, "There's our parking place, and it's right by the tea room. I don't know about you but I'm famished!" Stephen maneuvered into the parking place and they made their way up the incline to the little restaurant overlooking the lake. Because of their dalliance this morning they were well past brunch; it was already noon. The fruit they had eaten before leaving the house had tied them over, but now it was time for some real food.

Deborah and her aunt, made their way slowly through the aisles of Wal-Mart after dropping off the prescription. For the next forty-five minutes, they chatted and picked up the needed items. When she was with her aunt, Deborah was often amazed with her own patience. If only she could be that way with her mother. Things had gotten much better in their relationship but her mother still triggered her. Thank God the ministry had prepared her for how to deal with past wounds. Now, when she felt overly angry with her mother, she could go to the Lord and ask Him to show her the wound. It was amazing how faithful He was. Before she knew it, there would be another childhood incident that had caused her pain. Sometimes, it would be something her mother actually did; however, Deborah soon discovered that the Lord used her Mom to bring up past pain someone else may have caused her. Poor Mom, she had become quite the catalyst for further healing. She was thankful that her mother, Daniel and Anne were patient with her.

There had already been several times when she had overreacted with Daniel, but he had been loving and steadfast every time. Through the incidents, she had received even greater healing from situations with her father and other men. She felt sorry for Daniel, though. He was so kind and loving even when her anger raged. The first time it happened, they were both shocked; it had been a simple incident. One day after work Deborah had run a quick errand and had forgotten to turn her cell phone back on until she got home. When he finally got a hold of her Daniel had said, "Where have you been? I was getting worried."

That had been enough to set Deborah over the edge. "I'm not going to have you controlling every minute of my day, and I'm not going to report in as if I were a child!" she had responded angrily.

"Wait a minute, Deborah. I was just concerned about

you," Daniel tried to explain. But, the next thing he knew, Deborah had hung up on him.

The phone call had shocked them both but Daniel gave her some time. The next she knew, the Lord had dealt with her pain, anger and unforgiveness towards her father and Tommie Lee relating to their control issues. She poured out her complaint to the Lord and then forgave them. Then she saw the memory of the day Tommie Lee had come home early and she had gone out for a walk. He had been enraged that he hadn't known where she was he had slapped her across the yard. As she asked the Lord to visit the memory, she saw Him picking her up and holding her. He gently touched her bruised cheek and said, "Daughter, one day I'm going to teach you the difference between control and concern. This is not the life I've chosen for you."

Suddenly Deborah knew that that was the day the Lord had chosen to set her free from issues of being controlled.. Daniel hadn't been trying to control her, he had just been concerned. She picked up the phone hoping that she hadn't ruined everything. Daniel answered and she told him what had triggered her anger and why. He was so understanding, "Deborah, I just pray that you will be open and honest with me. If you'll do that, there's nothing we can't work through. With everything you've gone through, I expect this to be a process that might take some time. I just pray I can have the patience and grace that you need."

Suddenly she heard her aunt saying, "I think that's everything, dear." Their shopping completed, they headed to the check-out counters and continued to chat as they stood in line. It was Saturday and pretty busy, but the cashier worked quickly and within minutes they were out the door. Pushing the shopping cart, Deborah tried not to walk too fast as they made their way to the car. She unlocked the car door with her remote and encouraged her aunt to sit down as she put the shopping bags in the trunk. That had gone smoothly and now they were both looking forward to lunch. But as soon as they were on the road,

Deborah suddenly felt that same chill and apprehension she had felt Friday night. She didn't want to ruin the afternoon and tried to shake it off as they proceeded to her aunt's favorite restaurant.

"I'm going to pull off at this next exit. There's got to be a Wal-Mart somewhere around here," Tommie Lee said. "We're just a couple of hours south of Deerfield. And I don't want to get too close before we change. He exited off the interstate and headed towards Carson City.

Their first stop was a gas station where they asked directions to the local WalMart. The clerk pointed down the street. It was only five blocks away. Tommie Lee was delighted with his choice. They pulled into the WalMart parking lot, unaware that they had just passed their target on the street, missing Deborah and her aunt by minutes.

Chapter Five

A Prayer of Protection

❧ ❧

Daniel let the children sleep in while he spent some quiet time with the Lord. After they woke up, they unanimously decided to visit the local fair; the weather was perfect for it today. Daniel had enjoyed his time with the Lord, but was now looking forward to spending time with David and Aimee. The family looked forward to the fair every year; it was held every summer about the same time. Everyone had a light breakfast knowing thcy would get their fill of apple fritters, candied apples, apple jam, apple butter, and anything else apple one might want, along with apples of every variety. Beside the food there were games for the kids and it seemed as if every artist from the region brought their latest creations to display.

"Grab a jacket, it might cool off later," Daniel yelled up the stairs.

"Okay, Dad, we hear you!" they called back to him.

"And, don't forget to brush your teeth!" he reminded them as the quickly scrambled around the house in all their excitement. In minutes David and Aimee were bounding down the steps and ready to go. Daniel knew they loved having his undivided attention; for a second, he wondered what life would be like when he remarried. It would definitely take the Lord to make it all work.

Once they got to the fair, David and Aimee nearly bounded out of the car almost before it was parked. Daniel bought their entrance tickets at the gate and the happy family began walking down the fairway. As he saw her walking towards them, Daniel groaned inwardly. It figured, they had only been at the fair twenty minutes and he would have to run into Andrea. As always she was impeccable. Her blonde hair had been recently shaped. And as always, she had just the right amount of tan to look like she had just stepped off a cruise ship. Her face lit up when she saw him and the children.

"Hi Daniel," she said walking towards them. She bent down to hug Aimee who tried to shrug away. "I've missed you kids so much," she gushed. "Where's Deborah?" was her next question. It was obvious that she hadn't gotten over her infatuation with him. For the past six months, he could still feel her piercing blue eyes every time he walked into church with Deborah. They were constantly praying against any of her soulish prayers.

"Deborah's visiting her aunt and I'm spending some special time with Aimee and David. Now, if you would excuse us Andrea."

But the woman never took a hint, "Well, this is just my luck to run into the three of you. I've been walking around this place all by myself. Could I just join you for a little bit?" she simpered.

Daniel was so aggravated! She always put him in the position of having to be totally rude or giving in to her. Trying to remain calm he replied, "Well, just as we walk through the art exhibits. Then the kids are going to enjoy some of the games."

As they walked and looked at the different artist's wares, Daniel felt himself getting angrier and angrier. Why couldn't he have just told her, "No, not today." He kept trying to keep plenty of distance between them, but every time he stopped for a moment to look at anything, she was at his side. Finally, they came to the end of the exhibits. "Well, it was nice seeing you Andrea, but we really have to go now. Come on kids, let's see what kind of games they have," he said abruptly; they were as anxious as he was to get away from Andrea and hurriedly ran ahead of him and Andrea. Today, he truly appreciated their exuberant energy. "Gotta go, Andrea, see you at church tomorrow," Daniel called back hurrying after the children. Secretly, he hoped they wouldn't run into her again.

Andrea was left fuming! When was Daniel going to realize that Deborah wasn't the one for him? God had already spoken and promised her that she was the one. And, she loved those kids more than Deborah! She felt a deep longing inside; all she wanted to do was to play with them today. Now she felt all alone. "God, help expose Deborah for who she really is. Let Daniel see that she just isn't right for him." After all, she had heard enough about Deborah's past to know the last thing those children needed was her for their mother. My God, she was an ex-alcoholic and drug addict! Only God knows what else she was involved in. What could Daniel possible be thinking? He's got to come to his senses soon. "I'm just going to have to be patient," she decided to herself and flounced away. Maybe they would run into each other again today; however, she knew better than to make it too obvious. Pastor Harrison had already warned her against pursuing Daniel, and church was the one regular place she was able to see him. Even if it was only from a distance most of the time, it was still better than nothing. She didn't want to push the pastor into asking her to find another church. No, she had better just bide her time. After all, God was in control.

After completing their shopping, Tommie Lee and Sanchez found the next rest area. There they would begin their transforming make-over in the men's bathroom. After changing, Tommie Lee looked in the mirror at himself and then at Sanchez.

Boasting camouflage pants with olive green t-shirts and new hunting caps on their heads, Tommie Lee smiled happily with the results. When they came out, they were careful not to let anyone see the patches on the leather jackets they had carefully stored under a false trunk bottom. The Chevy might be getting on in years, but it sure came in handy. At some point, someone had spent a pretty penny outfitting it as a drug running car. In the back seat were jackets and the mandatory bright orange hunting vests. "We're going to blend right in, buddy," he said with a grin.

Sanchez pulled his hat down low and said, "Si, senior!"

It didn't take long for the men to change and get back on the road. A couple hours later they were pulling into Scranton. They found a little motel on the edge of town-it was perfect; it had little efficiencies rooms with a fridge, microwave and cable TV.

Tommie Lee sent Sanchez in to see if there were any rooms left. Upon returning Sanchez grinned slyly, "We're in luck; we just got the last room and it's on the backside of the place." They drove around looking for their room. The paint was somewhat worn and faded, but they parked in front of what appeared to be unit number nineteen. The motel was outdated and still used old-fashioned room keys with the plastic holder and number imprinted on it. "Home sweet home," Tommie Lee said as he opened the door. Anything other than his prison cell looked good to him. "Let's get some rest and wait till the sun goes down before we cruise into Deerfield," he said heading for one of the beds in the room. They were both coming down from the small amount of crystal meth they had used the night before. Before they knew it, both men were snoring loudly on their beds.

The sun was starting to set as Stephen and Lydia loaded the last shopping bag into the car. It was finally time to head home. It had actually been a very enjoyable day. The view of the lake was beautiful, and, as they had ate together and strolled through the town, it had given them a chance to talk and catch up with each other's lives.

"Honey, remember its family dinner tomorrow," Lydia said as they got in the car. It had become a once a month ritual to have the family over after church. She was looking forward to spending time with her grandchildren and updating with Marie and Diana. "Can we make one more stop on the way into town? I just need to pick up some fresh salad and vegetables," she asked tentatively, not wanting to press Stephen past his limits. He had endured the day of shopping very well and she didn't want to push it.

"How about if I just drop you off so you can start putting stuff away and then I'll just run out for you?" he asked.

Lydia quickly responded, "That would be awesome. I have to admit I'm a little worn out now, even though it was a great day. It feels so good to have most of my Christmas shopping done. I know the next couple of months are going to fly by. Thanks so much for being such a sweetheart today!" Thanking the Lord for the wonderful husband he had given her, Lydia leaned back in the seat of their Nissan and closed her eyes. The next thing she knew they were pulling into the driveway of their townhouse. She had fallen asleep and slept the whole way back.

Lydia and Stephen gathered the shopping bags and carried them into the house. Purposely, she had left her cell phone at home so she and Stephen could have some uninterrupted time. Now, it was letting her know she had several messages. First, however, she needed to put up the spoils of the day.

It was already seven o'clock by the time Deborah left her Aunt Liberty's and drove out of Carson City. She still had two hours on the road before she got home. As she hugged and kissed her aunt goodbye, Liberty said, "Deborah, make sure you take care of yourself, and trust in the Lord. No matter what happens, He will be with you. Don't lean to your own understanding. I pray for ministering angels to protect you." Her aunt's dark brown eyes had glistened with tears as she spoke. Her aunt had always prayed for her before she left, but this time it felt different—it was as if her aunt knew something she didn't. Her words kept ringing in Deborah's ears.

Again apprehension rose within her. She quickly reached for her cell phone and called Daniel. This time he answered and they talked for over thirty minutes as she drove. David and Aimee were watching a movie and settling down for bed. From Daniel's description, they had had a great time over the weekend. Deborah was looking forward to seeing them all at church the next morning. It still hadn't been the right time to talk to Daniel about everything she had learned from her aunt. Hopefully, she could hold it until Sunday evening. That's when Daniel had promised her they would have some time alone together. She felt better after talking to him and tried to put her aunt's prayer out of her mind.

She put in a new CD she had bought earlier that day at the Christian book store. It was called, *The Father's Love.* Just what she needed! She listened carefully as the speaker shared that when we accept the Father's love, His perfect love for us casts out all fear. We no longer need to fear for our protection or provision.

She prayed as she drove, "Father, please help me receive a greater revelation of Your love. I want to be able to totally relax and trust You in everything. I repent for my unbelief and doubt at times. I know I need to trust You more." A peace washed over her, as she heard the Spirit of the Lord say, "You will my daughter, you will."

REDEEMED

Chapter Six

Sunday

ॐ ॐ

Saturday night had not turned out the way Tommie Lee had thought it would. Now he needed another plan. He and Sanchez had headed to Deerfield after nine o'clock. They weren't very many bars in the whole town, and he figured the best chance of finding Debbie was to check the local establishments. He figured she was probably working as a cocktail waitress. It was her usual way of making a living. That's where they would start their search.

Tommie Lee folded up one of Debbie's pictures so that only her face showed. He sent Sanchez into the smoke filled bars-he didn't want to take any chances of her seeing him first. He had instructed Sanchez to search the bars for any sign of her; if he didn't see her anywhere, he was supposed to show her picture to the bartender to see if anyone recognized her. The story Sanchez was told to relay was that Debbie had been a friend of his sister's who was dying. He was the messenger sent to find her. After six failed attempts, Sanchez came out to the car. "No one knows her, no one's seen her. And I don't think they're lying. Do you want to go in and have a drink?"

Tommie Lee, feeling a bit frustrated, pulled his hunting cap down low and said, "Why not, isn't that what hunters do after a long day in the woods?"

The men shot pool and drank till nearly one o'clock in the morning. They were very careful when they talked even though no one seemed to pay any attention to them whatsoever. A couple of girls at the bar had caught his eye, but he knew this wasn't the time or place. Tommie Lee just lowered his head and kept from meeting their gaze. He caught Sanchez looking at one of them and tapped him hard with his pool cue. Sanchez quickly got the message and turned his attention back to the pool table. He wasn't ready for another lecture tonight.

As Stephen and Lydia entered the sanctuary Sunday morning, Joyce was there to greet them. "Did you get my message last night?" Lydia suddenly realized that after glancing at her cell phone on the way in that she had never checked her voicemail.

"No, actually I didn't. We went to Lake Moore shopping and by the time we got home and put everything up, I just forgot to do it. What's up?"

Lydia could see the concern in Joyce's eyes as she told her about her previous day. "I took a nap Saturday afternoon and had a dream about Deborah. It was a little scary. Can I run it by you after church? The service is getting ready to start now."

Lydia thought about the dinner she had to prepare but knew this could be important, especially since Deborah had also been on her heart the day before. "Just find me after service. I was thinking about her yesterday morning." After her brief conversation with Joyce, it took Lydia a little while to focus her attention to what was going on up front. Soon after, the worship music began and she was lost in the presence of the Lord.

Deborah and Daniel met in the church parking lot. Dressed in a dark brown pants suit with turquoise and silver jewelry, Deborah looked beautiful as always. Once again, just like it used to over eighteen years ago when he would see her in the halls at school, Daniel found his heart beating a little faster.

Aimee was already running towards her. Deborah scooped her up in a big hug. "Hi, sweetie, I missed you this weekend but it sounds like you and your Dad and David had a great time. You'll have to tell me all about it at lunch." David was a little more reserved in his greeting. He gave Deborah a quick hug as they walked towards the front door of the church.

Slipping his hand over Deborah's, Daniel said, "You look beautiful this morning. I'm looking forward to this evening..." he began, but interrupted by Andrea who had just walked up behind them.

"Daniel wasn't the Apple Fair fun yesterday? I had such a good time with you and the kids. So sorry you missed it, Deborah," she blurted out. And with that, Andrea walked passed them and into the sanctuary.

Daniel said quickly, "It's not what it seems. Let me explain at lunch what really happened. Trust me Deborah, the woman is just trying to make trouble."

The morning greeters were already welcoming them at the door and Deborah had no other choice but to wait until lunch for Daniel's explanation. She could feel Andrea's gaze follow her up the aisle. Fighting the urge to turn around and confront the woman, Deborah made her way up the center aisle of the sanctuary and settled in next to Aimee.

Deborah and Daniel were careful not to sit next to each other and positioned the children between them. Pastor Harrison had encouraged them to spend time together rebuilding their friendship but to be very careful with physical intimacy. Right now, she was glad. She wanted to trust Daniel, but every man she had ever met had lied and cheated on her. It had started out to be such a good day and now this! Deborah grasped for her Godly Belief "I can trust the Lord to give me discernment and wisdom to know who I can trust and to what degree. He will never fail me." She repeated it to herself several times. She began to feel calmer and was finally able to turn her attention to the service, which was just beginning.

Sunday morning found Tommie Lee, sitting on the bed switching from channel to channel. A little hung over and still upset that no leads on Deborah had turned up the night before, h was trying to figure out their next move. He knew better than to try another break in at a probation office. That was out of the question. He had just been so sure someone from one of the bars would have known or seen Debbie. He finally let out a yelp that startled Sanchez, "That's it, tomorrow we're checking out the banks. There can't be that many in town and if she's got a legitimate job, she's got to be putting her money somewhere. Get me a beer, Sanchez. Today we're just going to relax."

As soon as the service was over, Lydia and Joyce made a beeline for one another. It had been a great service but Lydia was ready to hear the dream. "Let's go in the prayer room so we can hear ourselves," she said over the din of people exiting the church. "Stephen, I'll just be a few minutes." Busily engaged in his own conversation, he nodded and waved her on.

As soon as the women reached the prayer room, Joyce began, "I had a dream about hunters; they were stalking Deborah like prey. They had on camouflage outfits and she was oblivious to what was happening. The dream was short but when I woke up my heart was pounding-it felt so real. I just don't know what to do. I didn't want to call and alarm her, but the danger felt so real. I hoped you would know what to do."

"Well, we definitely need to start with prayer right now. Lord, I pray for your divine protection over Deborah. Expose every strategy and plan of the Enemy, now, in the name of Jesus. Lord, give us wisdom if we're to call her or if this is just for prayer. I pray that she would be covered and hidden under the shadow of the Almighty and that no weapon formed against her would prosper."

Joyce continued Lydia's prayer, "And Lord, I pray that Deborah would be the head and not the tail, the hunter not the hunted, and that the victory would be Yours. I bind every spirit of murder, death and destruction, in the Name of Jesus."

Lydia could tell the dream had clearly shaken her friend and co-counselor. "I'm still not sure if we're to call Deborah yet, but let's stay vigilant in prayer. If you get anything else, please call me." Joyce nodded in agreement. They left the prayer room knowing at this point they had done all they could do.

Andrea walked out of church that morning satisfied that she had shaken Deborah's confidence. She wondered why no one else could see what a Jezebel Deborah really was. It seemed like she had just waltzed into church that Sunday morning, six months ago, and put everyone under a spell, even the pastor and his wife. For just a second, she felt a child's cry of desperation within her. It left as suddenly as it came. Now her head was beginning to hurt again. She would have to go and lie down. Yesterday the same thing had happened; afterwards, it left her feeling fuzzy and disorientated. She probably needed a check-up. But, since she had just received a promotion at work, it would need to wait a month or so.

Chapter Seven

The Family Secret

ॐ ॐ

It was Sunday evening before Deborah and Daniel had a chance to talk. They were very careful not to spend time alone in Daniel's house, so Missy, Aimee and David's babysitter from next door, had agreed to come and stay with the kids for a couple of hours. She was sixteen and always ready to earn a little extra spending money.

Daniel had already gotten Aimee and David ready for bed when he heard a knock on the door. It had to be Missy. He went to the front door. "Hi, Mr. Worthington," Missy said as Daniel ushered her in, "what time are you going to be home?"

"I'll be home by ten-thirty," Daniel said while slipping on his jacket. "Aimee's in bed already and David's finishing up his homework; he's supposed to be in bed by nine. Thanks so much, Missy, your money's on the counter." David hurried out; he was anxious to see Deborah. Even though they had lunch together after church, this would be the first time they could really talk without the children listening to every word.

Deborah's mother, Elizabeth, had graciously allowed them to use her front room as a place of courtship. It gave them a safe place to get to know one another while avoiding all appearances of evil. He was glad it was only ten minutes away.

As Deborah was getting ready for Daniel's visit, she thought about how glad she was that Anne and her family had gone to lunch with them that afternoon. Before she and Daniel even had time to discuss Andrea, Anne had said to her, "I saw the way Andrea was looking at you and Daniel in church. I don't want to scare you Deborah, but that woman is still obsessed with Daniel. Yesterday, we ran into him at the Apple Fair. He told me to pray because earlier Andrea had tried to join him and the children uninvited. Daniel said that he had to be outright rude to get away from her. I don't understand why she just can't get it. Daniel is just not interested in her and has never been interested in her!"

The conversation had relieved any residue of mistrust she had been experiencing, and lunch turned out to be a wonderful family affair. Everyone was laughing, talking, and sharing their weekend fun. At one point, Deborah looked around the table wondering how she ever ended up being included with such wonderful people. "Lord, I pray that this will never end. It will just get better and better. Thank You for setting the solitary in families," she prayed silently to herself.

Meanwhile that evening, after sleeping off another drunken stupor, Tommie Lee decided it was time for another shopping trip. After asking the clerk at the front desk where it was, he and Sanchez drove to the local Wal-Mart, which he knew would still be open. Tommie Lee and Sanchez needed to buy new clothes; checking out the local banks would require a little different look.

Tommie Lee sent Sanchez in with orders to pick out slacks, a tailored shirt, and a pair of shoes. For himself, he requested khaki work-clothes, boots and a work hat. If the need arose, he wanted to be able to look like an everyday service man, able to blend in anywhere. As he peeled several hundred dollars from the bank roll the Renegade president had handed him as they left, Tommie Lee was happy that the one thing he didn't have to worry about this trip was stealing or dealing to finance it. It was obvious, the Renegades wanted revenge as much as he did. What he didn't know was what would be required from him afterwards. There was no free lunch even riding in an outlaw gang.

Sanchez reached out his hand for the money, "Anything else you want, boss?"

Tommie Lee shook his head, "Tomorrow we're going to find her. I can feel it in my gut," he said out loud watching Sanchez make his way into the store. Totally unaware that the only audience he had was several demons assigned to their every move, Tommie Lee lit another cigarette.

The Enemy wanted Deborah just as bad as the Renegades, and he had a plan. Now he just needed these two dimwits to help him execute it. He laughed to himself, "Did Tommie Lee really think he was that smart or the Renegades that generous?" These guys were puppets on his string and they thought they were so tough and free! "Free! That's the last thing they were and they didn't even know it." But he did admit, he was looking forward to tomorrow as much as Tommie Lee. He just loved when a plan came together!

It was a chilly evening but Deborah asked Daniel if they could sit outside on the small patio. She couldn't believe that she had been able to wait as long as she had to tell Daniel what she had learned from Aunt Liberty. Maybe she was growing inpatient! She didn't want to take any chance of her mother overhearing their conversation, even though she was already in her bedroom. She had no idea if her mother had any knowledge of what she was about to tell Daniel. When Deborah had asked her aunt if her mother knew, Aunt Liberty had responded, "I would be surprised if he had ever breathed a word of it to anyone. There was just so much shame."

As soon as Daniel sat down on the patio chair, Deborah started talking and didn't stop until the whole story had been poured out. "When I got there on Friday night, Aunt Liberty had boxes of pictures and photo albums all over her living room. After supper we started looking at them. Just a few minutes after we had began looking at them she turned to me with tears in her eyes and said, 'I've got to tell you something that I had vowed to take to my grave, but Deborah you have to know the truth. I was a part of something that I never fully forgave myself for, and it's affected everybody's life including yours. It's hard to even know where to start. On your last visit, you asked me about your grandfather's, the Judge's, relationship with his secretary. Well, there's more to the story.'" Deborah remembered feeling her chest tighten, as she had leaned forward, wondering what her Aunt was going to tell her next. She didn't know how much more the box of family secrets could hold. Liberty continued, "There was a child born out of that relationship."

"So my father had a half-brother somewhere?" Deborah interjected.

Liberty hesitated for a minute and said, "No Deborah, that child was your father."

Deborah gasped, "But how...?

Chapter Eight

The Exchange

કેરુ જાં

Daniel sat transfixed as Deborah went on with the story. It sounded like one of those made for television movies, but it explained a great deal about her father, Theodore Noble.

Her aunt told her the story: "At the time, we all thought we were doing the best thing for everyone. My brother, the Judge, came to me and asked for my help. I knew how miserably his wife, Regina, always treated him and I felt sorry for him. The only reason Regina agreed to the plan was because he had threatened her with divorce. Back then, it was different than it is now; divorce was something very shameful and forbidden. My brother was willing to throw away his whole judicial career if necessary, but Regina's pride wouldn't allow it-reputation was too important to Miss High Society!" Her aunt caught herself for a moment, "You know, I may still have some unforgiveness issues there I need to work on, but I'll tend to that later."

Deborah inquired, "But how on earth did they manage to pull that off in this small town?"

Liberty responded, "Well, it wasn't as difficult as you would have thought. It was not unusual for Regina to go abroad in the summer months. This time she left for the south of France after announcing her pregnancy. Louise, your grandfatehr's secretary, on the other hand had been doing everything possible to hide hers. The story was that Louise's grandmother was sick and dying and she had to go take care of her. The Judge brought in some temporary help to cover her position. He convinced Louise that this would be the best for the child. The child would be raised with everything he needed, from social acceptance, educational opportunities, and unlimited provision. Otherwise, the only things the child could be was her bastard child because there would be no way he could ever claim the baby as his own.

The next thing my brother did was ask me to exchange the child for him." At that point she broke down in tears. "I'm so sorry, Deborah, for my part. I was just so young and I didn't know the Lord, yet. But I know there's no excuse. I think the hardest thing I've ever done in my life was to take that baby out of Louise's arms," then she began to sob as if her heart would break.

Deborah slid closer and put her arm around her aunt and held her gently as she cried. "Its okay, Auntie, it's going to be okay." She didn't quite know what else to say, and she felt her own heart breaking for her father in ways she never had felt possible.

Daniel was still trying to process everything that he had just heard. "So your grandmother, Regina, was not your father's real mother. What about his real mother, Louise, what happened to her?"

"Auntie said that Louise continued to work for my grandfather when she returned but that she had to watch her son grow up from a distance. I can't imagine how painful that had to have been for her. But Daniel, that's not all of it."

Now, Daniel could tell that Deborah was really getting uncomfortable. "It's okay, you can tell me anything. Just relax and take your time." He reached over and patted her hand.

"It's no wonder my father was so twisted. He never had the love of a mother. I knew Regina never fully embraced motherhood, and she was never a grandmother to me. But I had no idea what my father really lived through until now. Aunt Liberty said that Regina was physically cruel to him and would beat him much the way my father did my older brother, Paul. Because she had such anger toward my grandfather and the failed marriage she had gotten herself into, she took it out on the child that was never really hers. Auntie said that my Dad was turned over to a nanny immediately when Regina arrived home with him. Supposedly she had returned to Deerfield after giving birth to the baby prematurely overseas. Liberty thought some people might have suspected something, but no one ever dared question the Judge and Regina. It sounds like they had too much power, and life just went on.

As a child, my father had no idea about the circumstances of his birth. All he knew was that his mother did not love him. Aunt Liberty said that he always looked older than his age. Daniel, what I'm about to say is so awful, I can hardly say it."

"It's okay, honey. I know this is hard for you but you have to talk to someone about it."

"God, Regina was a sick woman, Daniel," Deborah held her head in her hands. "She seduced my father. You know she had a drinking problem. She got him drunk and seduced him. He was only fourteen. Afterwards, she informed him that there was no problem because after all he was never her real son. Can you imagine?"

Now, it was Daniel's turn to feel sick to his stomach. He too had wondered what could have happened to the woman to cause her to be so cruel.

"Of course, Regina immediately told the Judge what had happened but made it sound like my father had over powered her; she was still trying to make her husband pay for his adultery by abusing my father. The Judge almost murdered Regina over what had happened. If it hadn't been for Aunt Liberty, he may have killed her that night. He called Liberty in desperation one night and poured out the whole ugly mess. After he told her what happened, she went to the house immediately. She found him sitting with one of his hunting rifles trained on Regina. She was still taunting and laughing at him in a fit of drunken madness. My grandfather was enraged. My father and his sister were both supposed to be out for the entire evening. Dad ended up getting sick and was dropped off early; he walked into the whole scene.

"Aunt Liberty said that it was a miracle that somebody didn't get killed that night. That was the night she said she discovered that there was a higher power; she didn't know what else to do but pray. Auntie began to call on the name of the Lord. Right away, Regina began to sober up and the Judge dropped the rifle and began to cry. My father just ran out of the house. Once Aunt Liberty got the gun away from her brother, she went out looking for my Dad. She found him out back beating his head bloody against the brick fence, nearly mad with the pain of it all.

"At least, according to Aunt Liberty, my grandfather believed my dad. Liberty knew though that in order to protect his son from Regina, my dad had to be out of the home. She took him home with her that night and that's where he stayed until he was shipped off to military school. I'm sure it broke Louise's heart, too, to see him leave; at least when he was in town she could still watch him grow up, even if it was at a distance. Auntie didn't know if the Judge ever told Louise what really happened. No wonder my father could live a double life so easily, that's all he had ever known.

"Aunt Liberty said that she wrote to him while he was in military school and always tried to keep in touch, but he never responded. That was why he always kept me from her-he knew that she knew the whole truth and he never wanted anyone else to know.

"You would have thought what she did for him would have brought him closer to her, but instead, he put up a wall of shame. When he came back to Deerfield and married, he never wanted to have anything to do with her. It really broke her heart. She showed me pictures, Daniel. I know it's true. She had a picture of Louise; there was some resemblance. I know I forgave my father for the abuse when I went for ministry in Florida, but what I feel now goes beyond forgiveness. He had to have been such a tortured soul. You wonder how he made it all those years living a façade of a life," Deborah's voice trailed off as she looked into the night sky.

All Daniel could do was gently pat her hand even though he longed to take her in his arms and comfort her. He thought about how hard it must have been for her to go through the whole weekend without being able to talk to anyone. Tears of compassion welled up in his eyes. Still, he knew that as painful as it had been for her aunt to relive it in the telling, and as hard as it had been for Deborah to hear it, truth brought freedom. Until tonight, he had never heard Deborah call her father, "Dad."

Their family had stayed a little later than usual and Lydia and Stephen were cleaning up after them. The newest edition to the family was just three weeks old. Little Britania had slept most of the afternoon, giving her mother time to rest. Lydia had bought a couple of good children's videos and that had kept the other four occupied as well.

"It went well, don't you think?" she asked Stephen.

"It was a wonderful afternoon. I had a great time watching the game with Chuck and Brad. Did you have a nice time with Marie and Diana?"

"In between interruptions," she chuckled. "It's kind of hard to have a real deep conversation with four children running in and out. But it really is nice to feel like we're becoming a real family. The girls are getting along so well. It's taken a lot of work but it's been worth it, hasn't it?"

"I wouldn't change it for a minute," he answered. Again Lydia's heart swelled with thankfulness for the man God had brought into their lives. Stephen had never had a family or children until they had married. She and Marie had been an instant handful. Then Diana came along but he had never showed a bit of favoritism. God had truly given her a special man. Just like Ruth, she thought, He sent me my own personal Boaz.

As they finished straightening up, Lydia shared the dream Joyce had had about Deborah. "What's your discernment, honey? Should I call or just pray? I don't want to alarm Deborah, but I know Joyce was very troubled."

"Well, I think you just need to wait until tomorrow. If you're supposed to call, you'll have more clarity by then. I know you well enough that if you really felt a prompting from the Holy Spirit, you would already be on the phone."

Lydia laughed, knowing he was right. It was good to have someone so practical and down to earth to help balance her out. "You're right—I'm going to sleep on it tonight. But, I am going to continue to pray and see if I get any more discernment. Joyce and I are ministering together in the morning so she and I can talk then. This week we're ministering to a woman who's coming in from overseas. She lives in Israel but she's actually from Brazil. That should be an interesting combination. She'll be staying on afterwards for several weeks of training."

Chapter Nine

Monday Morning

❧ ❧

Deborah's hand was shaking as she put down the phone. "Who was that, dear?" her mother asked from the kitchen. She quickly replied, "That was Officer Brenda. You know she calls every once in a while to check on me even though I'm off probation." She felt guilty for not telling her mother the whole truth but right now she had to process the information she had just received. She hoped her mother didn't hear the quiver in her voice.

Fear like Deborah had not known in a long time gripped her as Officer Brenda shared with her that the probation office had been broken into over the weekend. Deborah heard her saying, "All the files under "W" have been stolen. Deborah, I'm concerned for your safety."

"Oh my God," Deborah gasped, "Could it have been the Renegades?" The thought gripped her with terror.

Officer Brenda hesitated and then replied, "Deborah, I hate to tell you this but I called to check on Tommie Lee and found out he was released on Tuesday. He cut a plea bargain with the D.A. about six months ago and received a reduced sentence. I really wish someone had notified me."

Slowly Deborah asked the question to the answer she was dreading, "Did my file have my address here in Deerfield?"

"Not your specific address, but it did have your probation officer's name and number there in Deerfield. I've already called Doug and let him know. He's making sure there's no record of your whereabouts left in his office. Your file was still under Debbie Lynn Webster." Officer Brenda's voice cracked, and she sounded ready to cry, "Deborah, I'm so sorry."

At that point, Deborah's knees went weak and she felt as if she was going to vomit. Knowing Tommie Lee had found out what city she was in frightened her beyond measure. Now, the feeling of apprehension on Friday night's drive to her aunt's made sense. Something had been going on! The old instinct to run flooded her. But right now, the only place she could run was to her room. She didn't want her mother to see the fear etched on her face.

Her immediate concern was for Daniel and his family. Precious Aimee and David, the thought of anything happening to them overwhelmed her. As much as she loved Daniel and the children, she knew for their sake, she was going to have to disappear.

This was unbelievable. Just when she thought her life was turning around for good, Tommie Lee was back. Just three months ago, under Pastor Harrison's supervision, she and Daniel had entered into courtship. Even though the relationship seemed to be moving kind of fast, everyone had a peace about what the Lord was doing between them. It just felt right. Until now, Deborah was amazed at how well everything had been going. She had fallen in love with Aimee and David, as much as they had with her. Through the restored relationship with Daniel, the Lord had given her more than she could ask for, just like His Word said. Intuitively, she knew that he was getting ready to propose any day now. She couldn't believe she was going to have to break his heart again.

How could she have been so stupid to think that it would be that easy to just walk away from everything and start a new life? She had really messed up this time, and now a whole lot of wonderful people could get hurt. She thought of going back and throwing herself at the mercy of Tommie Lee, but knew she'd rather be dead than go back to her old life.

Deborah, lay on her bed, a ball of agony. Once her mother had finally left, she cried the cry of a wounded animal. There was no holding it in; she just couldn't imagine having to give up Daniel and the kids. And the more she thought about it the more she cried. However, knowing what Tommie Lee and the Renegades were capable of, she couldn't imagine staying in Deerfield and having one of them harmed. Her mind was swimming with emotion and confusion. She knew there wasn't' much time—she was going to have to move fast.

She started to pray, "Lord, I need your strength to leave. Please give me a plan. What do I do about Daniel? Should I warn him or just leave, and where can I go?"

The heavens seemed like brass. All Deborah heard was a resounding silence.

At the same time Deborah was learning of the break-in, Tommie Lee was anxious to get on with the next part of his plan. He had Sanchez practice the story a couple of times: Debbie was a friend of his sister's who was dying. They had lost touch and his sister had sent him to find her. Once Tommie Lee was satisfied with Sanchez's performance, the men left for breakfast. They had found a little hole-in-the-wall restaurant right around the corner from the motel. After they finished eating, the men hit their first stop. It was a little branch bank on the outskirts of Deerfield.

Tommie Lee was in his work uniform wearing a hat pulled low and sun glasses. Sanchez looked a little like a used car salesman in his black slacks, light blue dress shirt and loafers. He had even gone as far as getting a tie to set off the ensemble. With his shirt sleeves rolled down and tattoos totally hidden, he cleaned up pretty good.

Sanchez walked out of the first bank, shaking his head-no one at the bank had seen or heard of Debbie Lynn. Tommie Lee wasn't concerned about it; to him it had just been a test run. "So, what did they say? Did they buy it?"

"They're girls, what do you think? They always love a sob story. I guarantee if they had known her, I would have got the info."

Their next stop was the Ameritrust Bank. Tommie Lee knew that they still needed to be careful not to arouse suspicion. Two guys checking out banks with an out of state license plate might get some attention. However, so far he hadn't even seen a cop car.

Arriving early that morning, Andrea was excited about taking over her new position. She had dressed with particular care that morning and it seemed as if it was a going to be a good day. Her head actually felt clearer than it had in days. Maybe she had just been dealing with some allergies.

As she was about to get up for her morning break, a young man asked if she could help him. "Well, are you planning on opening a new account?" she asked.

"Well, not exactly ma'am, but I do need some help."
He smiled almost flirtatiously at the good looking blonde. Sanchez held out his hand saying, "My name is Juan, Juan Santore, and I need some help." He allowed himself to choke up a little. "You see, my sister is dying, and I'm on a mission for her." He saw the young woman lean towards him. She was buying it. He continued, "She lost touch with a close friend who grew up in this town. I've come all the way from Chicago to see if I can track her down. There were some things that happened, and my sister just wants to make it right."

"Well, I'm not sure I can help you. I didn't grow up here. What's her name?"

"It's Debbie, ma'am. Debbie Webster."

Andrea started shaking her head, "I'm sorry, but that name doesn't ring a bell. I wish I could help you but..." she started to rise from her desk.

Sanchez quickly pulled the folded over picture out of his pocket. When she looked down, Andrea couldn't believe her eyes. Without thinking, she said, "That's Deborah Noble, her name isn't Debbie Webster."

"So you know her?"

Andrea hesitated, "Well, actually—yes, I do."

Now Sanchez knew he needed to tread carefully. He

didn't want to shut her down without getting more information. Tommie Lee sat in the car watching the street and tapping the steering wheel. This was the longest Sanchez had been in any bank. Hopefully, he just wasn't flirting with the tellers. "Can you just tell me this, ma'am?" Sanchez continued. "My sister heard that she had moved back home. Is Debbie still around here?"

Andrea was transfixed by the picture and trying to decide what to do next. She didn't want anything to mess up her new job. She had just been made the manager of new accounts and it had felt great to leave the teller window. She saw the assistant bank manager walking towards her.

Speaking in a hushed tone, she said, "I'm taking a break, there's a coffee shop two blocks that way," she pointed. "Meet me there. It's called Lucy's Place." Sanchez nodded and walked out of the bank. As soon as he saw Tommie Lee, his thumb went up in the air. He had hit pay dirt!

That same morning the phone rang as Joyce was getting ready for work. Figuring it was probably Lydia, she hadn't even glanced at the number.

Hearing his voice, she nearly dropped the phone. It was her ex-husband, Bill. "I know it's early there. I hope I didn't wake you. I just finally got the courage up to call. If you want to hang up, I'll understand."

Not knowing what to say or do, Joyce paused and then finally said, "No, go on."

"I know this isn't the right time to talk but next week I have business on the East coast. I'm going to be in Atlanta. I was just wondering, if I came to Florida, would you be willing to see me? There are some things I just feel I have to say and I'd like to do it in person. But, I don't want to put any pressure on you."

At that point, all Joyce could muster up was, "Let me

pray about it. I have your number on caller ID. But, I'm not sure, Bill, I just don't know," she hesitated, not really wanting to give him any hope.

He simply said, "I'll understand," and hung-up.

Joyce stood with the phone in her hand wondering if she had been dreaming. "Why now? My life is just getting back to normal," she thought. She felt shaken and angry. It was the phone call that she had been waiting for; it was just two years, too late.

"What a day to run late," Joyce thought as she made her way through traffic. The phone call from Bill had shaken her so much she wouldn't even dare mention in to Lydia. Her co-counselor had long since established that personal lives and issues were put on hold for the person receiving counseling and ministry. With only a week to deal with a person's lifetime of pain, there was no room for distractions. Joyce began to pray in the Spirit hoping that, after their morning session, Lydia would be available to talk. She knew this was one of those times her soul was so involved that she needed some wise counsel. She would also want to talk to Pastor Rick. When she pulled into the parking lot at His House, she was relieved to see Lydia was already there, at least they both hadn't run late.

She walked up the steps, took a deep breath, and opened the front door praying, "Lord, I trust you to keep my mind focused, and I put my decision in Your hands. I choose to trust You over everything that concerns me." She prayed softly in the spirit as she walked down the hall and opened the door to the Restoration Room.

After her morning devotions, Anne started cleaning and forgot to turn her cell phone on. Now it was almost noon. She quickly turned it on hoping no one had really needed her.

When she went to check her messages, the first one was from her brother, Daniel. "Hey, sis, what are you doing for lunch today? I need your help with something, call me."

She quickly called his office, "Hi, Irene, Daniel called earlier has he left for lunch, yet?"

"No, honey, he's still in his office. Can I get him for you?"

"Please, he called earlier but I forgot to turn my cell phone on this morning," Anne confessed.

Before she knew it, Daniel was on the line. "I've been hoping you would call. Have you had lunch yet?"

"Not yet, what do you have in mind?"

"I really just needed a woman's opinion and thought I could bribe you with some lunch."

Right away Anne realized what her brother was up to, "Are you looking at rings? That's what's going on, isn't it?"

"Well, I've had all weekend to think about it. Friday afternoon, I just happened to see a sale sign at Tiara's Jewelry Store downtown when I went out for lunch. Before I went back to work I decided to check it out. I think I found the perfect ring for Deborah. I'd really love your advice before I buy it. Do you have time this afternoon?" Daniel really wanted his sister's opinion.

"Absolutely! For a ring, I'll make time!" Anne replied excitedly. "Where should we meet?"

"Let's just meet in front of Tiara's and then we can have some lunch. How soon can you get there?"

Anne responded quickly, "Give me thirty minutes and I'll be there."

As their call finished up, Daniel once again thanked the Lord for the awesome sister he had. He wondered what Anne would have to say about the ring. If she had any check in her spirit, he was going to have to be smart enough and patient enough to trust it. Even though last night had made him even more anxious to ask Deborah to marry him, she had been so vulnerable. Everything in him wanted to protect her and make her feel safe, but he also trusted Anne. That was one great thing about his sister; no matter what anyone else said or did, when she knew that she had heard from God, there was no moving her. He could always count on her and he was so glad that she and Deborah were friends. But right now, he had time to review one more account before lunch, so he turned his attention to the computer screen.

Chapter Ten

The Meeting

ॐ ๑

As Sanchez climbed into the passenger's seat, he said, "Hurry up, man. I don't want her to see you." The car was already running and Tommie Lee quickly put it in drive. Sanchez began to tell him what had just transpired. At the first intersection, Tommie Lee turned right so that they could circle back to the coffee place where Andrea would be waiting. They quickly decided that it would be best at this point if Sanchez handled it all alone.

Tommie Lee pulled into a parking lot and hopped out of the driver's seat as Sanchez slipped in behind the wheel. "I'll wait for you over there," he pointed to some benches in front of what looked like a government building. Sanchez nodded and the green Chevy pulled away. Tommie Lee wished he could have gotten some more information; but for now he was going to have to trust Sanchez.

As Andrea walked into Lucy's Place she immediately spotted an open table towards the back. The coffee shop resembled a fifties diner and was full of "I Love Lucy" memorabilia. She was a regular there and the waitress brought her over water and coffee without even asking. Andrea said, "Hi, Lindy, I have someone joining me, can you please bring a menu and some water?" The waitress nodded as she saw Sanchez walk through the door and directly to Andrea's table. For some reason, he made her feel uncomfortable. Lindy and Andrea went to the same church, but she had never seen this man before. Without thinking, she began to pray to herself.

Sanchez slid into the booth opposite of Andrea. He politely said, "You don't know what it means to me ma'am that you're willing to talk to me."

Without any pleasantries, Andrea said, "Can I see that picture again? I want to make sure it's really her. Sanchez reached into his shirt pocket and pulled it out. He didn't want her to see the rest of the picture. He hung unto it awkwardly as Andrea reached for it. For a second, they had a quick tug of war, but when he didn't release it, she let go.

Studying the picture, she said again, "Yes, that's Deborah Noble. She goes to church with me." Sanchez nearly choked on the water he had just started to drink. Debbie in church? Wait till Tommie Lee heard that one!

"So are you and her friends?" Sanchez asked.

At that Andrea's eyes clouded over, "No, not really. I know who she is. That's about all."

Lindy came by and took the rest of their order while Sanchez continued with his tale of his sick sister, Maria. He told Andrea how his sister had been best friends with Debbie until a man had come in between them. The man was long gone and now Maria was dying of uterine cancer and just wanted to make things right.

Out of nowhere Andrea said, "Well, that doesn't surprise me. So did Deborah steal your sister's boyfriend?" her face now looked like she could cry any minute.

Taken aback for a minute, Sanchez responded, "Well, I don't really know the whole story."

"Well, I know how your sister feels. She waltzed back to

Deerfield and stole the man God promised to me. It's like she cast a spell over him or something."

Now Sanchez couldn't believe his good fortune, a woman scorned, could it get any better? He reached and patted her hand, "I'm so sorry, do you want to talk about it?"

That was all she needed to pour out the whole story. Suddenly she glanced at her watch and realized that she would be late if she didn't get going. "I'm sorry I really need to go," she said, "I know I've just talked your ear off."

Sanchez knew he still needed some valuable information and continued to try and act compassionate, even though he was getting quite impatient with the woman whining in front of him. "It's alright ma'am but can you tell me one more thing? How can I get in touch with Debbie?"

"She works at the Worldwide Travel Agency downtown. I'm not sure of the address, but it'll be in the phonebook." At that point Andrea went to stand up, but earlier on she had opened her purse for a tissue and hadn't closed the clasp. Its contents spilled on the floor. As Sanchez bent to help her pick them up, the photograph fell out of his shirt pocket. Exposing Deborah in a provocative pose straddling a motorcycle, Andrea gasped as she saw it. "Is that her?" Now she was hanging on to the picture. Sanchez reached for it, but Andrea drew back, opening the picture and taking a moment to study it. "I knew it. I knew it," she kept repeating to herself. "I have to save Daniel and the children." She looked at Sanchez, who didn't know what to do at this point, with her big blue eyes and said, "I need your help. Can you meet me after work and bring this?" she asked with the picture in hand.

Not knowing what else to do Sanchez, nodded and said "Sure, you've helped me, now I'll help you. Where do you want me to meet you?"

"Do you remember seeing the lake with the little picnic area on your way into town?" she asked.

Sanchez vaguely remembered and nodded, "Is it on

Highway 22?"

"Yes, it's about a half mile before the city limits. Meet me there at five-thirty."

At that point, Sanchez thought it might be best if Tommie Lee got involved, "I have a friend who was supposed to drive over from Columbus and meet me for dinner, is it okay if I bring him along?"

Andrea hesitated for a moment, but didn't want to miss this opportunity, "I guess that's okay."

As the two of them left the coffee shop, Lindy had an uncomfortable feeling, she almost felt sick to her stomach. As Sanchez paid the bill, his hand had touched hers for just a second. Everything in her had wanted to recoil. She wondered who he was and what Andrea was doing with him.

The Enemy was jubilant as Andrea made her way out of the coffee shop. Deborah was being tormented by fear at this very moment-she had just learned of the break-in. He was playing Tommie Lee and Sanchez like a violin, and Andrea, she was another story all together. He had held a part of her since she was a child, putty in his hands! If only he could shut-up those praying women! Deborah's Aunt Liberty was a royal pain in the butt! And those two other ones, Lydia and Joyce, he was just going to have to work over-time to stop them!

Tommie Lee was excited to learn that they now knew where Debbie worked; but as Sanchez went on with the story, he became a little concerned. He just wasn't so sure they should meet Andrea later. They couldn't afford any of this getting back to Debbie. He did know one thing: this afternoon they were going to have to find a car and pull a license plate. He didn't dare risk driving around town all day with a Louisiana plate. Then they would either have to move from the motel or change it back before returning. You just couldn't be too careful.

Tommie Lee wondered if tonight would be the night. All they had to do was follow Deborah home and then they could map out their strategy. He would make the decision regarding meeting Andrea later. He didn't want to make the woman mad, and if something happened to Debbie she could finger Sanchez. But if she was involved somehow, then she would have to protect her own neck. He would have to give this one some thought. However, he did know he was going to have to keep an eye on Sanchez. He obviously was having other thoughts about the woman. Tommie Lee knew that Sanchez had a reputation for raping what he called "gringo" women: blond hair, blue eyed, just like Andrea. Now was not the time for that. He didn't know if the stories were true, but he could tell by the look in Sanchez's eyes that something had gotten aroused the man.

Chapter Eleven

The Ring

ॐ ॐ

Deborah had finally got herself together enough to call the travel agency and let them know she wouldn't be coming in to work. Mrs. Mitchell had sounded concerned. She didn't want to lie and told her employer that she just wasn't in any condition to come in to work. Her voice was weak from fear and crying. Deborah thought how awful it was that she would have to leave them with no notice or warning. She thought about all the relationships and people she now really cared about. How would her leaving affect them? What could she tell them and when? Even if she just disappeared from their lives, she knew everyone would be worried about her.

She knew Daniel would never understand that it was because she loved him so desperately that she was going to have to leave. He had no idea what lengths the Renegades would go to in order to seek revenge. She was so thankful that her mother was working with hospice today. The woman she had been taken care of the last couple of weeks had just been given only hours to live. She didn't know when her mother would be back home. She could just see her mother, Daniel and Anne on one of those twenty-four hour news channels appealing for help to find her.

Praying for God to give her a plan, she pulled out her suitcase and started packing. As she tried to sort out what to take with her, tears continued to stream down Deborah's face. Thank God she had put a little money aside. Two thousand dollars wasn't much but at least it could get her out of town and sustain her until she found a job. She kept praying for the Lord to show her where to go.

———

Lydia and Joyce had finally finished their morning session. It had taken a little longer than the usual three hours. Theresa Diaz had a very complex generational history and her childhood had been quite abusive. She was one of those individuals who really loved the Lord; however, upon becoming a Christian, she had basically stuffed away all of her past pain and threw herself into works. The ministry had medicated the pain for a number of years but now, in her late thirties, things had begun to unravel. Lydia hadn't remembered her, but Theresa had actually attended a workshop she had conducted in Jerusalem on her last visit.

Theresa had shared earlier on in the morning that the only reason she had gone to the class was to appease a friend; but, something opened up within her as Lydia taught on soul restoration. She began to experience an intense desire for more healing and freedom. She had decided then, that if God made a way, she would go to the United States for more ministry. It had taken nearly two years, but she was finally there.

As they had started the interview, Lydia could tell that Theresa was almost scared to talk about her past; it was as if the two women might dig up her old man causing her to lose her salvation. Even though she had attended a workshop and really wanted the ministry, the counselors had to take some time to reassure her that Jesus was truly her Healer. He really wanted to comfort her and minister to her pain. He hadn't saved her just to say, "Now go to work and follow me." No, He had saved her to draw her into a relationship so that He might fulfill Isaiah chapter sixty-one in her life. He truly wanted to heal her broken heart, give her beauty for ashes, repair the desolation of many generations and give her double honor for her shame. She finally started opening up and then the details of her childhood came as if a dam had broken and a torrent of pain poured out.

———————————

Anne was delighted as Daniel showed her the ring he had found on Friday. It was perfect. Over lunch, they discussed Daniel's meeting with Pastor Harrison. "Anne, I know you believe Deborah and I are to be married, but do you feel this is the right time to ask her? You know I could always buy the ring and hold on to it," Daniel tentatively asked.

"I believe Pastor Mark is right. Deborah needs you and the children. It's not like you just met six months ago. Our family has known Deborah ever since we moved here and it's very obvious that she's had a true conversion. She was coming to my Bible study and went to Palm City for ministry before that day at the altar when the Lord brought her back into your life. And remember what the Lord had spoken to Mom years ago. I think you need to talk to them and if you get their green light, ask her. Actually, Daniel, I'm so excited I can hardly stand it."

Daniel broke out in a big grin, "I feel the same way, Sis, but every once and awhile I'm afraid it's too good to be true. But I'm going to call Mom and Dad tonight. Pray that if I'm out of timing at all, they'll help put on the brakes."

"What about the ring?" Anne wondered. "Are you going to buy it today?"

"Well, I trusted the Lord over it this weekend, so I'm going to wait until tomorrow morning. I want to hear what Mom and Dad have to say. The sale lasts until Friday, but I'll be there bright and early tomorrow morning if it's a 'go' with them."

"It's a gorgeous ring. I know she'll love it! Oh, Daniel, I'm so happy for you! God really does turn our mourning into joy. I know this has been such a hard season for all of you." Then she added softly, as she reached out and patted his hand, "This is what Susan would have wanted. Don't feel guilty for being happy."

Tears filled their eyes as they thought about Susan's struggle with cancer and the promise she had required from Daniel as death approached. She had wanted him to have a wife, and the children, a mother. At the time, the promise to take another wife had been hard to make but he knew she had been right. The house had never seemed right since she passed away; an empty hollowness remained. He and the kids kept busy, sometimes actually avoiding home; however, Deborah was so different from Susan that he wondered how they would all adjust.

As if reading his mind, Anne said, "I know they are as different as night and day, Daniel, but I know Susan would have liked Deborah. It's really okay for you to be happy with her."

He breathed a sigh of relief. It was just like Anne to know exactly what to say at the right time. It reminded him of that scripture in Proverbs: "A word fitly spoke is like apples of gold in settings of silver."

As she returned to work, Andrea couldn't get the photograph of Deborah out of her mind. If only Daniel could see it, it would finally convince him that Deborah was not the woman for him. She just knew that this was the answer to her prayers. "I just have to get a copy of that photograph," she thought. She decided to make a withdrawal before she left work just in case it took some money to convince Juan to let her make a copy of the picture.

Business began to pick up after her break. She decided to go to lunch by herself. She needed a plan. Would it be best to let Deborah know she had the picture and convince her it would be best to leave town or should she go directly to Daniel? She could hardly wait until the end of the day. She sure hoped Juan would show up later that evening. Her major concern was that he would give Deborah the message from his sister this afternoon and head out of town. She hoped the afternoon would go by as quickly as the morning had.

70

Chapter Twelve

Intervention

ﰰ ﰱ

It seemed like it had taken her forever to sort through her things as she packed and cried. It was already afternoon when her cell phone rang. She checked the number and saw it was Lydia. For a second she almost didn't answer it, but knew it was probably no accident she was calling at this precise moment. She tried to answer it as normally as possible, not knowing what she was going to tell her, "Hi, Lydia, how are you?"

"Well, actually, I was wondering that very same thing about you. Joyce had a dream on Saturday afternoon about you. We've prayed about it, but at lunch the Holy Spirit put it on both of our hearts to call. Are you okay?"

From the first day Deborah had sat on the couch at His House, the anointing had caused her not to be able to hold anything back from the woman on the other line. "I don't know where to start. I'm packing. I have to get out of here. I'm so scared. Officer Brenda called me this morning. He's out of prison. Someone broke into her office. I can feel it-he's coming for me. I can't tell Daniel where I'm going. I can't believe I'm going to have to hurt him again. I don't know where to go."

Lydia said, "Whoa, slow down a minute. Tommie Lee is out of prison? I thought he still had a number of years left.

Deborah, can I put you on speaker phone. We're private, but I think Joyce needs to hear this. Can you just take a couple of deep breaths and blow out slowly? And then let's start from the beginning."

Deborah could not believe the timing of the Lord. Maybe He had heard her prayers. She was surprised at how fast all of the information had poured out of her. She took a couple of deep breaths and then shared in more detail everything that had happened that morning.

Lydia and Joyce were almost holding their breath on the other end. Every once and awhile they would look at each other and shake their heads. The Enemy was up to no good. Thank God that He had given Joyce the dream and they had already been praying.

As Deborah shared, Lydia was trying to seek discernment on whether she needed all the details of the dream. They didn't want to frighten her any more than she already was, but this was serious. She wrote on her notepad to Joyce, "Do we tell her the whole dream?"

Joyce was praying in the Spirit, still not quite sure. Then she wrote back, "I think we have to." As much as Lydia hated to, she agreed. Deborah needed to know.

As Deborah finished with the story, Lydia said, "Deborah, I don't want to alarm you any more than you already are but I think you need to hear the dream Joyce had Friday night. Just remember, the Lord has gone before this and we've already been praying."

Joyce began with the details of her dream. "Hi, Deborah, the dream wasn't very long, Deborah. There were hunters in it—they were dressed in camouflage. You were totally unaware, but they were hunting for you."

Deborah gasped, "That's exactly how I feel. I wouldn't be surprised if he's here already. I don't want anyone else hurt; I have got to get out of here!" She broke down again.

Lydia said, "You can always come to Florida. We've got

room at the ministry house right now. But before any of us do anything, we need the mind of Christ. I know it's hard, but I want you to start praying in the Holy Spirit, right now."

They all prayed for several minutes. Deborah said, "I have been praying about where to go, but I haven't heard anything all morning."

Joyce said gently, "But have you prayed about if you're supposed to leave or not?"

Deborah immediately responded, "That's out of the question. I can't just stay here like a sitting duck. You don't know Tommie Lee. What about my mother and Daniel and the children? I wouldn't put anything past him. I couldn't live with myself if anyone got hurt."

Joyce replied knowingly and in a confident voice, "I just have to tell you what I heard, 'Stand still and see the salvation of the Lord.' I know that's easy for me to say, I'm not in your shoes. I just had to tell you what I heard."

Lydia added, "The only thing I've been getting is that you need to call your Pastor. He has spiritual authority in that geographical area and over your life. Plus, he also knows Daniel. I think God will give him the key."

Before she could stop herself, Deborah blurted out, "Right now, he's the last person I want to talk to. I'm so ashamed I got myself and Daniel into this mess. I should have never let myself get involved with a decent man!"

Lydia had had enough, "Deborah, I know you're scared and I know it looks messy, but God has not brought you this far to leave you now. Remember the vision you had of getting married and what the Lord did between you and Daniel after you were here. Our God is bigger than Tommie Lee and all the Renegades. We just need to trust His strategy. Remember Jericho, remember the Valley of Jehosophat, remember David and Goliath, remember Gideon's army? God's strategies looked foolish but they always brought victory. You've made a decision to walk with God and you have to do that in the good times and the bad. This is no time for you to fall back to the flesh. Now, we are going to continue praying, but I want you to hang up right now and call your pastor. When you're finished, call me back immediately!"

It was enough to shake Deborah, "Okay, I'll call. I don't know what he can do, but I'll call. I do trust that you both hear from the Lord, but right now everything in me wants to just throw my suitcases in the car and start driving."

"We understand, honey, but it's no accident I had that dream and that we called you right now. So just do what Lydia asked you to do. Give your Pastor a call and then let us know what he says," Joyce added softly.

"Okay, okay, I will, but I have to hurry, Deborah said. "Please pray."

"We are. We'll be waiting for your call. We love you," Lydia reminded her before hanging up. They both looked at each other and started praying.

Over lunch they had gone over Theresa's interview and prepared for tomorrow's session. Joyce had just been ready to tell Lydia about the call when the topic of Deborah and the dream had come up; she now knew that this was not the time to share about Bill's phone call. Right now it was more important that Deborah had been alerted. Cold chills went up and down her spine as she remembered the terror she had felt as the hunters stalked Deborah in the dream. Thank God they had called her. She hoped it would give Deborah confidence to know that God was on the throne even in this frightening situation.

Lydia stopped for a minute, "I think we need to call the prayer chain at church." She reached for her phone and then said, "Can you use yours? I don't want to miss Deborah's call.

Joyce reached in her bag for hers. Katie Jo, the church secretary, picked up the call right away. Joyce was glad not to have to leave a message. She started by explaining the situation. She finished saying, "Mainly, we need prayer for wisdom and God's protection. Also, the young lady is really battling fear right now, as you can well imagine. Please get the intercessors on this immediately. If they get anything specifically from the Lord, have them call us direct." She and Katie Jo said their good-byes and then she picked up the check and paid the bill.

Lydia was already outside, pacing back in forth in the parking lot, still interceding. "I just feel like we need to stay together. Do you want to just go back to His House until we hear from her?

Joyce nodded in agreement. They both got into their separate cars and headed back to the house on Magnolia Avenue. As she drove, Joyce tried to keep her mind on Deborah, but the phone call from Bill had really thrown her. She was glad a person could pray in the Spirit when you didn't know what else to pray. Even though the day Bill had been arrested and his sexual addiction had been exposed had been a couple of years ago, Joyce had received a great deal of healing since then; however, the memory was still very real and very painful. Her whole life had been turned upside down back then, and now out of the blue, he wanted to talk. She would have given anything to talk when everything had first been exposed, but today was a different story. She had been working so hard to put it all behind her. She thought of the day after everything had been exposed. It felt like she woke up that morning married to a stranger; now, Joyce didn't think she wanted any more involvement with that stranger. She wondered what Lydia would have to say when she finally got an opportunity to talk to her.

Chapter Thirteen

The Phone Call

಴ ಴

When the phone call came, Pastor Harrison was in his study preparing for the mid-week service. He was having difficulty concentrating and wasn't quite sure why. He heard the home phone ring in the background and waited for Christina to answer it.

There was a slight knock on the door and his wife handed him the portable phone. "I can't make out who this is, but it sounds like an emergency."

He put the phone to his ear and said, "This is Pastor Harrison." All he could hear on the other end were sobs and words so garbled he couldn't understand them. "Who is this?" he asked.

The only thing he could make out from the caller on the other end was, "have to leave... Daniel... need to see you right away."

Suddenly he realized who it was. "Deborah, is that you? What on earth is going on?"

She couldn't believe that she had broken down again. Pastor Harrison was going to think she was crazy. She had to get a hold of herself. She took another deep breath. "Yes, Pastor, it's me. I'm sorry, let me try to slow down and explain everything. I just got off the phone with Lydia, my counselor in Florida. She felt I needed to call you. I really hate to bother you."

"Deborah, it's no problem, just take your time. What's going on?"

Once again she related the whole story. In some of their conversations as he counseled Daniel and Deborah about courtship, he had heard bits and pieces about her former life, but he had never thought that it would invade Deerfield. He was especially concerned when she shared the dream that Joyce had had, and also about her own sense that something was wrong on the previous Friday night. As she continued the story, it was as if an alarm was going off inside of him. Obviously, the Holy Spirit wanted him to take her seriously. This wasn't just an emotional reaction. From what he had seen of Deborah in the last six months, she seemed pretty emotionally balanced and wasn't one to get rattled at every little thing. He could hear her concern for the well-being of Daniel, the children, both of their families, and even the couple she worked for, the Mitchell's.

Pastor Harrison tried to listen to both Deborah and for wisdom from the Lord as she continued to talk. What advice should he give her? Now, she was telling him about the Scripture verse that Joyce had received, "Stand still and see the salvation of the Lord." That was all well and good, but they still needed to know exactly what that meant.

"Please, Pastor Harrison, whatever you do, please don't call Daniel. I don't want him involved in this. I just can't believe I've messed up his life again!"

He could hear her weeping on the other end of the phone. "Deborah, here is what I need you to do. First, give me Lydia's phone number. Second, I want you to stay right where you are. Don't leave the house. Make sure the doors are locked. And Deborah, please don't run. I'll be right over."

Deborah said, "I just can't let you do that Pastor Mark. You have a family to take care of, you don't understand these men. They don't care about anything or anybody."

"Please, Deborah, I know what the Holy Spirit is telling me right now. On my way over, we'll keep praying and see what the next step is. All I know is that right now you don't need to be alone and we need a plan. I'll be there in fifteen minutes. I hate to pull rank, but I am your pastor. The Word says that He holds me accountable for your soul. Right now the Enemy is just pulling out all stops. You've come too far, Deborah. Remember the True Identity you received in Florida that you shared with me. Pull it out and start reading it over and over until I get there," with that he hung up, not waiting for an answer.

"Honey, get my jacket! I'll call you as I drive and explain what's going on.

As Christina handed him his jacket, he said, "I don't know when I'll be back." With that he was out the door and in the car. Christina had never seen him pull out of the driveway as fast and as furious. Something major must be happening. As she went into the kitchen to finish putting the rest of supper in the oven, the phone rang. It was her husband. For a minute, fear gripped her as he shared the story. Then she began to quote Scripture to herself, "God has not given me a spirit of fear, but of power, love and a sound mind."

As he finished, she asked, "Mark, can I call the prayer chain at the church?"

For a minute, he hesitated, "Okay, but I think it's best if we just have them praying protection for us and all church members. That will include Deborah and her mother, Daniel and his family. I just don't want to give out details without having talked to Deborah first. Tell them to beseech the Lord for warring angels to be sent into the situation."

"Please be careful, Mark," she cautioned, "call me when you know more."

"I love you, honey. Don't worry everything is going to be okay. If you get anything in prayer, call me."

They said goodbye and Pastor Mark turned his attention

to calling Lydia.

She answered the phone immediately. "Thank you for calling. Is it alright if I put you on speaker phone so that Joyce can hear, as well?"

"That's fine. I just want you to know that Deborah just called me. I'm on the way over to her house right now. She told me everything."

Lydia choked up as she said, "Thank God. She needs someone with her. I don't know how much you know about Tommie Lee, but from what Deborah shared during her ministry, there's no telling how far he and the Renegades might go to take their revenge. They have a perverted code of honor and when one of their own turn on them, especially in a legal situation, they like to make an example out of them. It puts fear in everyone else. Did she tell you about the dream Joyce had?"

"Yes, she did. I believe we have to take this seriously. I'm praying for the Lord to give us a strategy. I promised Deborah I wouldn't do anything until she and I talked and prayed in person. I'd like to call the police but I want to talk with her first."

"Just so you know she's welcome down here. If she needs to get out of town, we have room available for her," Joyce added.

"We'll be praying for you, Pastor. Thank you for helping her. We feel a little helpless down here, but I guess there's no greater power than the power of prayer."

"That's right, ladies. If the Lord shares anything else with you, please don't hesitate to call. I need all the help I can get."

After they had hung up, Lydia said, "I like him; you can sense his humility, yet confidence in the Lord. I know Deborah has had nothing but good things to say about him, but I feel better already."

Joyce nodded in agreement, "So what do we do next?"

"I think we need to just hold tight until they have time to

talk. I'm sure he'll call us with what they're going to do next. Is that okay with you?" Lydia asked.

"Sure, I don't think I could concentrate on anything else, anyway," Joyce agreed. Now all they could do was wait and pray.

––––––––––––––––––––

Tommie Lee was fuming. They had driven by the travel agency several times throughout the afternoon and hadn't seen Debbie once. Visibility was pretty good though the large plate glass window, but the only people they ever saw was an older man and woman. Maybe there was another back office, or maybe the woman from the bank didn't know what she was talking about. Well, that made up his mind. He was going to have to meet the bank lady himself. He stationed Sanchez where he could watch the back door of the agency and then pulled around front to see who came out. They would just have to wait and see who came out at closing time. If Debbie was there, they would just follow her home.

He was glad they had taken time earlier to pull some Ohio tags. It had been a piece of cake. They had driven out of town and found a house where it looked like no one was home. There was a car pulled up alongside the garage that hadn't moved in a while. They knocked on the door just in case. A dog was barking inside. No one came to the door, so they just quickly checked the back plate and found it was still good. In minutes, it was on the green Chevy, and they were heading down the road.

Chapter Fourteen

War in the Heavenlies

ॐ ॐ

The prayers of the saints were reaching heaven. Warring angels were being dispatched. If anyone could have seen into the spiritual realm over Deerfield, they would have seen hoards of demons descending on their town. Evil had been unleashed. The Enemy had been mounting this attack for some time now and the war was almost upon the town of Deerfield.

Satan was pleased at how many Christians this one would affect-collateral damage was his specialty. He was going to have to move fast though. The Spirit of God had alerted those women in Florida and now their prayers were joining with the prayers of Deborah's aunt. Demons were already falling, bound from carrying out his plans. But he had dispatched plenty for this job, so wave after wave they came.

He sent a demon of affliction to try and shut the old woman up, but she made quick work of him. He would have loved to just put her out of her misery but God had her days numbered and right now he had no legal ground to take her life. Suddenly, he felt hit by a blinding blow. "What was that? Oh, no! Somehow there were higher level prayers being sent in his direction. He would have to find out where they were coming from immediately.

As they headed to the lake to meet the lady from the bank, Tommie Lee growled, "This better not be a mistake!"

Sanchez responded, "Trust me, man. This lady doesn't like little Debbie, and I smell money. Where are the copies of the pictures we made?"

Tommie Lee drew them out of his jacket pocket and hesitantly handed them over to Sanchez.

"See, she's already there waiting on us. Remember, you're my friend, Lee, from Columbus," Sanchez said as they pulled alongside Andrea's parked car.

Tommie Lee was still not sure if he liked this whole idea. "I just don't want to sit out here in the open. Do you think we can get her in the car?"

Sanchez smiled and said, "They don't call me a ladies man for nothing. Just watch," he said as he opened his door.

"Hello, it's nice to meet a punctual lady," Sanchez smiled and bowed, slightly. This is my friend, Lee, he said as he pointed into the car.

Andrea gave a slight wave in Tommie Lee's direction and then asked, "So, did you find Deborah today?"

"No, ma'am, I didn't. She wasn't working today. Are you sure she still works at the travel agency?"

Andrea looked confused, "I'm pretty sure she does. I can't imagine why she wouldn't have been at work today. I'm sorry about that."

"Ma'am would you mind sitting in the car for a bit, the mosquitoes up here are pretty vicious, and I'm highly allergic," Sanchez said pointing to the back seat. Andrea looked a little apprehensive, but Sanchez immediately pulled the pictures out of his pocket swung the door open and slid into the back seat. Hesitating for a minute, Andrea followed. She just had to see the rest of the pictures of Deborah.

Christina had called the members of the prayer chain at the church. She tried to sound calm as she requested prayers of protection for her husband and church members, and then she called her mother and told her everything. When she hung up the phone she felt much better. Her mother was a praying woman who had lived on the mission field in South America during her teens and early twenties. There wasn't a whole lot that scared her. She was so glad her mother wasn't a worrier, and that she was able to share everything with her.

She put on praise music and began to sing and worship, thinking of testimonies her mother had shared with her as a child. She loved the one about how rebels, who had been known to kidnap American missionaries for ransom money, had surrounded the car her mother's family had been traveling in one day. Christina's grandfather had said immediately, "Praise the Lord, now!" The whole family had burst into song and within minutes the rebels had turned away from the car and made a hasty retreat. Later they had heard that the rebels had thought an earthquake had started; they had all felt the ground moving and shaking, yet, the family in the car had felt nothing. They knew it had been a great miracle. So Christina had grown up with her mother often saying, "Praise the Lord, now!"

As a child, she had sometimes thought her mother was being foolish, but today she sang with all she had. By faith, she believed that the high praises of God were inflicting damage on the enemy. If she could have only seen in the spirit realm, she would have known just how effective her worship and her mother's prayers were becoming.

———————————

Anne couldn't wait for Robert to get home that afternoon; she was looking forward to telling him about her lunch with Daniel. It was so exciting to know that Daniel was getting ready to propose to Deborah. She knew that Robert had been as concerned as she was for Daniel and the children.

As part of the church prayer chain, Anne received the call from the church to pray for protection for the pastor and church members. It sounded a bit strange and she tried to get more information so she could pray specifically, but to no avail. She wondered what was really going on and began to pray in the Spirit; maybe when Robert got home from work he would know what was happening. He was quite close to Pastor Mark. As Anne prayed, Andrea, kept coming to mind. She didn't know if it was because she had just been thinking of Daniel and Deborah, or what. It felt a little confusing and she found herself praying, "Lord, I bind every strategy of division that Andrea is devising. I pray that it would be exposed and torn down and that no weapon formed against Daniel and Deborah would prosper." As she waited for her husband to get home from work, she continued in prayer.

Now the Enemy was getting angry. Demons were being pummeled over Deerfield and he was actually beginning to feel some of the effects himself. He quickly launched demons of fear and confusion to those that had been newly enlisted onto the side of the saints. He also decided to create some diversions.

Christina suddenly began to feel an intense headache coming on; she knew instantly that it was part of the warfare. The Enemy also released spirits of infirmity into Anne's son, Joshua, who walked into the house after school and told his mother that he wasn't feeling very well. Next, he used someone Christina's mother had been ministering to and she called for help; that should tie her up for a while, he thought. He knew the time he had bought wouldn't last long, but at least the intensity of the battle had decreased and it gave him time to reorganize the troops.

Andrea couldn't believe her good fortune. Not only did Juan have the seductive photographs of Deborah, he also had nude ones. She began to get the feeling, however, that he was lying to her about his dying sister. Right now she really didn't care-all she wanted to do was get her hands on those photographs. She decided to be direct and asked "So what would I have to do to get a copy of these pictures?"

Sanchez replied, "Well, Ma'am, this trip has been expensive and I've had so many extra expenditures because of my sister. What would they be worth to you?"

Andrea decided to offer him five hundred dollars.

Tommie Lee cleared his throat up front and Sanchez knew that wasn't enough. "Ma'am my sister would kill me if she knew I even had these with me, much less, giving them to someone else. I just don't know if I can do it. I understand your predicament, but I just don't know."

Quickly she said, "How about a thousand dollars? Would that be enough?"

"Well, that's a hard offer to turn down. How about this? One thousand dollars and the address of where she's living right now."

"That's a deal. I'll work on getting the address tonight. I think the area where she stays with her Mom is called Lancaster Fields. It's a little subdivision on the south side of town. She drives a silver Honda Accord. Where can I get in touch with you or where can I call to give you the address as soon as I get it?"

"Ma'am, why don't you just give me your number and extension at the bank, and I'll just call you in the morning?"

She nodded affirmatively and pulled a card out of her purse. "Well, what about the pictures, if I write you a check now, can I have them?"

Sanchez quickly said, "No, checks could be incriminating. We'll just wait here. You can use your ATM card and bring us the cash."

"If I promise to get you the address tomorrow, will you

give me the pictures tonight when I get back with the money?"

"Sure, I trust you. I know how important it is to you to help your friend. I'll call you sometime after your morning break for the address."

As Andrea drove away, she began to suspect that either Juan, or the man called Lee, might have more of a personal interest in Deborah than what they were sharing. Either way it didn't matter to her. As soon as she returned with the money, she would have the pictures. And if Deborah knew what was good for her, she would leave town and spare everyone the embarrassment.

Chapter Fifteen

The Plan

ॐ ॐ

As soon as Andrea drove off, Tommie Lee remarked, "You know, I didn't like the idea of getting anyone else involved but this is going to be the perfect alibi. Everyone is going to think the bitch left town and disappeared because of the pictures. We're just going to have to be real careful to not leave any evidence. I think we need to be ready to just throw her in the trunk and get her out of town before we get rid of her. We'll have to make sure we give Andrea some advice on how to handle those photographs when she gets back with the money. And if Debbie gets a call about those pictures, she'll know I'm close. That will get her running scared."

Sanchez laughed and said, "Right boss, let's make sure Andrea tells everybody that she hired a private investigator because she was concerned about that guy and his kids, and he turned up with the photographs."

Tommie Lee lit a cigarette, feeling a whole lot more relaxed now that the plan was coming together. "Sounds good." Give me that map we picked up today. I think we'll need to take a trip to Lancaster Heights tonight.

Twenty minutes later, Andrea returned with the money. Immediately Sanchez began to coach her, "The first thing you need to do is call Debbie and let her know you have the pictures. Tell her you hired a private investigator because of your concern for Daniel and the kids. Tell her if she leaves town and disappears you won't show them to her boyfriend; but, if she doesn't, he'll not only see them, you'll post them on the internet and make sure all of her new church friends have the opportunity to see them."

Andrea was getting more excited. She just knew this was what was going to help Daniel see just how much she loved him. She knew that "Miss Goodie Two Shoes" wouldn't be able to stand the heat of her past. She couldn't believe that Deborah had the nerve to throw herself on a good man like Daniel. Andrea could hardly wait to get home to make that call. Her only problem was getting Deborah's cell phone number; she knew calling Daniel or Anne would be trouble. Then she thought of the Mitchells, they would have it. She could express concern about Deborah being out today and see if she could get it that way. She hurriedly said goodbye to Lee and Juan, promising to have Deborah's address for them the next day. I can get that from the Mitchells, too, she thought triumphantly.

Tommie Lee and Sanchez picked up some beer and headed back to their motel room. They decided that it would be best to wait until dark before exploring Debbie's neighborhood. Craving crystal meth, the two got high and discussed their good fortune of running into Andrea at the bank that morning. It seemed like days ago. Tommie Lee just loved when a plan came together.

Pastor Mark arrived at Deborah's house in record time. When he knocked on the door, identifying himself first, she opened it with the chain still in place. When she saw it was him, she opened the door and fell into his arms weeping. "Pastor Mark, I'm so scared. Help me!"

He held her and prayed until she began to calm down. "Deborah, I understand your fear and concern for everyone's well-being, but we have to make sure we follow God's leading in this. I need you to trust me, okay?"

Her eyes still filled with fear, she nodded apprehensively and said, "I'm trying."

"Okay, here's what I need you to do quickly. Pack an overnight bag and enough clothes for a few days. Where's your Mom?"

"She's staying with a lady who's dying," Deborah told him. "I really don't want to scare her."

"Will she be coming home tonight?" he asked.

"I don't think so."

"Okay, first things first, get what you need and let's get you out of this house," Pastor Mark ordered. "I need to call Christina," he said as he dialed the phone. "Honey, I'm here with Deborah, she's fine but I felt the Lord said that I was supposed to bring her home with us for right now and then He would show us the next step. Are you okay with that?"

"I was just getting ready to call you, I was feeling the same thing," she explained. "I called Mom and she's praying, too. I've already freshened up the guest room."

He hung up thankful for the wife God had given him. The next call he made was to Lydia and Joyce; he explained the first step of the plan.

Relieved that there was a plan in motion, Lydia said, "I'm so glad to hear she's okay. We might be going overboard, but it's better to have her protected than to be sorry later. Please keep us posted. We'll continue praying."

As she came out with her things, Pastor Mark told Deborah, "I feel like we're supposed to put your car in the garage. Can I have the keys?" Deborah dug them out of her bag and handed them to the Pastor. As he walked toward the garage he told her, "You wait here until I'm done. Write your Mom a note and let her know you're spending the night with us just in case she comes home."

Deborah was feeling a whole lot calmer; it felt good to have Pastor Mark step in and take charge. She remembered her ungodly belief, "You can't trust anyone." Well, this was surely a test. She said her new Godly belief out loud, "I can trust the Lord to give me discernment and wisdom on who I can trust and to what degree. He will never fail me."

They slipped out of the house quickly, throwing her things in the back seat. "I just want you to rest a bit, and we'll talk more when we get to the house," Pastor Mark said as he turned the worship music up just a bit. As he drove towards the house, he continued to pray softly in the spirit, wondering what the next step was going to be.

After the phone call with Pastor Harrison, Joyce asked Lydia, "Do you have a little while longer? I need to tell you something."

Lydia sensed it was important, "What's going on?" she asked.

Joyce proceeded to tell Lydia about her early morning phone call with Bill.

Lydia said, "I can't believe you held that all day. I'm so sorry I wasn't more sensitive."

Joyce said, "Well, a couple times it was a little hard. This has ruled my life for so long I just wasn't going to let it affect our work today. I really don't know what I should do. I think I should talk to Pastor Rick, too."

"That's a good idea. I'm pretty close to this, too. You know that God's given me a heart to pray for Bill. I guess I've ministered to so many men trapped in the prison of sexual addiction that it's given me compassion for them. I've even counseled guys who talked about castration if it would help them and others that truly wanted to pluck their own eyes out. Lust is a cruel master, and it destroys so many lives, but that's neither here nor there. The main thing right now is, are you supposed to see Bill? I'll pray, but I think this one is going to have to come from your own heart."

As Joyce left His House, she was glad that Lydia had used wisdom related Bill. She didn't know how she would have responded if Lydia had adamantly said that it was God and that she had to see Bill. She would call Pastor Rick the first thing in the morning. Tonight she was going to get some rest. It had been a draining day. She was thankful that Deborah was safe in Pastor Mark's hands.

The Enemy had to make plans of his own. How was he going to get Deborah out of Pastor Mark's grasp and into the hands of Tommie Lee and Sanchez? It would take something special. It was one thing for Deborah and the whole church to suffer fear and embarrassment. However, because he knew the plans God had for Deborah's life, he wanted her dead even more than Tommie Lee and the Renegades. He had to put a stop to everything now before she fully understood her destiny. Before it hadn't mattered-she had been too weak even as a Christian to do much damage to his kingdom. Now she was starting to become a danger to him. Previously, it wouldn't have been hard to cause her to backslide. She had caught him off-guard by going to that ministry in Florida; how he hated that place and every other place just like it! It was bad enough when people got saved, but then when they got free it was a whole other story. He surveyed the battle scene over Deerfield. They still had a chance. He dispatched several more demons of deception to Andrea's home just to insure that she didn't come to her senses as he calculated his next move.

Chapter Sixteen

The Threat

ॐ ॐ

As she drove home that evening, Lydia wondered what decision Joyce was going to make. She had never met Bill, but had prayed a great deal for him. She hoped that the Lord would make the answer clear to her friend.

It had been a long day. At least she and Joyce had finished up Theresa's paperwork while they had waited on Pastor Mark's call. He seemed like such a nice man. So many times the women had ministered to wounded sheep and had to send them back to environments where there was very little care. So many shepherds were incredibly hurt and wounded themselves, and they weren't really equipped or interested in doing more than building a church of numbers, regardless of the condition of their sheep. Lydia caught herself before she went any further. There was a fine line between honestly evaluating the situation and moving into judgment against other ministers. It was just hard sometimes to see the true condition of God's sheep and knowing that, in most churches, very little was being done about it.

She began to pray, "Lord, I pray that you would give your people shepherds after your own heart. Open their eyes so that they can see the wounds of your people. I pray that they would no longer heal the wounds of your daughter slightly as you said in Jeremiah, but that they would seek to heal people deeply and completely. Thank you for those like Pastor Mark and Pastor Rick who bring life and hope into the Body of Christ."

As she pulled into her driveway, she saw that Stephen was already home. She smelled something cooking as she walked into the house. Her husband was already preparing dinner—it was an unexpected surprise, but one she needed after a day like today.

After supper Deborah and Christina cleaned up the dishes. The children were off doing their homework and Pastor Mark was back in the study working on his message. Everything seemed so normal, it was almost surreal.

Deborah couldn't believe how much better she was feeling after everything she had been through that day. The Harrison's house was warm and inviting. She had called her mother to let her know where she was. She could tell her mother was preoccupied-Mrs. Simpson's entire family had traveled in to be with her in these last hours. She told Deborah that she definitely planned on spending the night and wasn't sure when she would be home. Deborah was relieved as she hung up the phone. Her mother hadn't asked any questions.

The grown-ups had decided to talk and pray more about Deborah's situation after the children were in bed. After the kitchen clean-up, Christina went into the family room to help the children with school work and Deborah went to the guest room. She had a message from Daniel on her phone. Earlier, she had been too emotional to answer the phone. Now, she knew it was probably time to return the call, but she still wasn't ready to tell him what was happening and she knew she couldn't lie.

Deborah sat looking at the phone for several minutes before finally dialing Daniel's number. Pastor Mark had left it up to her to decide how much information she shared with

Daniel right now. He had just said, "Deborah, I trust the God in you and know you'll use wisdom and discernment when you talk to Daniel. I just pray you won't be motivated by fear."

Deborah dialed and was relieved to hear Daniel's voice mail. "He must be helping the kids with their homework," she thought. She tried to keep her voice from quivering as she left the message. "Hi, honey. Give me a call later. I'm over at Pastor Mark's and Christina's for some fellowship and ministry. Mom wasn't going to be home tonight, and they've asked me to spend the night. I just might take them up on it." She tried to sound light but wasn't sure how effective she had been. Daniel was very good at sensing when something was going on with her. But for right now, she didn't want to worry him-not until she had been able to discuss her strategy with Pastor Mark and Christina.

Suddenly her cell phone rang. She almost answered without checking the number, sure that it was Daniel returning her call. Something stopped her. She didn't recognize the number on the caller ID so she just let it ring. A few moments later she was alerted that she had a message. When she dialed her voicemail she heard Andrea asking. "Hi, Deborah, do you know who this is?" It continued on for another minute.

Tommie Lee and Sanchez were flying high from all the crystal meth. The Enemy wanted them totally out of their natural minds so that he could completely take them over. Tonight was not a night for a conscious. He didn't want anything to stand in the way of his plans.

The men finally made it out to the old Chevy and decided to start looking for Lancaster Fields. Sanchez was ready to get back to his old lady and hoped this would be the night to finish the job. They cruised down the highway laughing and sharing exploits from the past, each trying to outdo the other by bragging about how "bad" they really were. At one point Tommie Lee patted the photographs of Deborah which were still in his pocket, "I can't believe we made a thousand dollars today with these. Wait till the guys here this one!"

Sanchez chuckled, "I told you, man, just leave it to me. I had that chick eating out of my hands. I'd still like to pay her a little visit before we leave." This subject had already been discussed.

Tommie Lee quickly responded, "You promised! Don't even think about it! No evidence, no crime. I'm not going back to the joint over this one. Don't even think about screwing this up on me! Right now, it's nice and easy. Everyone will think Debbie left town because of that bitch's little blackmail scheme. Just don't let me forget to have Debbie write her goodbye note for everyone. Man, what a great alibi."

After hanging up the phone, Deborah felt like she was going to throw up for the second time that day. Now she was experiencing even greater panic than she had felt that morning. The voicemail message had made it quite clear that Andrea had, and was ready to show everyone, the pictures of her from the past to Daniel. She even threatened to put them on the internet for the whole church to see unless Deborah left town. Hearing Andrea's syrupy, sweet voice, as she described the photographs in detail, gave Deborah chills up and down her spine. What scared her even more was that she really didn't believe Andrea had got them through a private investigator. Tommie Lee was the only person Deborah knew who would have had access to them. Did this mean he was already in town? But how on earth could Andrea have ever gotten hooked up with him? Without a doubt, Deborah knew she had to get out of town immediately!

Not wanting Pastor Mark or Christina to try and stop her, Deborah called for a cab to meet her at a convenience store down the road. She hated running away but she was going to have to just slip out and go for it. She was convinced it was best for everybody, but how could this have happened? Twenty minutes ago she really had thought everything was going to be okay. She quickly got her things together and listened by the door.

Everything was quiet as Deborah slipped out to take a look around. The children and Christina were all in the family room, and Pastor Mark was nowhere to be seen. Quietly, she picked up her belongings and made her way to the front door. Within moments she was outside felling empty and lost as she walked away from the environment that had felt so safe and secure. The night air was even colder than she thought it would be. She knew she needed to hurry to catch the cab. It wouldn't be long until Pastor Mark and Christina would be putting the children too bed. She started slowly jogging down the road.

That evening Bill called his counselor. "Well, I called her but I didn't get much of a response. She said that she would pray and let me know. I don't think the chances are very likely."

"At least you did the right thing and made the call," Evan responded. "You sound a bit discouraged. What did you expect?" Bill and his counselor had been working a great deal on the unrealistic expectations that addicts have with themselves and others.

Slowly Bill said, "You're right, I hear you. She just sounded so cold. I guess even if she did see me she would never believe I've changed anyway."

Evan nailed him again, "There you go from unrealistic expectations to hopelessness. Remember, there's something in between."

"Yeah, I know, realistic faith. It's just so much easier to say than to do," Bill admitted. They talked for several more minutes and then Bill asked Evan if he would pray for him. Evan prayed that if it was the time for Bill to repent to Joyce, the Lord would speak to her heart and she would agree to see him. It was a heartfelt prayer. Both men knew that it would be a big step in Bill's own healing process if he could face Joyce and truly repent for his unfaithfulness, and do it without placing any hopes or expectations on Joyce. Over the past six months, Evan had come to really care about the man who had come to him for help. He had overcome sexual addiction in his own life and was now helping others like Bill get free. It had become his passion.

Chapter Seventeen

The Discovery

ॐ ॐ

Tommie Lee and Sanchez eventually found the entrance to Lancaster Fields. It was a zero lot line subdivision where the yards were all neatly manicured. Most of the houses looked pretty much the same. They were small, charming Victorians all painted a different pastel color. They cruised slowly up and down the streets, trying not to look to suspicious. The old, green Chevy already looked out of place in this quaint little suburb.

"Keep driving, I want to cover every inch of this neighborhood," Tommie Lee said to Sanchez.

"Maybe, she's just not home yet," Sanchez said. "She's probably out with her boyfriend."

With that Tommie Lee slapped him on the back of the head, "Shut up and drive!" Sanchez realized that he had hit a vein of jealousy in Tommie Lee, but didn't say a word.

Sanchez wondered if Tommie Lee was just full of hot air. "This better not be a wild goose chase," he thought to himself, "I came up here for some action." They continued to drive slowly up and down the neighborhood looking for the silver Accord Andrea had told them about earlier that evening.

Nearly twenty minutes had gone by. Frustrated, Tommie Lee snapped angrily, "Let's get out of here. If we drive around anymore people are going to start noticing. His mood had turned ugly ever since Sanchez had made the comment about Debbie and her boyfriend. "I need a bottle," Tommie Lee said. "I'm tired of drinking beer. Find a liquor store."

Sanchez, regretting that he had opened his mouth earlier, decided to keep it shut now. Obediently making his way down the street, he made a right turn and headed silently back to the subdivisions main entrance. He knew he couldn't say anything; it was one thing to get high, another to get wasted. He hoped Tommie Lee would come to his senses. If he got drunk tonight, they could miss their opportunity to nab Debbie. He drove slowly hoping the man would come to his senses.

Because of his time in prison, Tommie Lee's normal ability to handle drugs and alcohol had diminished. He was already more messed up than Sanchez knew, and now a blind rage was coming over him. "Pull in over there. You almost drove right by it, you stupid idiot. Go in and get me a bottle of Jack Daniels," he ordered Sanchez as he opened the passenger side door. "What are you looking at? I'm going to drive. Now get me the damn bottle!" he barked at Sanchez.

Lydia spent the evening updating Stephen on the events of the day. They prayed for Deborah's safety, as well as for the decision Joyce was going to be making concerning Bill.

"I don't know what's going on," she told her husband. "Earlier I was feeling pretty peaceful about everything, but now I'm starting to feel uneasy. I think I'll just give Deborah a quick call and see how she's doing. Is that okay, honey?" she asked Stephen.

"Sure, I've got to write out some bills tonight anyway. He knew his wife well enough to know that if she didn't have peace, it would be hard for her to just go to bed. It would be better for her to call Deborah and find out if everything was okay.

Lydia dialed Deborah's number; it rang several times and then went to voicemail. Sitting in the back seat of the taxi, Deborah said softly to herself, "Sorry, Lydia," as she saw the name and number on the screen. She just couldn't take the chance of answering the phone now. She also knew it probably wouldn't be long before the Harrisons discovered she was gone. They were such precious people—she hated putting them through all this. She was going to have to live with the fact that by running, she would be a terrible impression. She hated it, but it was still better than the hurt and embarrassment those pictures could cause Daniel and the whole church.

Daniel finished tucking Aimee and David into bed. Afterwards, he went to call Deborah. He really had missed her today and was looking forward to chatting with her. There was only one message and he decided to get it out of the way. When he heard Deborah's voice, it made him feel good that she had actually called him. Most of the time, she left the initiating up to him. It had to mean she was getting more comfortable with him.

Even though Daniel thought it was a bit strange, he was glad that Deborah was spending the night over at the Harrisons. It still worried him though; it just didn't seem like Deborah. He hit speed dial only to get her voicemail. "Deborah, it's me returning your call. I'll be up for a while, please call before you go to bed. I really missed you today." "Maybe they're having a time of ministry," he thought as he hung up the phone. He grabbed his briefcase and pulled a couple of files out that needed reviewing before tomorrow and started reading.

Christina knocked softly on the guest bedroom door but there was no answer from Deborah. She went into the study and said to Mark, "I think she must have fallen asleep, she's not answering the door. Should I just let her rest a little while longer? She's got to be exhausted from today."

Still preoccupied, Pastor Mark nodded. He was glad for the extra time to finish his message. "Let's give her thirty more minutes. I should be finished by then."

Christina slipped out of the study and went to the laundry room to fold another load of clothes. She wondered how long Deborah would end up staying with them. It really didn't matter, but for Deborah's sake, she hoped this would all blow over quickly. She had to remember to call her mother in the morning and let her know everything was okay. Christina was so thankful that her parents had instilled faith in her as a child. She thought about how hard it must be for Deborah to believe when so much of her childhood was so contrary to God's heart and Spirit. Deborah had shared enough testimony with her to give Christina compassion for the young woman. She had been through an awful lot, but it was so exciting to see the love that had sprung up between Daniel and Deborah. Christina could hardly wait to start planning the wedding. In some ways, it reminded her of the story of Hosea. She was just glad that they didn't have to worry about Deborah being unfaithful at this point, unlike the prostitute the Lord had called Hosea to marry.

She thought about the first time she had ever read that book of Hosea. The prophetic picture of God's unfailing love for an unfaithful people had touched her heart immensely. Deborah had shared enough of her testimony to give Christina compassion for her. Many times, Christina had reminded herself of Hosea's story when she was just about to give up on someone; it would always help her to reach out one more time.

"Deborah," Christina called softly and knocked on the door. There was still no answer. She knew they needed to talk tonight and decided to check the door. It was unlocked, and she gently pushed it opened. "Deborah, it's me, wake up, honey."

The room was quite dark and she walked carefully to the bedside table to turn on the small lamp. She had decided that the overhead light might be a shock to Deborah. Instead, she was the one who was shocked when she discovered an empty bed.

Deborah was nowhere to be found!

REDEEMED

Chapter Eighteen

The Notes

ॐ ॐ

Frantically, Deborah packed her car. She was so thankful that her mother wasn't home tonight. When she was finished, she sat down at her mother's little desk in the corner of the living room to write four notes. As she wrote the first one, tears streamed down her face:

Dear Daniel,

I am so sorry to do this to you again. I know you probably won't understand, but I am leaving town for your sake. You and the children deserve much more than I can ever be. I really thought I could walk away from my past, but it has found me once again. I know this might be hard for you to understand at this point, but I'm asking you to trust me in this. I know it's better and safer for everyone.

I will always treasure the time we have had together. Thank you for always loving me. Please don't try to find me, just let me go in peace. I know this will be hard to explain to David and Aimee, but I know in the long run, it will be better for them. I will always love you. - Deborah

As she wrote, Deborah remembered the first time she left

home after graduation. That time had been easy. She had been angry at everybody. Her heart had been hardened and there were no ties. This time, her pain was so great she could hardly stand it. And to make matters worse, she kept seeing the vision of herself walking down the aisle of the church in a wedding dress with Daniel standing at the altar. It was the same vision that she had had as she returned from the ministry in Palm City. Now it seemed like a cruel joke, taunting her with a promise that would never be fulfilled. As she continued trying to write the next note to her mother, tears stained the paper. Their relationship had been growing over the past six months and Deborah knew this was going to be painful for her mother, as well. Hurting her again was the last thing Deborah wanted to do, but there seemed to be no other choice.

After finding Deborah gone, Pastor Mark immediately jumped into his car to try and find her. Christina searched the yard just in case she might have gone out for some fresh air, but to no avail. Deborah had vanished. Christina started praying fervently as she went back inside. "Lord, please protect Deborah and Mark. Give Mark wisdom on what he should do. Show him where Deborah is right now. Help us Lord!" She continued pacing and praying in the Spirit.

As Pastor Mark drove towards town, he scanned the sides of the road looking for any trace of Deborah. He was going to call her, but felt a check in the Spirit; it might just alert her and make her more difficult to find. He wondered what on earth could have happened to make her run like this. Praying as he drove, he saw a picture in his mind of Deborah packing her car and suddenly felt an urgency to call Daniel. He picked up his cell phone and called Christina to get Daniel's number out of the church directory. Christina's heart leapt as the phone rang, maybe he had found her.

On the other end, Mark requested, "Christina, I need

Daniel's number. I feel like the Lord wants me to call him. I know Deborah didn't want to involve him, but he lives much closer than us and can get to her mother's house quicker than I can."

Christina ran to get the church directory and gave her husband the number. She was feeling the same fear she had felt earlier today, "Please be careful, Mark. Call me when you get there." Pastor Mark hung up quickly and dialed Daniel's number, hoping he would answer quickly.

Liberty had just crawled into bed when the unction to pray came upon her. She had already said her goodnight to the Lord and was a little bit surprised as she began to pray in the Holy Spirit. "What's up Father?" she asked the Lord. "Where is the mission tonight?" She had truly loved all the years of intercession, feeling like a secret agent for her heavenly Father. Suddenly Deborah came to her mind. "Oh, no, you don't, Satan," she prayed, "that girl has come too far and I have prayed too many years for her for you mess up God's plan for her life. Lord, send your warring angels to Deborah where ever she is right now. Let no harm befall her, let no weapon formed against her prosper."

Liberty grabbed her little notebook from the bedside and wrote down the time and the day: October 23, 9:45 p.m. – prayer for Deborah. It would be interesting to find out from Deborah the next time they talked what had been happening. Of course many times when an intercessor did her job, people weren't even aware of the things that had averted by the power of prayer. Deborah might not even have a clue what was going on. Still, she wrestled with the Enemy earnestly in prayer.

Deborah had finished her notes to her mother, Pastor Mark, and Lydia and Joyce when suddenly she thought of her

Aunt Liberty and Anne. She couldn't even consider not writing a note to them; she reached for more paper. She knew that she needed to get on the road and this process was gut-wrenching, but she had to honor the people who had helped her so much through this time. In her note to her mother she had asked her to contact the Mitchells at the travel agency. She really hated leaving them like this.

This past year had been a taste of the goodness of the Lord's redemption and Deborah was thankful as she wrote. Some people never experience in a lifetime the love and support she had received from all of these people in such a short while. And there were others, but she knew that there wasn't time for any more notes. Deborah prayed that the Lord would give them all understanding and that they would be able to forgive her for leaving. She wished that she would have known that this weekend would have been the last time that she would ever see them again. She tried to fight back the tears, praying that the Lord would forgive her, too. What a mess she had made of everything!

Suddenly her phone rang. Thinking it was probably Daniel, she let it go to voicemail again. She just couldn't talk to him now. But glancing at the number, she saw it was another call from Andrea. She quickly redialed her only to get Andrea's answering machine. "Don't worry, Andrea, I'm leaving town tonight, and I'm begging you, not for myself, but for Daniel, my mother and the church, please destroy those pictures. I promise, I'll never return to Deerfield again. Just please destroy the pictures." As she hung up the phone, Deborah started getting angry with herself. How had she been so stupid to pose in those photographs for Tommie Lee? She had been so under his control and the influence of drugs. She cried out, "Oh God, forgive me, forgive me of my sins!"

The still, small voice in her heart said, "I have my daughter, I have. You are My redeemed. I have bought you with a price. Do not run daughter, stand still and see My salvation."

The Enemy was ready. As Deborah thought for a moment about what she had just heard from the Lord, he brought a picture to her mind. It was similar to the vision that she had remembered earlier. This time, though, she was naked, walking down the aisle of the church with everyone pointing and laughing. The feelings of humiliation and embarrassment were overwhelming. The picture totally removed any thought of trying to stay and work things out.

———————

Daniel had fallen asleep when Pastor Mark's phone call woke him. "Daniel, this is Pastor Mark. I hate to call you like this, but it's Deborah. I need your help."

Thinking that Deborah was still at their home, Daniel replied, "Sure, Pastor, what can I do."

"Deborah's in danger. I need you to drive straight to her house. Tommie Lee is out of prison. He may be in the area. I'll tell you more later. Daniel, do you have a gun?"

Daniel hesitated and then remembered his hunting rifle, "Yes, I do. Is it that serious?"

"I'm afraid it might be. I feel an urgency in my spirit. Go quickly Daniel, I'll be there shortly and explain more."

Daniel dialed the neighbors as he went to the locked closet where he kept his hunting rifle. "Hi, Mrs. Burke, is Missy there? I'm sorry to bother you but this is an emergency. I'll explain later. I need her to come and sit with the kids. She can sleep in Aimee's room. I don't know when I'll be home."

Missy's mom was surprised and concerned. "Yes, Missy will be right over. Is there anything we can do, Daniel?

"No, Ma'am, not right now. Just pray. I'll explain more later. Tell Missy, I'll pay her double time."

"You don't have to do that Daniel," she said but then realized he had already hung up. She wondered what on earth was going on as she went upstairs to get Missy.

From Missy's bedroom window Mrs. Burke could see

Daniel walk to his car with a rifle in hand. Not wanting to alarm her daughter, she knew better than to say anything; but, she continued to wonder what on earth could be going on at this time of night.

Chapter Nineteen

Prepared for Battle

ॐ ॐ

Sanchez had never seen Tommie Lee like this. He had finished off almost half a bottle of Jack Daniels. The car was weaving back and forth and, despite Sanchez's protest, Tommie Lee insisted on driving. "Let's just go back to the hotel, man," Sanchez suggested. "You're wasted. We can take care of this business, tomorrow."

Slurring his words, Tommie Lee refused, "No way. She has to come home sometime, and I'm going to be waiting when she does."

"At least let me drive. You're going to get us pulled over."

"Just shut the hell up. I'm getting sick of your whining." With one hand on the wheel he pulled a blade out of his boot that Sanchez did not know he had. The blade glistened as they drove under a street light.

"Take it easy, man, take it easy. I was just trying to help," Sanchez said trying to calm him down. All he needed was for Tommie Lee to go loco on him now. He reached for the radio for distraction and tried to find an Oldies station that Tommie Lee seemed to enjoy.

Within a few minutes, they were back in Lancaster Fields

once again cruising up and down the streets looking for the silver Accord. The small homes only had one car garages, but Sanchez said, "Maybe she's already home and her car is in the garage."

Tommie Lee responded, "No, she would let her Mom park in the garage and she would park in the drive. I know Debbie." Not wanting to get the man upset again, Sanchez just kept his mouth shut and scanned the homes as they drove up and down the streets. He didn't feel good about being there again like this. It was the kind of neighborhood where people watched out for each other; and, if things looked suspicious, they were the type of people to call the cops. This was the kind of area where if you had to do business, you did it quickly and got out fast. He reached for another cigarette and resigned himself to the fact that it was probably going to be a long night.

Meanwhile, there was another mother down on her knees praying. She was crying out for her son. In her arms, she held a picture. It was a photograph of Sanchez when he was eight-it had been taken right before his father died.

Over Deerfield, the spiritual battle continued to rage. Demons were falling from the sky like lightning, just as Jesus had shared with his disciples years ago. The prayers of the saints were going forth empowering the Army of God. Jesus personally surveyed the battlefield with satisfaction. A Man of War, Jesus took great delight in bringing defeat to the Enemy's plans and purposes. He, Himself, continued to make intercession on behalf of Deborah and those engaged in the warfare. Within the midst of it all, His agenda was not just to protect Deborah, but to add to the Kingdom of God. He heard the cries of a mother's heart and wept with her, crying out to the Father to turn the heart of her little boy.

Daniel raced to Deborah's mother's house. He was wide

awake now. He hoped that Pastor Mark might be overreacting but the man was pretty level headed. He couldn't believe Deborah hadn't told him what was happening. No wonder she had been at the Pastor's home this evening. It hurt that she hadn't reached out to him first, but right now all he wanted to know was that she was okay. He hated to alarm his sister, Anne, but she was one of the best prayer warriors he knew. He hit number two on his phone.

"Hi, Daniel, what's up?" Anne wondered. "It's awful late. You didn't propose tonight did you?"

"No, Anne, but I just got a call from Pastor Mark. He's on his way to Deborah's and so am I. Tommie Lee is out of prison, they think he might be in the area. Anne, he asked me to bring a gun. I don't have any more details, but please pray. Pray for all of us."

Anne could hear the fear in her brother's voice, immediately she said, "Daniel, God has not given you a spirit of fear, but of power, love, and a strong mind. I will continue to pray. Drive safely!" She hung up the phone, not wanting to believe what she had just heard. She, probably more than anyone, knew how much Deborah had been controlled by Tommie Lee and how much she had feared him. Her only comfort had been that he was still in prison and did not know where she was. Anne wondered how he could have found out where Deborah was living. "Robert, Robert," she called upstairs, "That was Daniel on the phone. Honey, we have to pray!"

Hearing the urgency in her voice, he quickly made his way downstairs. Anne gave him the limited amount of information she had received, and they both began to cry out in prayer. In a few minutes, Robert began to sing a song of the Lord; about Him being a mighty Man of War, ready for battle, victorious and glorious. The song energized Anne and gave her a sense of peace that the Lord was truly in control.

———————————

Deborah had completed her notes and took one last look around the house she had shared with her mother. "Lord, why did you give me a taste of the goodness of life just to rip it all away?" Heaven was again silent.

Thoughtfully, she took her house key off her ring and put it on the table. No sense in her mother having to have another one made. As she walked over to the table, she saw a car drive slowly by. Somehow it didn't look like it belonged in the neighborhood. It was older and much bigger than most of the smaller, gas efficient cars used by the retirees in Lancaster Fields. Deborah felt a cold chill wash over her. It was the same sort of feeling she experienced on Friday, a sense of great evil. It still seemed unreal that there was a possibility that Tommie Lee was patrolling the streets of her neighborhood. Within minutes the car had passed. "It must have been someone visiting down the street," she thought to herself. She shut off several lights, leaving a smaller lamp on and turning on the light out front. She didn't want to leave the whole house dark with no one at home.

Deborah walked through the kitchen and out the side door to the garage. There, her car was awaiting her packed up with some of her things. She had instructed her mother to give the rest of her things away. Once again she would be starting over, but this time she had no idea where or how. She hit the garage door opener and began to back slowly out into the driveway.

———————

As the high praises of God began to hit the camp of the Enemy, demons were being bound. Yet the skies were still full as a fresh wave of evil forces flooded the skies over Deerfield. The Commander of the Armies of the Lord, said, "Michael, it is time. My army has been assembled."

Michael bowed before his Lord in humble salute. He drew his sword from its golden sheath, "I am ready, my Lord." The handle of the sword was encrusted with jewels and the blade was of heavenly material. Laser beams of light burst from the two-edged sword with every movement the warrior angel made. In times of old, Michael and Lucifer had warred together. Back then they had been on the same side. He still couldn't believe that Lucifer's pride had risen to such heights that he would dare to confront the Ruler of all Rulers, the Lord of Heaven and Earth. From heaven he had watched his old friend being expelled out of the heavenlies; Lucifer had been cast down to earth. Not one to question his Lord, Michael had never asked why Satan hadn't been sent straight to the abyss. The only thing he could figure out was that God wanted to humble him further my making him subject to humans. If only they would realize the fullness of their power, this war could soon be over. The sooner the kingdoms of the world became the Kingdom of the Lord's, the better it would be for everyone, including himself. Yes, he knew the fallen angel well; he was crafty and an experienced warrior. Michael did not take his assignment lightly. He wondered what human had created such a stir in heaven.

As he left heaven, Michael heard the sound of a great roar. The Lion of Judah had spoken. It was a roar that shook heaven and earth in the spiritual realm; a roar that could even make Lucifer freeze in his tracks. As Michael made his way to the battlefield called Earth, the roar continued to reverberate throughout the heavenlies.

REDEEMED

Chapter Twenty

Surprise Attack

Before Deborah pulled all the way out of the drive, she realized that she still had the garage door opener in her car. She shifted into park and decided to leave the opener in the garage and run underneath the door before it closed. She didn't want to leave it anywhere outside where it might be misplaced.

What she didn't see was the dark green Chevy that had just turned the corner. Tommie Lee saw the car first, "There it is-the one with the garage open. Is she coming or going?"

Alert now, Sanchez saw what Tommie Lee was talking about. Sure enough, there was the silver Accord they had been looking for all night. The headlights were still on but it didn't look like anyone was in the car. "Back up before she sees us," he said to Tommie Lee. Easing the car into reverse, Tommie Lee pulled around the corner. Sanchez was already half-way out of the car before it stopped. He wanted to get her before she got into the house. No telling who else was there.

While in the garage, Deborah remembered a box that her Aunt Liberty had given her of old family pictures. She decided to find it and take it with her. With the car running, she couldn't hear the man as he approached her from behind. Suddenly his arms were around her. She was too scared to even scream, and she had no strength to struggle. He turned her around and she found herself looking into Daniel's penetrating eyes. He put his hand under chin and tilted her face to his. He saw the fear written all over her face. "Deborah, what's going on? Where are you going? Pastor Mark called and said that you might be in danger." He wrapped her in his arms saying, "I'm so sorry I scared you. I'm not mad, Deborah. Just help me understand what's going on here."

Still unable to speak, Deborah was shaking in his arms. Suddenly, Daniel received a blow to the back of his head and fell to the floor. Now, Deborah was looking into the eyes of Satan himself. She pulled back as he grabbed for her.

"Your old man has a message for you: don't make this hard for us, or everyone is going to have to pay," Sanchez told her his eyes shifting to the unconscious man on the floor.

Deborah couldn't believe her eyes as she spied the same car she had seen earlier move slowly down the street and pull into the yard. She saw Tommie Lee's grinning face at the wheel. All she could think of was getting out of the garage fast before he saw Daniel.

She started to walk past Sanchez but he grabbed her arm, "Where you going little lady, please let me escort you." Obviously, she wasn't going to put up a fight.

She walked directly to the car where Tommie Lee was sitting, "What do you want Tommie?" she asked.

"You," he said simply. She couldn't believe the boldness and confidence she was feeling right now. Tommie Lee had always made her cower in fear. Maybe it was that she didn't have anything else to loose. What she didn't see was the two angels standing on either side of her with their swords drawn.

She stood there as the two men discussed their options. "I'll drive her car," Sanchez said.

Deborah responded calmly, "The keys are in the

ignition."

Tommie Lee couldn't believe his eyes, Deborah looked more beautiful than ever. There was something different about her—it was as if she was glowing. It almost scared him to know that she was standing there with no fear of him. He decided that tonight he would have his fill of her and then tomorrow he would turn her over to Sanchez. Sanchez motioned for him to pop open the trunk. Deborah, realizing what was going to happen next, said, "Tommie Lee that's not necessary. Let me ride with you."

He hesitated and Sanchez shook his head, "no." Tommie Lee hit the trunk latch; he just couldn't trust himself or her. Sanchez reached in for the rope. Scanning the neighborhood, he motioned to Deborah to walk towards the back of the car. It had been easier than they thought; she hadn't put up any struggle.

All Deborah could think of was Daniel lying in the garage. She hoped he wasn't dead. She prayed that Tommie Lee would not go near the garage; he seemed to be quite content to sit in the car leering at her. Like a cat with a mouse, he was enjoying toying with his prey.

The prayers of the saints were reaching heaven in unison; Lydia and Joyce had also joined in with the others. They hadn't called or talked to each other, but neither of them could go to bed. The prayer warriors paced and prayed, each feeling alone in their own private battles. Some of them had information; others only had the stirring of the Lord. Each could feel the leading of the Holy Spirit urging them to continue. Whatever was happening was not over yet; the intensity of the battle was increasing.

Deborah's mother had even been alerted. At first she had thought that she was interceding for Mrs. Simpson but then Deborah came to mind. She wasn't quite sure what was happening, but in obedience she began to lift up her daughter in prayer.

Christina found herself bowed over in travail on her living room floor crying out to the Lord to protect her husband. Anne and Robert continued in their warfare praise; wondering why Daniel hadn't called yet, neither one of them were going to stop until they heard from him. Surely he should have been at Deborah's by now. The battle raged as demons smelled the opportunity to spill human blood. That was their purpose—to kill, steal and destroy!

Deborah walked slowly to the back of the car hoping someone would drive by. The neighborhood was so quiet-not even a dog was barking. As she turned towards the trunk she saw Daniel staggering out of the garage. "No, Daniel, run!" she screamed. Sanchez cursed and pulled his gun on Daniel. He hadn't wanted it to come to this. He liked jobs that were nice and clean. This was getting messy. Daniel stopped in his tracks, first looking at Sanchez, and then at Deborah. He felt like he was in a bad dream and just couldn't wake up. His head was killing him and he was so dizzy he could hardly stand up.

Chapter Twenty-One

The Rescue

A demon of mechanical failure had been assigned to Pastor Mark's car; he was having trouble keeping it running. If it wasn't for the angels propelling him forward he would have been left on the side of the road. He hoped Daniel had made it to Deborah's. He didn't want to bother Christina any more than he had to, and he was upset with himself for not getting Daniel's cell phone number when he had called her last.

He decided to dial Deborah's number. Daniel had to be there already-Pastor Mark hoped he had gotten there in time. The phone rang and rang. For whatever reason, Deborah was not answering it. He was relieved to finally see the entrance to Lancaster Fields. It wasn't as far as he had thought.

When Pastor Mark Harrison came around the corner he couldn't believe his eyes. There was a man with a gun trained on Daniel, another man in an old green car, and Deborah standing by an open trunk. He had to think fast. "God what do I do?" he asked. Suddenly he sprang into action. He blew his horn loudly and stepped on the gas. The car which he had been having so much trouble with sprang into action. He raced down the street, and at the last minute, ran through the neighbor's yard ramming the car that Tommie Lee was sitting in. Everyone was thrown off guard. The impact knocked Sanchez off his feet; the gun flew into the air. Deborah had seen him coming and had backed into the street. She was unhurt but still shocked.

In the meantime, Daniel ran towards his car yelling, "Deborah, run to the neighbors and call the police!" By this time lights in the neighborhood were beginning to turn on-the crash had sounded like a small explosion. Pastor Mark's airbag had opened up and he was trying to get out of his car.

Suddenly, Tommie Lee threw the Chevy into reverse, almost running over Deborah as she started for the neighbor's house. The old green car lurched forward and sped down the road. Sanchez came to, but as he opened his eyes a lion roared and put a paw on his chest. He couldn't move; it was as if he was paralyzed. Then the warrior angel, Michael, cast the spirit of murder out of him and sent it into the abyss. The Lord removed the veil between the natural and the spiritual and, for an instant, Sanchez saw a giant of a man with a huge sword in his hand. The angel plunged the sword into him. As he did Sanchez heard a voice, "This night your mother's prayers are answered. From this day forth, you will serve the Lord." A strange peace passed over Sanchez as he lay on the concrete driveway. Maybe he had died. He wasn't sure, but this didn't seem like hell. When the angel's sword of light had passed through him, the darkness had to flee. Suddenly, he began to weep and repent of his sins. The next time he looked up, there was only a man with a hunting rifle standing over him—no lion, no giant man with a sword.

Daniel was as confused as Sanchez as he watched the man who had knocked him out weeping and repenting for his sins. The next thing Daniel knew, Pastor Mark was by his side saying to the man on the pavement, "Son, are you ready to give your life to the Lord?" From the pavement Sanchez nodded. They both helped him to his knees. As Deborah returned from the neighbors, she saw Sanchez giving his life to the Lord in her driveway. As the neighbors came out and surrounded them, they weren't quite sure what had just happened.

Deborah said, "He just got saved," and burst into tears.

Within minutes the police were there taking down information. Sanchez was handcuffed and loaded into the back seat of the police car. They were quite the spectacle: Daniel with his hunting rifle and blood soaked hair, Pastor Mark with bruises on his face from the air bag, the neighbors trying to figure out what had happened, and Deborah trying to explain the whole mess to everyone.

Before the police car pulled away, Pastor Mark asked if he could talk to Sanchez for a minute. "What's your name, son?"

The man still had tears streaming down his face, "Sanchez, sir. I am so sorry for what I've done tonight. Let me tell you where Tommie Lee and I were staying. He might go back for his stuff. It's the least I can do." He proceeded to give Pastor Mark the information.

"I have visiting rights at the county jail. I'll be there next Thursday. I'll try to see you then. Ask them for a Bible," Pastor Mark instructed.

Sanchez nodded. As he did, once again he saw the giant angel standing behind the man, looking very intently at him. Sanchez wanted to prostrate himself and the angel, knowing his thoughts, said, "Don't worship me. Worship the one who created you."

At that moment heaven opened up and Sanchez had a vision of Jesus sitting at the right hand of the Father. He cried out, "Jesus, have mercy on me."

The Lord spoke back to him, "I have. Now, go and sin no more. I have called you to be a witness for me and to win souls for the Kingdom of God. You are now a new creation, born of the Spirit. I have redeemed you for my purposes." Sanchez shook his head. If this was all a dream, it was time to wake up, but somehow he knew it wasn't. These were the kind of things he had heard other ministers talk about as a child growing up in his mother's church, supernatural events that changed the course of one's life. At the time, he had thought they were just full of it. Now, he realized the course of his life had been altered forever. His mother's prayers had been answered. It would be the first phone call he would make.

Tommie Lee raced down the road cursing his bad luck. He hated leaving Sanchez behind but he had panicked. There was no way he was going back to jail. The old Chevy was moaning under the pressure he was putting it through. He made a decision not to go back to the motel, but to head in the opposite direction. There was just a little bit of dope, but that could easily be replaced. He was glad to have the thousand dollars Andrea had given him in exchange for the pictures. He was going to have to figure out how to ditch this car and steal another one. After the crash, there was no telling if the neighbors had seen the car or gotten his tag number. He had to stay calm and not lose his head. He cursed the day he ever met Debbie Lynn Webster. She had brought him nothing but trouble!

The intercessors felt the battle turn but knew it wasn't quite over yet. Even though the Enemy had tried to put a spirit of slumber on some of them, they shook it off and continued to pray.

Christina heard the phone ring. She heard her husband's voice on the other end. "Honey, there's been a bit of a situation but we're all okay. I'll explain more when I get home. It still may be a little while yet. We have to fill out a police report."

His wife gasped, "A police report, are you sure you're okay? What about Daniel and Deborah?"

"We're all okay, but keep praying. Tommie Lee is still on the loose. By the way, the car is smashed. Daniel has offered to give me a ride home."

"The car? We're you in an accident?"

She heard someone in the background calling his name. "Pastor Harrison, we need your statement now."

"I'll explain everything, but I have to go now. I love you, Christina. Everything is going to be okay."

Baffled by what had taken place and what she still didn't know, Christina hung up the phone relieved, knowing at least that her husband was okay.

Chapter Twenty-Two

The Proposal

ॐ ॐ

Most of the neighbors had returned to their homes. The tow truck was loading up Pastor Mark's car and the police were finishing with the crime scene and reports.

Deborah's teeth had started chattering from the cold night air and the shock of everything that had just transpired. Daniel opened his trunk and pulled out an extra jacket. He wrapped her in it and then held her tightly. He couldn't believe that he had almost lost her tonight.

He asked Officer Pulowski, "Can I get Deborah in the house? She's freezing out here."

"Sure, we'll be there in a minute to get your statements. Sorry this is taking so long," the officer said apologetically. "This is a little out of the ordinary for our department. Haven't had this much action in a long time."

As Daniel started to walk Deborah towards the house, he heard the Lord say, "Propose, propose now and take away the shame and fear." He shook his head. It was the last thing he would have thought of at this moment. But then he heard the voice again, "Propose." It sure wasn't the romantic evening he had planned, but Daniel had learned to be obedient to the voice of God. All of a sudden he put his hand in his coat pocket. He couldn't believe it—he had forgotten to take the ring out of his coat pocket when he came home from work. He had been so busy with Aimee and David, it had slipped his mind. Only the Lord would have known that he had it with him. It had to be His Voice encouraging him to propose because it would have been the last thing he would have thought of doing at this moment.

Suddenly, he dropped to his knee and took her hand. As he reached into his pocket, Deborah gasped putting her hand to her mouth. Surely he wasn't going to propose now! Not after everything she had put him through tonight.

Pastor Mark was just finishing his statement, when to his amazement, he saw Daniel dropping to one knee amidst the broken glass of the driveway. The flashing police car lights gave the whole scene a surreal look. A hush settle over the area, as everyone stopped to watch the proposal.

Daniel took a deep breath, "I bought your ring today, and I want you to know no matter what happened tonight, I want you to be my wife. Deborah Noble, will you marry me?"

She couldn't believe it. After everything he had been through, knowing that she had been ready to leave town and that Tommie Lee was still on the loose, he was still asking her to marry him. There was no one like him. She heard herself saying, "Yes, Daniel. Yes, I'll marry you." Tears were flowing down her face as she accepted his proposal.

Suddenly, the remaining officers and bystanders started applauding. Deborah pulled Daniel to his feet and they embraced. This had been a night like no other night. She looked down at the ring he had slipped on her finger. It was beautiful and fit perfectly.

Daniel put his arm protectively around her and together they walked into the house. Everyone at the crime scene got back to the business at hand.

———————————

Tommie Lee found a back road that seemed to be heading

south. It had very little traffic, and rather than stopping to find another car, he flew through the night. So far he hadn't seen any sign of the police. They were all just a bunch of small town losers.

He had the window down and began to sober up from the night air. Now he regretted getting drunk. What a mess this night had turned into! What had gotten into him? He pounded the wheel in frustration. He couldn't believe what had just happened. Deborah had not only slipped from his grasp, but he had also run out on Sanchez. That just wouldn't fly with the Renegades. Now all he could do was keep driving.

Once he had Deborah settled inside, Daniel figured he had better call his sister. He dialed Anne's number, "Are you sleeping yet, sis?"

"Sleeping, how could I be sleeping? We've been praying and warring. What on earth has been going on?" Daniel started sharing some of the highlights of the evening's events. Anne could hardly believe her ears. At one point, she interrupted, "Do I need to be there, Daniel? She can't be left alone. Even better, when you're through, bring her over here. I'll get the guest bedroom ready."

Daniel couldn't believe his sister; it was so Anne to have a plan. She was always helping and making sure everyone was okay. He hadn't even thought of where Deborah would stay tonight. His sister was always so practical and so unafraid.

"Sis, you're the best. I'll talk to Deborah and see what she wants to do. This is probably going to take a while. I know where the key is, you and Robert just get some sleep. We also have to make sure Tommie Lee isn't in the area. We can't have him following us anywhere. Pray that he's apprehended soon! He is one evil man."

Suddenly he was interrupted by Officer Pulowski, "I think we've got him. There was an accident out on Highway 24.

They're trying to put the fire out, then we'll know for sure; we hope we've got him. Sounds like there's not much left of the car."

"They may have got him, Sis," Daniel said returning his attention to his sister. "There was a crash. We should know for sure in a little while. I'm sorry, I have to go. They're ready for me now."

Anne was left holding the phone wondering how she was going to explain to Robert everything she had just heard. Everything sounded so bizarre, but thank God everyone was okay. When she returned to their bedroom, Robert had already fallen asleep. She decided not to wake him; he was already sleeping so soundly. Everything had turned out okay and he really needed the rest. She quietly shut the bedroom door and went back out to the kitchen.

She turned on her electric tea pot and reached for her favorite china cup. Robert had purchased it in London for her. She always said that it made the tea taste better. It was gracefully decorated with English wildflowers and gold around the rim. She chose a chamomile tea from her tea box and added a bit of honey to the bottom of the cup. The water heated quickly and in no time she was cuddled up on the couch under her favorite afghan.

She just wanted to digest everything that Daniel had just shared. She also wanted to spend some more time praying about Tommie Lee. She didn't want to take any chances—maybe he had died in the crash, but maybe he was still on the loose. This was serious business and right now all she could do was pray.

Chapter Twenty-Three

The Evidence

క్ర

As the police were taking Daniel's report of the night's events, Pastor Mark found Deborah in the living room. "Deborah," he said still concerned over her decision to leave with absolutely no discussion, "I'm not mad at you, but what made you leave our house tonight the way you did?"

She hesitated a moment and then said, "This is really hard for me, but I might as well face it. Here listen to this." She reached for her cell phone and pressed the phone number to retrieve her messages and handed him the phone. His surprise, when he heard Andrea's voice, turned into shock when he heard her threaten Deborah with the pictures from her past.

He turned to Deborah and said, "I can hardly believe this. I knew she was desperate but I would have never thought she was capable of this. I am so sorry this happened to you."

Tears of relief began to roll down Deborah's face, she said, "I know I just panicked, but I didn't know what else to do. I just didn't want to hurt anyone anymore." She began to choke up as she said. "Pastor Mark, thank you so much for coming after me." She glanced at Daniel, "There's no telling what might have happened if you hadn't come to our rescue. I'm just so sorry to have caused so much trouble."

Pastor Mark reached out to give her a big hug, "Honey, we love you. You're part of our family, and God loves you. This is just the Enemy working overtime to try and keep you from your destiny. This is not your fault. But I am personally going to have a talk with Andrea and get those pictures from her. We may even have to report this to the police."

Deborah said, "There's actually another message from her. I didn't have time to listen to it. I was packing and just let it go to voice mail."

"Let me listen to it now," Pastor Mark said, "Just don't erase them. I want to keep them as evidence." The voice Pastor Harrison heard on the next phone message had sounded strangely male. The call was threatening, "Get out of town, Deborah, or you're going to get hurt. We've got the pictures, and we've got a gun. If you're not out of town in the next twenty-four hours, you're a dead woman." The record showed that the message had come from Andrea's cell phone. It was the same number that the previous call had come from and the voice sounded somewhat like Andrea's, yet deeper. It sounded like she was trying to distort her voice into that of a man's.

Pastor Harrison tried convincing Deborah to allow the police to listen to the messages; she was still so ashamed about the pictures and really didn't want to talk to the authorities.

When Daniel finished giving his report, he listened to the Andrea's messages as well. He agreed with the pastor that Deborah had no choice but to report this. If there was someone else involved and they were threatening bodily harm, they needed to be apprehended. And if it was Andrea, she had gone way too far. Finally, Deborah succumbed. The police immediately went to work on a warrant for Andrea's arrest. With everything that had transpired this evening, they weren't taking any chances, either.

After it was all over with, Deborah wrote her mother a note saying that she would explain everything the next day. With skid marks in the driveway, tire tracks in the front yard, and police tape marking off the area, it would be somewhat of a shock for her mother to come home and see it all. Deborah hoped that she would be able to contact her first. She just didn't want to disturb the Simpson family tonight.

Deborah decided to take Anne up on her offer to use their guest room. There was no way she wanted to stay at home by herself tonight, and it wouldn't be appropriate to stay at Daniel's. She insisted on taking her car because it was already packed with her things, and she would need it in the morning. Daniel followed her over to Anne and Robert's amazed at how brave she had been through all of this.

Anne was still awake in the living room when she saw the headlights in the driveway. They were finally here. She went to the kitchen and unlocked the back door. Daniel and Deborah were gathering some of her things from the car. After they had made it into the house, she threw her arms around them, "I'm so glad you two are okay."

Daniel had tried to clean up the blood from the cut on his head but his hair was still matted; Anne made him sit down so she could take a look at it. She tried to talk him into going and getting some stitches but he refused. Anne acquiesced and brought out the peroxide and some butterfly bandages and went to doctoring. As Anne worked on his cut, he proceeded to recount the details of what had transpired earlier saving the best part for last, "I proposed tonight and Deborah said, 'yes.'" Daniel told her how it happened. "When I left the house, I had put on the jacket I had worn to work. The ring was still in the pocket. I couldn't believe I had forgotten it there but the Lord reminded me. I heard Him say it was time to propose. So, if you have a problem with it, Sis, you'll just have to take it up with Him."

Anne let out a little scream and then put her hand over her mouth. She gave her brother a big hug just as Deborah walked out of the bedroom. Anne said, "It just wasn't the romantic evening I was imagining at lunch today."

"Me, neither, but it worked and she said yes."

"I'm so excited!" she exclaimed as she went to hug Deborah. "Let me see the ring."

With an awkward smile on her face, Deborah put her hand out for Anne to see. "It was a little unorthodox, but we'll never forget the night we were engaged," she said with a laugh. "You should have seen him, Anne, down on his knees in the middle of everything. The police and rescue crew were still there and they all cheered. It looked like something you would see in the movies."

Anne shared about the intensity she and Robert had felt as they had entered into spiritual warfare. Daniel and Deborah thanked her profusely. It was obvious that the Lord had protected everyone, and the picture of Sanchez confessing his sins and giving his life to the Lord in the middle of it all, was incredible. Now, they all hoped that the next call they received would be the one telling them that Tommie Lee had been apprehended.

By this time, all the events of the night had left Deborah exhausted; and she was ready for bed. Daniel hated having to leave her, but he knew that he needed to get home for Aimee and David. As he put his coat on he told the women, "Now you two ladies have a wedding to plan, but not until we all try to get some sleep. Deborah, call me when you get up." He walked over and gave her a gentle hug. "It's going to be okay, I promise you." Then he laid hands on her and prayed, "Lord, I ask you to remove all trauma of this night and allow my betrothed to sleep peacefully. I pray against all nightmares and torment." He took her hands and looked deep into her eyes, "Today when I bought this ring, I knew I wanted to marry you. But after tonight, I know I'm ready to lay down my life for you, and I don't ever want to think of losing you again."

As Deborah gazed back, she was reminded of the day she had come home and had asked for his forgiveness standing in front of the church. She could see the unconditional love of God pouring out of him now in the same way it had then. She said, "Thank you for being so understanding. I didn't really want to leave, I was so torn. I just didn't want anyone to get hurt. No more running. You don't have to worry anymore. I don't know if you felt it, but I know something happened to me tonight when I confronted Tommie Lee. It was the first time I wasn't' afraid of him. I want you to know whether they catch him or not, I feel free."

Anne watched the scene with tears in her eyes. She was so happy for both her brother and her friend.

As Daniel his left his sister's, he made a decision—a difficult one. His next stop was going to be Andrea's. He had decided to confront her and get those pictures before the police did. He knew it could be considered evidence tampering but at his point, he didn't care. He wasn't going to have them hanging over Deborah's head.

Andrea awoke to someone knocking on her door. Wondering who could be at her door in the middle of the night, she grabbed a robe and headed down the hallway. When she looked through the peep hole, she saw Daniel standing on her step.

She quickly opened the door, "Daniel, what's going…

Interrupting her, Daniel said, "Andrea I'm here for the pictures you have of Deborah, and I'm not playing games. Where are they?"

"What pictures, what are you talking…"

He interrupted again, "Andrea, I'm in no mood. You have no idea what we've been through tonight. I can't believe you would have anything to do with the likes of Tommie Lee. Now hand over the pictures!"

Andrea looked very strange for a moment and then put her head down. When she looked up, the confusion was gone from her eyes. "Okay, but you're a fool, Daniel Worthington. All you have to do is look at those pictures to know she's not the woman for you." When she finally handed him the pictures, Daniel could tell she relished doing it.

Without even looking at them he began to tear them up. "The police know about the phone calls, Andrea. I don't know what's going to happen to you, but I'm warning you, leave Deborah alone."

Andrea was crushed that he hadn't even taken a look at

the pictures. "Daniel, don't leave, can we please talk?" she asked desperately and reached for him.

Daniel looked disgusted and pushed her away. "Andrea, stop already. You need help." He turned and walked out the door. Weeping, Andrea fell on the floor in a crumpled heap.

Chapter Twenty-Four

The Arrest

ॐ ॐ

Christina was waiting up for her husband who arrived home in a police car. She threw her arms around him when he walked through the front door. "Thank God, you're okay. What happened tonight?"

"Let's not wake the kids. I need a quick shower and then I'll tell you everything. Can you fix me a sandwich? I'm starved." Christina quietly went into the kitchen as Mark took his shower. Being a pastor's wife had certainly taught her patience over the years. She was dying to know everything that happened. As he showered, she made him a ham and cheese sandwich and heated it in the toaster oven.

Dawn was breaking when Mark finally finished sharing the details of everything that had happened. Knowing Christina, Mark made sure to tell her everything. She hated having to pull information from him. They held each other tightly thinking about what could have happened tonight. Their bed felt safe and warm. Christina finally said, "Honey, you get some sleep. I'm going to get the kids lunch ready for today and get them off to school. Then I'll come back and join you." Because they lived out in the country, the bus came early. Christina slid out of bed and, within minutes, Mark was fast asleep.

Andrea woke up with a terrible headache. As she was getting ready for work she heard banging on her door. When she went to answer it was she saw two police officers. She opened the door, "Can I help you?"

"Are you Andrea Kline?"

"Yes, I am. What's the problem officer?"

"Ma'am we have a warrant for your arrest." He began to read her rights. As the officer finished, she started to protest, and then he said, "We'll allow you to get dressed, but you'll have to let us in."

Andrea was in shock. It felt like she was in a bad dream. She had no idea what these men were talking about, but they appeared to be dead serious. They followed her as she went into her room to get things to change into, and one of the officers checked the bathroom to make sure there were no windows. They allowed her to get dressed. She quickly brushed her teeth and ran a comb through her hair wondering who she should call for help. This had to be some kind of mistake.

By the next morning, Joyce had made her decision. She was going to see Bill when he was in town. She knew Lydia would probably be shocked, but last night the Lord had given her a dream. It had been a simple one, but it had settled it in her heart.

The dream was about the night Bill had been arrested. In it, he had come home and said, "I need your help." She had seen the Lord standing behind him and beckoning to her. As she moved toward Bill, the Lord was nodding in agreement. She didn't know if they both just needed the closure, or what. But she had made up her mind to trust the Lord in this. He had looked so reassuring in the dream. At least this morning, the pressure and unrest were gone. She felt peaceful and decided to call Bill this morning and let him know her decision.

In his jail cell, Sanchez was just finishing his breakfast. It was hard to believe what happened the night before. When he closed his eyes he could still see the lion that had come out of the night: the eyes were fiery, and it emanated power. He knew that he had come in contact with the Lion of Judah. He remembered hearing songs in church about the Lion of Judah when he was a child. It had all seemed like fairy tale stuff back then. But now, it was as real as anything he had ever experienced.

He had called his mother the previous night when they had brought him in to the station; he hadn't talked to her in years. She wept as he had shared what happened. He knew he was going to be doing some serious time, but he really didn't care. He wondered where Tommie Lee was now. He hoped someday, he could witness to him. Everything had changed. The only thing that mattered now was the peace he felt inside. The other guys in the holding cell were running their mouths. Before he would have been the loudest one, bragging about the crimes he had committed. Now, he felt unusually quiet. He thought about what it had felt like when the sword of light had been thrust through him. How could he ever explain it? He had felt the darkness leave and his heart had been changed. Now, he knew what had happened to Saul on the road to Damascus. It had been no less dramatic last night. He had been apprehended, arrested by the Lord and for the first time since he could remember he wasn't angry anymore.

As she was being booked, Andrea kept trying to tell anyone who would listen to her that everything was all a mistake. At one point, she started sobbing like a little girl saying, "I want to go home now. Let me go home."

"What a nutcase," the booking officer said as they took

her back to strip search her. At that point, Andrea began to sob convulsively; she cried so hard that she started hyperventilating. She felt so confused and disorientated. What was going on? Why had she been arrested? Nobody was telling her anything, and her head was hurting so bad she could hardly think.

By the time, she was put in the holding cell, she was shaking uncontrollably. There was only one other woman in the cell and she said nothing; she just watched suspiciously as Andrea went and sat on the bunk near the opposite wall.

Andrea was intently trying to remember the night. Had she dreamt about Daniel? Something about him and some pictures? Nothing was clear. She pulled the rough jail blanket up to her neck rocking back and forth, trying to comfort herself.

Chapter Twenty-Five

The Aftermath

෨ ෪

The whole town was buzzing with information, and misinformation about the events that had taken place Monday night. The next day, Deborah heard about Andrea's arrest from Officer Pulowski who called and also informed her that Tommie Lee was still on the loose. They had identified the crash victim, and it was a seventeen year old from the next county who had been drinking and stole a car. Because of the fire, it had taken some time to identify the body. She was surprised at how calmly she took the news. That meant Tommie Lee was still on the loose. It was as if he had vanished—they hadn't received any reports of him or the green Chevy.

Hearing the news about Andrea, she actually felt bad for the woman and wondered how she had ever got involved with the likes of Tommie Lee. If Andrea was arrested, the pictures were probably now in the hands of the police. It was just so embarrassing!

Deborah stayed at Anne's on Tuesday and rested and made phone calls. Daniel had gone to the office for the afternoon and then spent the evening with Aimee and David.

Pastor Harrison and Christina were trying to respond to inquiries while trying to keep the congregation from moving in to a place of gossip and judgment. That was something that wasn't always easy. But over the years, they had developed the philosophy of being as honest and open as possible, while still walking in love and integrity when it came to the lives of others. This one wasn't easy!

Deborah's mother received the whole story late Tuesday morning from her daughter over the telephone. That afternoon, when she went home for a brief nap and a change of clothes, she was very glad Deborah had prepared her for what awaited. The front yard was still a mess, but she was so thankful that everyone was okay that it didn't even matter.

Aunt Liberty had called and left a message for Deborah early Tuesday morning. She wanted to know if everything was alright because of the prayer burden she had felt the night before. Originally, Deborah wasn't going to call her because she didn't want to upset her, but it was obvious she was being more protective of her aunt than God was. She called Aunt Liberty Tuesday afternoon and shared the whole story. Afterwards, she teased her aunt that it sounded like she was more excited about the part of Sanchez giving his life to the Lord than Deborah being rescued. "Both, dear. Both give me great joy! I am so glad you're okay. It's a shame about the one young boy who died in the crash. I hope he had a conversation with his Maker beforehand. Hell is an awful place for anyone." Deborah hung up the phone thinking about how much she loved her aunt and how thankful she was for her prayers.

Deborah called Lydia next and they rejoiced together. The Word of the Lord had been correct, "Stand still and see the salvation of your God." Deborah admitted she hadn't been very good at the "stand still" part, but she had learned another valuable lesson: trust in the Lord no matter what the circumstances. Lydia rejoiced with her over the news of the engagement and promised to tell Joyce as soon as they saw each other. They ended the conversation with Deborah promising to let her know when the wedding was going to be. When Lydia hung up, she was amazed at how calm and confident Deborah sounded even with Tommie Lee still on the loose.

Daniel called his parents with the news of his and Deborah's engagement. He knew how word got around and figured it was important to share the highlights of the night before himself. He had been a little concerned about how they would respond, but his parents actually took it all in stride. They were just thankful that everyone was okay. The main thing his mom wanted was a go ahead to start planning the engagement party.

―――――――――――――――

By Wednesday morning, people's lives were starting to get back to normal. Deborah was back at work when Daniel called asking if they could meet for lunch. The last thing she felt like doing was eating but she did want to see him. They hadn't seen each other since he had dropped her off at Anne's.

For lunch that afternoon, Daniel and Deborah decided they would meet at a deli they both enjoyed downtown. Driving to the restaurant, she found herself looking in the rearview mirror repeatedly, but all she saw was the unmarked car following her. She wondered how long this was going to have to last.

The little restaurant was nothing fancy, but the soup was always homemade and the sandwiches fresh. After they ordered, Daniel decided to tell Deborah about the pictures. "I need to tell you something. I hope you won't be upset with me," Daniel started.

She looked at him curiously, "Why do you say that?"

"I went by Andrea's last night on the way home."

"You what?"

"I got the pictures and destroyed them. I couldn't stand the thought of you being tormented by them any longer. I know they could be considered evidence, but I had to do it. I burnt them in the fireplace before I went to bed."

"Did you?"

He interrupted, "I never looked at them, Deborah, that's not who you are anymore. I never knew that person. That's not who you were when we went to school together, and it's not the woman I am in love with now. I wouldn't do that to you."

Tears of relief filled Deborah's eyes. "It's been so hard thinking about the police finding them or having them used as evidence in a hearing or trial. It's one of the main reasons I didn't want to report Andrea."

"I knew that, but for everyone's safety we had to tell the police. She acted very strange as always last night. I can't believe that she actually thought those pictures would make a difference in how I feel about you." Daniel reached out and patted her hand reassuringly.

"I don't know how to thank you. I can't believe you did that for me," she said.

"You deserve a clean slate, Deborah, and I'm not going to let the devil throw the past in your face."

"I know this sounds strange, Daniel, but I've actually been praying for Andrea today. I know she's treated us badly but I hate to think about her being in jail. I've been there before, and it's hard to think I've put someone there. I think she needs some help. It's obvious that you've become an obsession for her. For some reason I can't be mad at her. She's so desperate."

Now it was Daniel's turn to be surprised, "After the way she's been treating you and now this, you definitely have more grace for the situation that I do. 'Love your enemies' is a little easier said than done sometimes. I wonder what she's going to tell the police about the pictures. I just hope they won't charge me with evidence tampering."

Deborah hadn't really thought about that possibility before now. "Oh, Daniel, I hope not. That would be awful. We better pray for mercy!"

"Whatever happens, it will be worth it. Those pictures needed to be destroyed. I'm going to give my attorney a call this afternoon to see if there's anything I should do next. But I don't want you to worry about this. That's why I waited until today to tell you. This has been hard enough on you."

By the time their order was ready, Deborah and Daniel were ready to change the subject. Daniel shared his mother's desire to throw them an engagement party. The family's kindness and acceptance was overwhelming at times for Deborah, but she graciously told him that a party would be fine with her.

———————————

On Wednesday evening, Daniel and the children joined Deborah at Anne's and Roberts for dinner. It was a lively affair. The adults were very careful not to talk about the previous night's events. Before they had left for dinner, Daniel had shared with David and Aimee that he had asked Deborah to marry him and had given her a ring. Because they had already talked on Friday, they didn't seem too surprised when Daniel shared the news.

Anne had already asked Deborah to spend another night, and Deborah decided to take her up on it. Her mother wasn't going to be home again and they still weren't quite sure who had made the second call from Andrea's phone. Deborah felt safe with Anne and Robert, and she knew Daniel would also sleep better. Looking around the dinner table that evening it was nearly overwhelming as she considered what she could have lost if she had left town. She had to choke back the tears while grace was being said.

Chapter Twenty-Six

The Delay

❧ ❦

After ministering Theresa's final session that Friday afternoon, Lydia went home to take a nap. She wanted to be refreshed when Stephen came home that evening. It had sure been a week of ups and downs. She wondered what kind of shape Joyce would be in after her meeting with Bill tonight. Joyce had promised to call her no matter what time it was and give a report. Lydia was praying that the Lord had truly done a work in his life. She didn't know what the Lord wanted to do in their relationship, but she did know that Joyce needed a true apology. Even though she had been able to forgive Bill and move on with her life, Lydia knew that it would help Joyce with closure.

As she was dozing off to sleep, she heard the Lord say, "Pray for the repentance to be received."

Lydia knew the Holy Spirit was talking about Joyce. "I pray that you soften Joyce's heart and allow her to receive Bill's repentance in Jesus Name." She fell asleep praying in the Spirit.

Joyce was on her way to meet Bill for dinner reflecting on the week. From Bill's phone call to the crisis with Deborah and then ministering to Theresa, the week had felt like a rollercoaster. And now she was facing her ex-husband in person!

Lydia had been overjoyed when Joyce had told her about her decision to meet with Bill. She had also called Pastor Rick to see what he had to say. He had felt a peace also. Joyce could tell that Bill was quite surprised when she called to let him know what she had decided; however, she knew she couldn't go as far as picking him up from the airport and was glad when he didn't even ask. Bill was flying into the Orlando International Airport. It was a little over an hour from where she lived. She had e-mailed directions to Bill on how to get to the restaurant they were going to meet at when he arrived. She didn't even dare ask how long he would be in town or where he was staying. She made sure the conversation had been short and to the point, not wanting to take the chance of getting too personal.

Bill's flight was delayed in Atlanta because of area storms. He had hoped to have time to get to the hotel and freshen up before meeting Joyce. Now it looked like he would have to rush straight from the airport. He went into the airport bathroom to freshen up a bit.

Even though he knew this was something he had to do, he still had mixed emotions about seeing Joyce again. She had to hate him for all the pain he had caused. Not only had he sacrificed their relationship, he had also cost her the relationships she had at church and in the community. Looking back, he couldn't believe how selfish he had been. He wondered if she would ever be able to truly believe how sorry he was. He had paid a high price for his sexual addiction.

When he had first left home after his arrest, he had went totally wild, indulging all his fantasies. But he found that it just left him even emptier than he already felt. Finally, one Sunday morning, he decided to get up and go to church. Hating his own hypocrisy, he decided to go to the church he passed on his way to work. The name of the church had intrigued him; it was called Redemption Chapel. The messages on the sign out front were new every week. On Monday mornings, he found himself looking forward to reading the word for the week. He knew from the sign that the service started at ten o'clock in the morning.

As he shaved, Bill looked in the mirror. The face looking back at him was gaunt and his eyes were blood shot. He had aged ten years since he had moved to California. His hand shook as he reached for his toothbrush. The sexual addiction hadn't been enough to dull his pain so he had started drinking every day. Then he thought of the message he had seen all week on the church sign. It had simply read, "Come home this week, Jesus loves you." Something in its simplicity had touched his heart and tears ran down his face every time he passed it. He had started thinking of his home with Joyce and their daughter, Rebecca, and then about his church, friends and everything that he had once held dear. He felt like the prodigal waking up in a pig pen and thinking about his father's house.

Now he looked into the mirror in the airport bathroom and the man looking back at him was clear eyed. And for the first time in a long time, he could look back. He said to himself in the mirror, "You can do this, it's the right thing."

Joyce's cell phone rang when she was about a half an hour away from the restaurant. It was Bill. "I was delayed in Atlanta, and I'll probably be about twenty minutes late. I'm really sorry, Joyce." They both knew she was irritated when she responded, "Whatever, Bill, I'll see you when you get there." Joyce had hung up abruptly and as she did inside she could feel rage begin to build. "Oh, no, not now," she thought to herself. "I thought I was over this." She began to pray and ask the Lord what had triggered her. It wasn't a hard one to figure out. The Holy Spirit brought back all the times Bill had been late coming home from work. Sometimes it was an hour, sometimes it might be four. He had always had an excuse. The Lord showed her she was not only mad at him but mad at herself for being so gullible. For years, she had believed his excuses only to discover that all those late nights he had either been on his computer looking at pornography, or stopping by some strip joint. It made her blood boil just to think about how many hours of her life she had spent waiting for him, and now he wanted her to do it again. What she really wanted to do was turn the car around and head for home. Let him sit at the restaurant and wait for her all night. Joyce decided to pull off at the next exit until she could calm down and decide what to do. She tried Lydia's number and her phone went to voicemail. She found herself in the gas station parking lot weeping and beating the steering wheel saying, "I'm not going to let him do this to me again." After several minutes, she was able to calm down enough to know that she needed to use the ministry process. She began to pour out her complaint to the Lord. It felt better even just talking it out. It took a little bit of time, but she was finally able to forgive Bill and herself. She released him from the debt of time that he had robbed from her and the peace of mind. Then she asked the Lord to come into the memory of one of the times it had been the most painful.

It had been a Friday night, and the entire family had all planned to leave for a weekend trip. It had been a night that Bill had promised to be home early, and he ended up being over four hours late. They had gotten in a huge argument and the whole trip had been called off. Rebecca had been so disappointed, and it had been a time when Joyce had been hoping there might be some reconciliation in their marriage. The Lord came into the memory and showed her that when she had been in their guest room weeping, He had comforted her. Then He had spoke to her and said, "Daughter, I'll redeem the time. I'll redeem the joy. And I'll redeem him."

Joyce's tears and anger had subsided. Her make-up had run and she felt like a mess, but inside peace had returned. She quickly dug in her purse and found her compact and some lipstick. After running a comb through her hair, she got back on I-4 and headed for Orlando. Now it looked as if she might be the one running late.

Chapter Twenty-Seven

Repentance

❧ ❧

Stephen and Lydia ate dinner alone at home that Friday evening. They had a busy weekend planned and just wanted some time together. After her nap, Lydia had begun dinner, preparing chicken with steamed vegetables. As they cleaned up the kitchen together, she began to share about Joyce meeting her ex-husband, Bill, that evening. "I sure hope it goes okay. Joyce is just finally getting settled. I know she was supposed to meet with him, but now I'm a little nervous for her."

"It'll be fine, honey. Joyce has received a lot of healing. Let's just pray she uses wisdom and discernment," Stephen said reassuringly.

The couple talked a little while longer about their week. Stephen had just lost one of his assistants and a good C.A. was hard to find. Janet had gotten married and her new husband had just been transferred. The office manager was going to begin the interviewing process next week. Lydia commiserated with his loss. "Did she like the bracelet I picked out?"

"She loved it. I wish you could have come by at lunch for the going away party, a number of patients came in. I think she was really surprised."

"That's great! I would have loved to, but I knew with

Joyce and Bill's dinner meeting tonight I couldn't move the session to the afternoon. Joyce needed that time to get ready."

"I understand and I know Janet did, too. We just like when we get to see you. I sure hope we find a good replacement. She was one of a kind."

"I've already been praying for you. So what would you like to do? Take a walk, watch a movie or what?"

Stephen replied, "Let's watch that comedy you brought home. I could use a good laugh tonight."

Lydia put in the video and curled up on the sofa. Stephen settled into his recliner. Both of them laughed till they hurt as they enjoyed the movie together.

Bill was glad that he had made reservations when he saw the restaurant parking lot. Joyce had suggested a place called Dundee's. She had said that it was known for its seafood and steak so then he could choose what he wanted. It hadn't taken him long to find the restaurant after he had landed, but he was still about fifteen minutes late. He gave his name to the hostess wondering if Joyce was there already. Joyce had sounded upset when he had called and said he was running late; he wondered if it might cause her to change her mind. The hostess seating him said, "Your other party hasn't arrived yet, may I get you something from the bar?"

Bill shook his head, "No, I'll just have some water."

"Your server will bring that right out to you. Have a good evening, sir." As she walked away, Bill realized that he hadn't even once looked at the young woman's body. That was exciting. Before he hadn't been able to control the lust; he had always wanted more. He had been subtle with his looks, but he had been in a habit for years of undressing almost every woman he saw. He wouldn't blame Joyce if she didn't show up; he had been such a cad. He didn't know how she had even put up with him for their eighteen years of marriage.

———————————————

Joyce arrived at Dundee's about ten minutes after Bill; she had gotten stuck in some heavy traffic that had delayed her even more. At least, now she knew she wasn't late out of spite. She was actually feeling pretty good. After her exit and prayer for a little more healing, she had put on some good praise music and tried to keep her mind on the Lord as she finished the drive. It sure beat playing imaginary conversations over and over again in her mind. She took one last look in the mirror after gathering her things. Her heart was racing just a bit, and she took several deep, slow breaths as she walked towards the entrance.

The hostess greeted her and when Joyce gave her name, she said, "Right this way." Joyce followed her through the restaurant. Her hands were beginning to sweat. She wiped them quickly on her jacket. The hostess stopped abruptly and said, "Here's your table."

Joyce turned and saw Bill. He started to get up, but she stopped him saying, "That's alright. Hello, Bill." She extended her hand.

Feeling awkward and not knowing what else to do he shook her hand briefly and slid back down into the booth. "Joyce, it's good to see you. I really appreciate you coming tonight." He hoped the rest of the night wasn't going to be as awkward. She looked great. Lightly tanned from the Florida sun, Joyce looked younger than he remembered. Her blue eyes looked bluer than ever, but instead of the blonde hair he always insisted on, she had returned to her natural color. He had to admit now that it really did become her. "You look wonderful," he blurted out.

She had been examining him, also. He had lost some weight. Bill's hair was a bit more gray around the temples, but what surprised her most was it seemed like his eyes had changed color. Before they were dark almost black, now they were a soft brown. They almost looked kind. She looked away quickly when she realized that she had been studying him.

"You look good, too," she said. "It looks like divorce was good for both of us."

She saw a quick look of hurt come over his face and then disappeared. She wished that jab hadn't come out, but it was too late to take it back.

Their server interrupted and Joyce was thankful for the reprieve. She already knew what she wanted and they both placed their order.

Bill decided to break the ice, "Can I start with telling you how sorry I am for everything that happened?"

Joyce just stared at him and nodded.

For the next hour and a half, he shared with her the depths of his sexual addiction and the help he had found at Redemption Chapel. They had a men's group that met weekly which specialized in sexual addiction. Joyce sat listening, wanting to pinch herself; it was Bill's body, but this man was engaged and talking to her openly and honestly. It wasn't the Bill she had known and lived with for eighteen years. He had always been so guarded. She made very few comments as he shared. When he was done, he asked her the question, "Can you and will you forgive me for what I put you and Rebecca through?"

Joyce was still trying to process everything. She said, "I've worked through a lot of stuff myself, and I have been forgiving you and I do forgive you. I'm sorry if I'm not jumping up and down. It's a little hard to see what I prayed for come true now when it's too late. Actually, I was wondering if this meeting was to inform me that you were remarrying."

Bill immediately replied, "Not at all. I just knew you deserved an honest apology. I haven't been seeing anyone. The last year has been intense work with my counselor and the group. I've actually been clean a year. That's why I'm here. I didn't want to come until I knew that I was getting victory. I just felt I had to come and let you know that all of those times I turned things on you it was just manipulation. I had the problem. It wasn't you. I had an addiction and nor matter how much love or sex you gave me; it wasn't going to be enough. Can you hear me, Joyce, it wasn't you. It wasn't your fault."

Her eyes were filling with tears. She reached for a tissue in her purse. All the times he had been angry at her because she wasn't sexy, or exciting enough, came back to her. She remembered the times he had called her a "nag" when all she wanted to know was where he had been. All she could say was, "But, you said so many things."

"Joyce, I need you to hear me. I just said and did those things so I could justify my sin. You were a great wife and mother and you didn't deserve any of it."

She couldn't believe her ears. Some of the things he had said back then still haunted her. Lydia had tried to tell her the same thing. She remembered her voice, "Joyce, that's what addicts do; they attack, blame and find fault so that they can distract themselves from the real issues. They have to justify what they're doing or they couldn't do it."

To hear the truth coming out of Bill's own mouth was almost overwhelming. She said, "That's what the lady who has been ministering to me kept saying, but when you hear it over and over, you start believing it really is you."

Bill's eyes filled with compassion, "I truly am sorry for everything I put you through." He reached out and patted her hand. She instinctively pulled back, looking at him warily. Even though she was hearing everything he was staying, her heart was having trouble believing it. He quickly said, "I'm sorry. I've gone on and on. Now, it's your turn to tell me about yourself and everything you've been doing." That really took her by surprise, once they had gotten married; Bill had hardly been concerned at all about her life. All she had been was someone to meet his needs.

Joyce slowly started sharing with Bill about the *Restore Your Soul Ministry* and all that she was doing. He actually looked at her and listened while she talked. She noticed that even when several attractive women walked by the table, he hadn't even glanced their way. She became more and more animated as she shared. It was obvious to Bill that she really loved what she was doing. The more they talked the more relaxed they each became.

As they finished up the evening and walked out to the parking lot, Bill told Joyce that his next step was to call Rebecca. He wanted to repent to his daughter as well. He asked Joyce how much Rebecca knew about what had happened.

"Well, I was pretty honest with her. I told her partly out of my own anger, and because I felt she was old enough to know the truth. She's pretty hurt, Bill."

"I understand. I would expect her to be. I'm not asking for anything to happen overnight. I realize I have to earn her trust and the right to be her father again. But I do sincerely want to apologize to her."

As they were standing in the now nearly vacant parking lot, she said, "So when do you fly out?"

"Actually, not until late Sunday, I was going to ask you if there was a good church in the area."

Joyce started to name a couple in Orlando. Then she felt the prompting of the Holy Ghost. "Those are all good, but if you would like I could give you directions to Grace Fellowship. Then you could actually meet Lydia and Stephen. Lydia has been very faithful to pray for you," she chuckled, "even when it made me mad."

Bill said carefully, "I wouldn't want to impose. Let me pray about it and if it's okay I'll give you a call tomorrow."

"That's no problem. I didn't invite you because I felt I had to, the Holy Spirit actually put it on my heart just now. I hadn't even thought of it before."

He looked at her intently, "Okay, then, how do I get there?"

"Hold on a minute, I have a church brochure in the car. It

has a map on it." As she opened her glove box, she was a little surprised at what she had just done. But so far, trusting the Lord had worked. She pulled out the brochure and wrote the extra directions on it. He had walked over to the open car door. She handed him the brochure and said, "I was really nervous about tonight, but I'm glad I came. It's good to have some closure."

He agreed with her and then said, "Good night, Joyce. I can't thank you enough for being willing to listen to me tonight. I know I was asking for something I really didn't deserve. God is teaching me more and more every day about what mercy and grace really mean. I will see you on Sunday." Bill then turned and walked away.

On the way back to Palm City Joyce called Lydia, "Guess who's coming to church on Sunday."

Lydia replied "Bill?"

"Yes, I can't believe I invited him. Lydia, he's really changed. It's almost scary, like another man in Bill's body. I just don't know if it's for real or not. He said that all he wanted to do was repent to me face to face. It sounds like he's been getting as much ministry as I have been. Now, I don't know what to think. But at least it feels good to be civil to each other. He wants to meet with Rebecca and repent to her, too. Maybe this will just help all of us get on with our lives."

When Lydia hung up, she was relieved that the dinner had gone as well as it had. "It looks like we're having a visitor in church Sunday morning."

"Who's that?

"Bill, Joyce's ex-husband. He asked her where a good church was and she told him about ours. I've heard so much about him. It'll be interesting to actually meet him. Something must have happened for Joyce to have done that. Her whole reasoning for meeting him in Orlando was that she didn't want him to know where she lived or anything about her new life."

"Don't be match-making now, honey. It's time for bed. I can see those wheels turning."

"You know, anything is possible. I've seen God restore marriages before, even those that did end in divorce."

"I agree, but I think it's a bit premature. They just had one dinner," he said. "I don't know about you but I'm ready for bed. I want to get up bright and early and get a few things done around the house."

It took Lydia awhile to fall asleep; she was rested from her afternoon nap but she also felt an excitement in her spirit. She could hardly wait until Sunday. Even though it might mean losing her ministry partner, she loved to see families restored. What a week it had been!

Chapter Twenty-Eight

Sunday Lunch

ॐ ॐ

Saturday had seemed like an eternity to Joyce. She wondered if she was crazy for inviting Bill to church; but, at the time, she had felt like the Holy Spirit was prompting her. She knew Lydia had family plans and didn't want to interrupt her. She had almost called her daughter to tell her about the dinner but then decided against it. That was between Rebecca and Bill. It was one of the areas she had to repent for during her own ministry. She saw how much she had emasculated him by always being in the middle of the two of them. Even as a child, she never allowed Bill to discipline Rebecca. Joyce now saw that it was because of what had happened to her as a child. At the time, it had been a big point of contention until Bill had just finally given up.

Joyce had begun to see that he had learned to love his daughter from a distance. No, this was one time she wasn't getting in the middle of things. In fact, if he showed up Sunday, it was something else she probably needed to repent to him about, also. She finally decided to give her apartment a good cleaning. It needed it, and it would help her work off some of her nervous energy.

That same Saturday morning Bill had called his accountability partner and gave him a report on the previous night's events. Dennis was elated to hear how good the meeting went and how well Bill sounded. At first, when he had heard Bill's plans of trying to see Joyce when he went out East, he had been a little apprehensive. The time he had tried to repent to his ex-wife hadn't turned out so well-she had informed him that there was a new man in her life and six months later she was remarried. Before hanging up Bill said, "One more thing before I let you go. She actually invited me to her church on Sunday morning. I was totally surprised. I'm not sure what her motivation was, but I figured it can't hurt."

"Well, maybe she wants to see if the changes are for real. Just move very slow buddy. Don't get ahead of yourself. Remember keep yourself emotionally honest and don't get yourself involved in dreaming up a fantasy. Whether it's an ex-wife or not, fantasy is fantasy, and that's what got us to where we're at. What are you going to do today? You've got a lot of time on your hands."

"I knew you would ask. Actually, I plan on driving over to Palm City this afternoon. That's where Joyce lives. I'll get a room over there and enjoy the beach. That way I won't be late for church. I almost blew it last night-my plane was delayed in Atlanta. Joyce sounded a little irritated when I called to let her know. The Lord showed me it was related to all of those times I called to tell her I was working late. Keep me in your prayers. Let Leon know everything worked out."

Leon was the head of their support group. He had been very instrumental in reaching out to Bill when he first started church. He was actually the first person to help Bill understand that he had more than a lust problem-he had an addiction problem.

Bill had never thought of himself as an addict before, perverted yes, but not an addict. He remembered the night that he and Leon had coffee after church. He had started telling him about his issue with pornography and how it had destroyed his marriage. When he was through, Leon began to share his own journey of recovery. That night, Leon opened Bill's eyes to the fact that he was battling a chemical addiction; he had never thought about the powerful chemicals released in his brain at the time of orgasm. Finally, Bill could see even more why no matter how hard he tried, he hadn't been able to stop. It was no excuse for his sin, but at least he understood it better. Leon had left him with one statement that night: "Until you find the pain you're trying to medicate, you won't get free. It's a love issue man, not a lust issue."

Bill had gone home and mulled the statement over and over again in his head. Never before had he thought of why he couldn't control himself sexually. Before, he had always just focused on trying to stop, feeling like a failure when he couldn't. It had finally gotten so bad he had just given up.

Leon had invited him to the men's group that met on Monday nights at the church. When he arrived that first night, he was impressed by the transparency and the understanding some of the men had. Leon had been free and clean for over seven years. It took Bill a while to believe that a man could truly live without being plagued by lust. One of the beliefs he had to work through was that it was just part of being a healthy male. But over time, he actually came to believe it was possible.

Leon introduced him to a great counselor and, between his individual sessions with Evan and the group meetings, Bill made a lot of progress quickly. He couldn't believe how uneducated and ignorant he had been about his problem. He began to recognize his stress triggers and started getting to the root of some of his childhood issues. Leon had been right: Bill had been trying to fix a deficit of love with lust. It hadn't been easy, but the more he dealt with his personal past, the easier and easier it was to resist temptation. He remembered the sense of victory he had the first week he had made it without masturbating. It was something he hadn't been able to do since he was twelve.

Joyce found herself dressing carefully for church on Sunday morning. First, she put on a deep blue suit with a cream colored blouse. It just looked too business like and boring. Next, she pulled out one of her favorite dresses; it was a lighter shade of blue. She had always liked the dress; it was softer and more feminine, and she always received compliments every time she wore it. Maybe she just wanted Bill to regret what he had thrown away. As she changed, she was almost irritated with herself for caring about what she wore. Her hands were a bit unsteady as she put on her earrings and she gave herself one last glance before heading out the door. She grabbed her keys and bag and shut off the bedroom light. If she didn't hurry up, she'd be late.

Service was extra special that day. Afterwards, Joyce introduced Bill to Lydia and Stephen. They were carefully polite. Even though Bill could feel them sizing him up, he didn't blame them. Of course they were going to be protective of Joyce. He would expect Leon and Dennis to do the same for him. The next thing he knew, Lydia and Joyce had headed for the bathroom, leaving him standing with Stephen.

Stephen said, "So what kind of work do you do?"

"I work for a company that creates software for the medical profession," Bill answered, "how about yourself?"

"I'm a chiropractor. So what does the software do?"

"It's actually a program used for insurance billing. We have a number of chiropractors who are using it now." By the time, Lydia and Joyce had returned, the two men were talking like they had known each other for years. The women just looked at each other when they saw them. During their trip to the bathroom, Lydia had wanted to know if they could invite Bill to join them for lunch. Joyce agreed and the next she knew they were all at the China Buffet.

The meal conversation was pretty light until Bill broke the ice. "I know you've ministered to Joyce a lot, and I want to thank both of you. I want you to know I take full responsibility for all of the pain I've caused her."

Lydia saw the tears in his eyes. "Well, we love her, and she's become a part of the family."

Stephen nodded in agreement. "She's also become Lydia's favorite ministry partner. It's a good thing I'm not a jealous man."

Before she knew it, Lydia bluntly said, "So what exactly are your intentions?" She could have kicked herself for opening her mouth. Joyce glared at her from across the table.

Stuttering, Bill replied, "Uh, my only intention was to repent to Joyce in person. I thought she deserved that."

Stephen quickly changed the subject, "So when do you leave for California?"

Bill glanced at his watch, "Actually, I probably should get going. My plane leaves around five." He picked up the bill, "My treat, and no arguments please, it's the least I can do."

Stephen and Lydia stayed in the restaurant as Joyce walked Bill to his car. On the way, she said, "I want you to know I do receive your repentance and do believe it's sincere. I wish you well, Bill."

"You've got great friends, Joyce, and a wonderful church. It's done my heart good to know you're okay. Thank you for allowing me to come today. Lydia and Stephen are special. You're blessed." He leaned over, "May I?" She nodded and he kissed her gently on the cheek. She watched the rental car pulling out of the parking lot, wondering if she would ever see him again.

Chapter Twenty-Nine

The First Visit

ॐ ॐ

At the end of the following week, Pastor Mark was summoned to the local jail. Andrea Kline wanted to see him. She had been charged with two indictments: extortion and threat to due bodily harm. It was hard to believe a member of his congregation could have left the messages Andrea had on Deborah's phone. If he hadn't heard them himself, he would have never believed it. This had been a nightmare for everyone. He couldn't believe what things had come to, and to be honest, even though she was a member of the church, he wasn't relishing this meeting. How she could have had anything to do with that Tommie Lee was beyond him. He was trying to work up some compassion, but he just wasn't finding any. It had been nearly two weeks but it still made him shaky to think about that night.

After going through the usual ritual of signing in and being patted down, Pastor Mark was escorted to a private room to meet with Andrea. That was unusual, most of the time he met with prisoners in the visitor's room. "Andrea's attorney must have pulled some strings," he thought to himself as he entered the room. There was a mirrored window to the right which he figured allowed for observation. Besides the table and two chairs, there was nothing else in the room.

He was completely shocked when Andrea walked in with a guard at her side. She did not look like the same woman; normally, Andrea was dressed and coifed to perfection. Now, he wouldn't have recognized her if he had seen her on the street. Her hair was pulled back in a ponytail, and she was dressed in a bright orange jumpsuit. With no make-up and her usual tanning bed tan fading, she looked like a bad "before version" in a beauty make-over.

She said, "Thank you for coming, Pastor," as she pulled out the chair and sat down.

Pastor Harrison wasted no time as he found his seat opposite of her, "What can I do for you Andrea? Your attorney called and said you wanted to meet with me." The church's jail minister, Sam, had already made a couple of visits since she was arrested twelve days ago, but this was his first.

Andrea started to respond, but then put her head down and held it as if in pain. Pastor Harrison assumed it was because of the shame she felt. He was in no way prepared for what happened next.

Andrea lifted her head and everything about her looked different, almost childlike. The voice that came out of her did not sound anything like her. "Pastor, we wanted Andrea to ask you to come, we're scared. We don't want to stay here anymore. We want to go home. You're the only one we could trust. We know you have a good heart."

Pastor Harrison blinked his eyes in unbelief. He wondered what Andrea was up to know. "Andrea, what are you talking about? Who's we? What is this all about?"

Andrea responded in the same little girl's voice. "Pastor, Andrea is asleep; the child people are here now. There are several of us. I am the Brave Girl. We need your help. We got Andrea in trouble and now we have to get her out."

The Pastor still couldn't believe his eyes or ears. Was this a demonic manifestation? He had always known Andrea was a little different but this was over the top.

He decided to go along with her. "Okay, Brave Girl, explain to me how you got Andrea into trouble."

She tilted her head as if listening and then began, "It's a long story but first you have to know that there are many of us. Andrea doesn't know about us, but we think we're going to have to tell her now."

As Andrea continued to talk in a little girl's voice, Pastor Harrison was transfixed. He still couldn't believe what he was hearing and seeing. He glanced at the window, praying that someone else was observing this. If he tried to tell anyone what was happening, they would never believe him. He kept his eyes on Andrea as she went on talking.

Brave Girl continued and tears started pouring down her face, "We were just looking for a Daddy, and we saw how good Daniel was with his children. We wanted to go live with them and let him take care of us. When the bad man left Andrea, we were all happy. But then we started getting scared. We didn't like being home alone, and we needed someone to take care of us. It was Baby Girl's idea first; she wanted to be best friends with Aimee. We all voted that Mister Daniel would be a good Daddy, and we got Big John to talk to her in his God's voice."

Pastor Harrison couldn't help himself, "Who is Big John?"

Brave Girl blinked several times and suddenly a deep, manly voice came out of Andrea. "I'll tell you who I am. I'm the one who protects all these little girls. It's important to have a man to take care of some things, you know." Now the Pastor, shook his head, could he be dreaming? If so, he really wanted to wake up. The voice sounded just like the one that he had heard on Deborah's phone. Big John went on, "I just talked to Andrea using my God voice. The girls asked me to. I never thought we would end up here. I just told her that Daniel was going to be her husband and even helped her have some dreams, but you know the story. Andrea really didn't have a chance. It was all of our faults. I don't like to ask anyone for help. But I'm asking you too, Pastor, can you help get Andrea out of here? The girls aren't doing too well."

Suddenly, Brave Girl was back, "We figure it's time for Andrea to know about us. She's going to be real mad. We've been trying to talk to her some but she keeps thinking we're just demons. She's really afraid she's going crazy."

Witnessing this, Pastor Mark was reminded of the movie, "Sybil." Could Andrea Kline actually have multiple personalities or was this a ploy so she could plead insanity against her charges? He had never seen anything like it before and a chill went up and down his spine. He prayed silently, "Lord, give me discernment. I need to know what's really going on right now."

Suddenly Brave Girl said, "Oh, oh, she's waking up. I've got to go. Please help us Pastor Harrison." Andrea's head bent back down, and suddenly she was back.

Her eyes, still looking somewhat confused, looked at him, "Pastor Harrison, I'm so glad you came. I'm sorry, I've been having these terrible headaches. I'm not even sure why I asked you to come. Pastor Sam has already been so kind, and I know how busy you are. I just felt I heard the Lord telling me to ask for you."

The two conversed for about ten more minutes but the conversation wasn't very deep. Andrea definitely wasn't her usual in-control self. Pastor Harrison felt it was best not to make any reference about what had just transpired until he had time to try and figure out what had just taken place. Needless to say, the conversation was pretty strained. Then the guard came to the door, "Time is up, sir. I need to take her back before the lunch count."

As Pastor Harrison walked out to the reception area, he asked the woman sitting at the desk, "Was there anyone in the observation area?"

She replied, "I don't think so Pastor, but the camera might have been on. Is everything okay?"

Pastor Harrison answered, "Yes, it's fine. But I'm going

to leave you my card, if my visit was recorded, could you please have someone call me." He walked slowly out of the jail wondering what on earth he was going to do next. Would anyone believe what he had just witnessed? He decided not to say anything to anyone until he had an opportunity to go home and pray with his wife.

Chapter Thirty

The Next Visit

ॐ ॐ

After his initial astonishing encounter with Andrea and her multiple identities, Pastor Mark had given Lydia a call and asked her if she had ever worked with anyone with such strange symptoms. Suspecting that Andrea might be suffering from Dissociative Identity Disorder, Lydia discussed her experiences with the condition and suggested several good books. She also gave Pastor Mark some advice from her first hand experiences.

Since then, Pastor Mark had done quite a bit of reading and research on Dissociative Identity Disorder; he had found out that it was not a form of mental illness, like schizophrenia. Even though an individual suffering from D.I.D. may appear crazy, he discovered that each of the individual's identities have a different reality and function: each one serving as a part of a very complex coping mechanism. Pastor Mark had also discovered that it only occurred in people who had been severely abused under the age of four or five years old. Often, the abuse continued as they grew older, so their psychological defense systems became quite complex creating different alters which held different memories, functions and emotions. Sometimes, as an adult, the occurrence of a traumatic event would cause blocked memories and situations to begin unraveling in the individual; feelings or memories from the past would begin to penetrate the wall of dissociation and make their way to the conscious.

Pastor Mark also found out that Dissociative Identity Disorder was much more prevalent in women than men, and, that often, it went undiagnosed until they were in their forties or fifties. Many times the person would have had other concurrent or previously diagnosed disorders such as bi-polar disorder, eating disorders, depression, addiction, sleep disorders, etc.

Pastor Mark wasn't sure if Andrea had ever been diagnosed with any of these disorders. It had started him thinking that, even though she had attended the church for a number of years, no one really knew her. He wondered if the trauma from her husband's sudden departure and her discovery of his homosexuality could have triggered some of her erratic behavior recently.

He had talked with Christina about Andrea's condition and they had prayed. Together, they had decided that he needed to go back for another visit. The first one had been too strange, and he needed to be sure before he approached anyone else about what he had observed.

The following Thursday Pastor Mark was back at the jail. He felt a little bit more prepared, but still apprehensive about his second visit with Andrea. After his usual pat down he was ushered back into the same room he had visited Andrea in the week before. This time, Pastor Mark had requested that the video camera in the corner of the room be turned on; he knew this had to be captured on tape for anyone to believe him.

To Pastor Mark, it almost felt like a repeat performance. Several minutes after he and Andrea conversed, she suddenly put her head down. When she picked it back up, she looked like another person again. Slowly, Pastor Mark asked, "How many of you are there?"

The voice responded, "There are five child people, then Big John, and there are several older helpers for Andrea. There are also some hidden people who won't talk to anyone. I'm not sure exactly, but I know there's more than twelve."

Pastor Harrison decided to play along, "What is your name and how old are you?"

She didn't hesitate to respond, "I'm Brave Girl. I'm ten. I'm the oldest and the bravest. I help Big John take care of the girls."

This time when Pastor Mark left the jail he was convinced: no one was that good of an actor. Brave Girl had even told him some of the memories she had about the abuse Andrea had suffered as a little girl. When the Andrea he knew resurfaced, he asked her a few questions.

"Andrea, do you suffer from bad headaches?" From what he read, headaches often happened as different personalities surfaced or memories began to come up.

"Yes. I have all my life and I think they're getting worse. Why do you ask, Pastor Mark?"

Not quite sure how to answer that he said, "Before I say anything more may I please ask you a few more questions?" She nodded affirmatively and he continued, "Do you ever find that time gets away from you? What I mean is, do you sometimes feel as if time has passed and you're not actually sure what happened during it?"

Now she looked uncomfortable, "Sometimes, but I just think it's from all the stress."

He continued, "Do you ever hear voices in your head?" She turned away for a minute and he could tell that this was a hard one for her to answer.

Finally she said, "Yes, but I'm not crazy. I know it's just demons, and I command them to leave and be silent."

"Andrea what do you remember about the Monday before you were arrested?"

"Well, it's kind of fuzzy but I do remember a man coming into the bank. He wanted to know about Deborah. I met up with him at the diner on my break and I saw some pictures of her. They were bad pictures. It felt then like something just took over and I really don't remember much more of the day."

Then he said a strange thing, "Who met with the men later in the day and paid for the pictures?"

She looked at him as if she didn't know what he was talking about and suddenly, she transformed again. A very tough sounding woman started talking. "I did, Andrea is such a wimp; she couldn't handle anything like that. She's scared to death of men. Always afraid they're going to rape her just like that S.O.B. Chuck did when she was little. I'm Adrian. I was the one that handled most of the details that night." Then she chuckled, "Except for the phone call, which was made by Big John."

At that point Andrea felt like she was going crazy. She could actually hear herself talking but it wasn't her. She didn't know anything about pictures or phone calls.
She felt overwhelmed by confusion and terror; then suddenly, she saw a picture of herself being abused by her step-father Chuck. She began to cry out, "No, no, don't hurt me again."

The next thing Pastor Mark knew, he was comforting a little girl in the middle of a traumatic memory. He felt like he was in over his head then remembered what Lydia had said: "just minister to each identity just like you would a person or child at that age." As he began to pray and comfort the little girl, she began to calm down and over time the sobbing subsided.

Then, Andrea was back and he now had enough evidence. Deciding to risk telling her and classifying her problems, Pastor Mark told Andrea, "I think you may be suffering from Dissociative Identity Disorder. I want to see if we can get an evaluation for you."

"One of the psychologists I saw before I got saved once said that to me but I thought he was telling me I was crazy. I never went back to see him again. What does it mean? I don't want to be crazy. I feel real scared and my head is killing me.

Please help me, Pastor Mark."

The first visitor Sanchez had at the jail was Pastor Sam from Deerfield Family Worship Center. "Pastor Mark really wanted to come but, because he may be called as a witness, they wouldn't let him visit, even though he has chaplain privileges."

"Pastor Mark? Who is that?" Sanchez questioned.

"He's the man who led you to the Lord in the driveway."

"He's a pastor? He just said his name was Mark. Oh, Lord, forgive me!"

Pastor Sam could tell that this new piece of information shook Sanchez. He was surprised at how much fear of the Lord he saw in him. For him, it was hard not to get jaded over the years; there were so many convicts in prison that simply used the visiting ministers. He had cut his teeth ministering in the prisons and had seen and heard just about everything, but this guy really seemed sincere. He hadn't just got religious; it appeared as if he had truly had a salvation experience.

"I brought you a Bible from Pastor Mark. They have to scan it and search it before they give it to you. The guards told me you'll have it by the end of the day. Inside is a Bible study guide that will help you get started. How have you been?" He listened intently as Sanchez began sharing about some of the changes he was feeling and how peaceful he was even though he knew he would be facing prison time. When Sanchez finished, he asked, "What about Tommie Lee, have you heard anything about him?"

Pastor Sam reported that there still was no news. They were still praying that he would be found soon.

Sanchez's eyes actually teared up, "I'm hoping I'll get a chance to tell him about Jesus someday."

"Well, keep praying for him, and remember there are plenty of others who need to hear your testimony. But right now, your main focus needs to be getting discipled. So many of the guys I've worked with don't have a strong enough foundation; they have a conversion experience, but then they don't get the Word into them and they won't get under God's authority. The next thing you know, they've backslidden; their witness is shot and then they give up on their dream of ministering to others.

Sanchez listened intently as the minister continued to share. He had wasted too much of his life playing the fool and hurting others. He wanted to learn everything he could from this man and anyone else who really knew God.

Chapter Thirty-One

The Engagement Party

ও ঙ

It was early November when Deborah and Daniel's engagement party was finally held. The Worthington's knew how to throw a party-it seemed like half of Deerfield was in attendance. They had always had a large great room where they had held home fellowship meetings years ago. Tonight, the room was filled with family and friends. Deborah was working hard at trying not to feel embarrassed at all of the attention she was receiving, especially since it had barely been a month since everything had happened. Suddenly, Daniel came up behind her and put his hands over her eyes. "We've got a little surprise for you." She wondered what could be next. Then, she heard the front door open. Daniel quickly removed his hands. Deborah gasped as the two men walked towards her.

Astonished, Deborah began to tear up at the sight of both of her brothers. She had talked to them on the phone since returning home, but actually hadn't seen them since she was seventeen. Her older brother, Paul, looked just like her father; so much so that, for a moment, she was taken aback. Paul was now about the same age as her father was when he had started molesting Deborah. She quickly recovered and turned her attention to Timothy, who was a combination of both her mother and father. She opened her arms wide, and they both were embraced by her hug. Tears were flowing freely around the room. Both of her brothers lived out west: Paul in California and Timothy in Arizona.

When Daniel knew the date of the engagement party, he had called Paul and Tim to invite them. It didn't take a lot of persuading. He had been ready to buy their tickets, but the brothers would have not part of that. He knew how much this would mean to Deborah. Restoring family relationships was high on her list of priorities. He was overjoyed when they had consented to fly in for the party.

"Just look at you, little sister! You're beautiful!" Paul said as he stepped back and admired her.

Deborah grinned and said, "You sound awfully surprised. What did you think you would find?"

Her mother laughed and interjected, "Now, don't you two start already."

Timothy said, "It's so good to see you, sis. You do look wonderful."

Deborah smiled with happiness, "I can't believe you're really here. I've seen Mom's pictures of you and your families, but they never seemed real because you've been so far away. I just keep picturing you both the way you were when I left home. But I guess you really have grown up!"

Mary Rachel, Deborah's younger sister, stepped forward to hug her brothers, "Don't forget, you do have two sisters."

Tim quickly turned and gave her a big hug then Paul picked her up and swung her around, "Don't worry, we could never forget you!" She began pounding him on the back, telling him to put her down, but the smile on her face said that she was loving every minute of it. Mary Rachel's husband, Jonathan, and their son, Nathan were next in line.

Paul said to Deborah and Daniel, "We understand that you have other guests to tend to tonight so we won't take up all your time. We're going to be in town for a couple of days, we'll have plenty of time to catch up."

"You better have brought lots of pictures with you. I hope this doesn't mean you won't be home for the wedding," Deborah said in the next breath.

Timothy replied, "No, Daniel already made us promise. We plan on bringing our families out in April. You picked a good date for the wedding-April fifteenth is in the middle of spring break this year so the whole family can come."

Now it was Daniel's turn to step in, he gave both of Deborah's brothers a hearty bear hug, "I'm so glad you could make it. I knew how much it would mean to Deborah. She's always talking about how long it's been since she's seen you. I can't thank you enough for coming."

As Deborah turned to greet new arrivals, Paul put his hand on Daniel's arm and said quietly, "Can we talk a minute?" The two men casually walked into the kitchen and out on the back porch. As soon as they were alone, Paul said, "What about this Tommie Lee, guy? Mom seems pretty upset. How dangerous is he?"

Daniel said, "I'm not going to minimize it. He's one bad dude. They were getting ready to put Deborah in the trunk of the car—Sanchez has since confessed that they had plans to kill her. I haven't told Deborah about the confession—she may still think that all they were doing was taking her back to Louisiana. I just found out and hadn't wanted to spoil the engagement party. Actually, she's been incredibly courageous in the midst of everything. Deep down she may have known their true intent but as strange as it may seem, we've just never discussed it."

Paul asked, "Do the police have any leads on this guy?"

"Not that we know it. They've been faithful in keeping a police presence around Deborah. Actually there's an unmarked car sitting across the street right now. I just don't know how long they'll be willing to do that. Surveillance is expensive, and Deerfield doesn't have a big city budget."

Letting out an expletive, Paul continued, "I'm sorry, I just feel helpless all the way out in California. I just wish I could get my hands on that S.O.B."

He was interrupted by his mother's voice, "Paul, Paul, where are you. There's someone here I want you to meet."

Paul looked at Daniel and said, "We'll talk more later."

As they walked back into the house, Daniel thought to himself, Deborah wasn't kidding when she said her brother was always very angry. He had felt the man's rage just under the surface. He tried to shake it off as he walked back inside.

That evening as the last goodbyes had been said, Daniel and Deborah returned to the kitchen to help with the cleanup. Anne and Robert were both still there and the four of them shooed the Worthington parents to bed. The Worthington's finally acquiesced and made their way up the stairs.

As they got ready for bed, Daniel's mother realized how happy she has been that evening. The party had been a great success, and both her and her husband had wanted to make Deborah feel welcomed and loved. She had been radiant this evening and it had been so much fun for everyone when they had seen the look on her face when she saw her brothers. Climbing into bed next to her husband she noted, "Deborah is going to be a beautiful bride, isn't she?"

"Yes, dear, but you need to go to sleep and not start planning the wedding tonight."

She chuckled, "You know me too well."

"Forty years of marriage should give me some clue," he countered. "But seriously, you did a wonderful job tonight. The food was great and everything looked beautiful. I could tell that Daniel was blessed by everything. All I know is that it feels so good to see him smiling again."

"Both him and the children. I think David and Aimee had fun tonight, too. It's so important to make them feel a part of everything right now. I'm just praying for a smooth transition. Right now everything's fine, but I wonder how they're going to do when Deborah actually becomes their step-mother."

"That concern will have to wait for another night," he said leaning into her. "I am beyond tired!" he exclaimed as he kissed his wife. "Besides, Deborah can hold her own. I think she'll do fine. Now let's get some rest, it's been a long day."

Elizabeth Millstone lay awake reliving the evening. She hadn't experienced such a sense of joy and well-being in years. She had enjoyed the engagement party very much and was so thankful for the Worthington's and how they had embraced Deborah. Actually, she could not remember when she had been so happy. It had been a miracle to have all of her children gathered together in the same room. She had kept in touch with them, e-mailing and talking often, but she hadn't seen either one of them in several years. For the first time in a long time she thought about her husband.

It was too bad Theodore had not lived long enough to see it. Because of his controlling personality, all their children had gotten as far away from home as they possibly could as soon as they were old enough; it had been such a shame. She couldn't believe how much Paul looked like him, and he had those high cheekbones like Deborah's. Theodore had been such a handsome man. For a moment, she almost missed him.

Elizabeth was still awake when she heard Deborah come in the back door. Tomorrow was Saturday and she was going to be making dinner for the whole family. As she lay there she thought about the groceries she would need to pick up in the morning and how it was going to be crowded with everyone there. Mary Rachel, Jonathan and Nathan had decided that they would stay the weekend as well. She wondered for a moment if they would all go to church together on Sunday. It had been years since her two sons had been to church, but she decided that she wouldn't be the one to ask. She knew Deborah had been trying to witness to Mary Rachel lately. All she could do was pray.

She thought about how her family was now, finally, coming together. She thought about Deborah and how afraid she had been when she had first come home. It seemed foolish now, but in the beginning, her own daughter had felt like a stranger who had suddenly moved in with her. Since Deborah's return from the ministry in Florida, however, the mother-daughter relationship had never been better. But, every once and awhile, Elizabeth still felt as if there was somewhat of a wall between her and her oldest daughter. It was almost as if Deborah wouldn't allow herself to get too close. Whatever it was, she didn't know what else to do but trust the Lord to take care of it in His time. She decided to read for a while to unwind; there had been too much excitement that night for her to just drop off to sleep.

———————————————

While Deborah started her bedtime routine, she reflected on the evening's events. It had been wonderful being reunited with her brothers; however, she couldn't help returning to the image of Paul's face and how much it shocked her that he looked so much like their father. She still had not told her mother about the molestation. But for some, she was fighting an urge to go and tell her everything.

Deborah knew there was still a barrier between her and her mother. Part of her didn't want to go there, but the other part wanted to be able to share with her sister and brothers why she had really left town years ago. The problem was that everyone was so happy right now and she didn't want to rob their joy or her mother's sleep. She began to pray, "Holy Spirit if this is you make it clear to me." Suddenly her cell phone rang; it was Daniel's ring.

When Deborah answered, he said, "Hi honey, I think the

Lord is putting something on my heart. Is it okay if I share it with you?"

She now felt the anointing of the Holy Spirit all over her. "Okay, but I have something I nccd to ask you about, too."

Daniel began, "I know this might be hard to think about right now, but I saw you talking to your family this weekend about what happened to you."

He heard Deborah take a deep breath on the other end. "That's exactly what I wanted to talk to you about," she said. "I've been fighting the urge to go into my mother's room and tell her everything; but it was such a wonderful evening and she seemed so happy—I didn't want to ruin it for her. The light was still on when I came into my room. She might still be reading. I was just asking the Holy Spirit for confirmation. But Daniel, I'm so scared." Her stomach was knotting up and her mouth was getting drier. "I just don't know what it will do to her. And what if she doesn't believe me?"

Daniel reassured her and then they began to pray together. Deborah decided if her mother's light was still on when they hung up, she would take it as a sign that she should do it tonight. Her insides were shaking as she hung up the phone. She put on her robe and went out into the hallway; underneath her mother's door she saw a crack of light.

Chapter Thirty-Two

The Talk

ॐ ॐ

Tentatively Deborah knocked on her mother's door. "Come in, dear. It's open." Her mother was sitting up in bed with her reading pillow tucked behind her. She peered over her reading glasses. "What is it, Deborah?"

"Do you feel up to talking? I know it's late," Deborah trailed off sort of hoping her mother would give her an out.

"Actually, tonight was so exciting I'm having trouble falling asleep. That's why I was reading. It was so good to see all of you children together in the same room."

Deborah smiled, "Yes, it's been such a special night and the last thing I would want to do is ruin it."

"What do you mean?"

"Mom, I wouldn't be doing this unless I felt I was supposed to; it just doesn't seem like the right timing to me. But, it seems that maybe the Lord thinks otherwise."

Elizabeth wondered if this was what she had just prayed about, she said tentatively, "Go ahead, Deborah, what's on your heart?"

Her first question was, "Mother, did you know?"

"Know what, dear?"

By the look on her mother's face, Deborah knew her first

question had been answered. Her mother hadn't known! One of her fears had always been that her mother had known. She didn't know how she would have handled it if that had been the truth. She began to slowly pouring out her story. Elizabeth was scared to move. Barely breathing, she kept her eyes fixed on her daughter as she shared the secret that had built the wall between them. For the next twenty minutes, Deborah shared the pain of being sexually abused by her father. Deborah ended her story with a question, carefully watching her mother's face for her reaction, "Do you believe me?"

Then the dam broke, Elizabeth began to sob, "I'm so sorry. I'm so sorry. I had no idea—no idea. Of course I believe you. It finally all makes sense."

Now it was Deborah turn to comfort her mother as she rocked back and forth, bent over in pain and grief.

Elizabeth felt so stupid; how had she not known? Had she just been blind because it was easier? It was going to be hard to forgive herself for this one. No wonder there had been a wall between her and Deborah.

She finally had enough presence to say, "It's hard to believe I was so blind. You must have felt terribly unprotected and all alone. I knew your father had problems, but obviously I didn't know the extent of them. Can you ever forgive me, Deborah?"

"Me forgive you? I've wanted to ask for your forgiveness all these years. He was your husband."

Elizabeth saw the guilt written on her daughter's face and sensed the burden she had carried all those years. "Deborah, I can't forgive you for something that was done to you. I don't believe it was ever your intention; but if you need to hear the words, of course I forgive you."

At that it was Deborah's turn to fall into her mother's arms sobbing. "I was so afraid you would hate me or that you wouldn't believe me. I've wanted to tell you so many times."

Her mom said, "Deborah, can you forgive me for not

recognizing the signs, for not protecting you and for living in my own world?"

"Of course, Mom, I really already have. I did have to work through some of my anger towards you when I was going through the ministry in Florida. I just don't know what I would have done if you had known and had just let it happen. I didn't want to believe it, but I have to admit at times I wondered."

Elizabeth responded, "I promise you, there were a lot of things I thought and knew about your father but I never saw this. I guess he was so religious and everything. He hid it well. I'm just glad he's already dead because right now I feel like killing him."

Deborah was shocked for a moment to hear her mother express that much anger, but part of it made her feel good to hear her mother's response. This was a conversation she had played over and over again in her head; it had actually turned out better than any time she had rehearsed it. Though she had been dreading this moment, it had actually taken less than an hour for Deborah to discuss what had bothered her for more than twenty years.

Even though it had all been hard to hear, Elizabeth still felt a sense of relief. She thought for a moment then said, "I think we need to tell the rest of the family tomorrow. Do you think it happened to Mary Rachel, as well?" her thoughts suddenly turning to her youngest daughter.

"I don't know for sure." Deborah admitted, "I haven't point blank asked her, but I have alluded to it. I guess a part of me really hasn't wanted to know. It almost feels like it would hurt worse than when happened to me."

Elizabeth decided, "Why don't we have dinner first tomorrow and then have a family discussion? I know this is hard especially when you haven't seen your brothers in years, but I believe it's time. No more secrets."

Deborah nodded and patted her mother's hand. "Okay, I guess if I could do this, I probably can do anything. Thank you,

Mom. Thank you for believing me and thank you for not giving up on me." She leaned down and kissed the top of her mother's head. "I think it's time we both get some sleep, and I need to call Daniel. I'm sure he's waiting up."

"Does he know?"

Deborah saw the flicker of shame across her mother's face. "Yes, Mom, I had to tell him. It affected him, also. It was the reason I dumped him. I was afraid he was just like Dad. After all, he went to church and professed to be a Christian. I just couldn't trust that, not after setting on a church pew with a father who was molesting me."

"It's okay, I understand. No wonder we always had such a battle trying to get you to church. You had to have been so confused. I'm so sorry, Deborah," she apologized again.

Seeing the sorrow in her mother's eyes Deborah suggested, "Let's try and get some sleep, I have a feeling tomorrow is going to be a long day."

Daniel had just dozed off when the phone rang. "She believed me, Daniel, it's going to be okay," Deborah said excitedly before even saying hello. He was so relieved at the sound of her voice. Tonight had the potential of devastating her. He was so glad to hear how well Elizabeth had handled the news. He had prayed intensely, but you never knew how people would respond. He had heard of a number of cases where mothers refused to believe their children, even when they were older.

"That's awesome. So she's really okay with you telling your brothers and sister?"

"She was the one who suggested it before I even asked. I only hope it goes as smooth with them as it did with mom. I can hardly wait to call Lydia and tell her I finally did it. It's as freeing as she said it would be. I feel free, Daniel, free!"

They talked for several more minutes and then said goodnight. Deborah then picked up her Bible and opened it to one of her favorite passages: Psalm 61. She loved How David wrote the part about mercy and truth preserving him. Tonight she had experienced both: mercy and truth. "Yes, Lord, I will sing praise to Your Name, forever and ever." God had been so good to her; more and more she was feeling an overwhelming desire to serve Him. She didn't know exactly what that meant, but she knew that she was willing to do anything He asked her to do. She was His-there was no turning back.

Chapter Thirty-Three

Preparation

৵ ৶

Elizabeth woke up early Saturday morning. After Deborah had left her room the night before, she had cried herself to sleep. This morning her eyes were still puffy, and she felt like she had barely slept at all. She was relieved to have learned the truth, and was so glad that her daughter had finally confided in her after all these years; but, it still was hard to digest everything. She could only imagine what Deborah had gone through all these years. Thank God, Theodore was gone. If he was still alive, she didn't know what she would do. She prayed that Mary Rachel had not been molested, also. She hoped that question would be answered today.

Elizabeth showered and tried to fix herself up as best she could. She had to go to the grocery store for a few things before she started preparing dinner. She slipped out of the house without seeing Deborah. She hoped her daughter had rested better than she had.

When Deborah woke up, the house was quiet. Surprisingly, she had fallen asleep quickly the night before and woke up feeling rested. It had felt so good to finally be able to tell her mother everything; it was like a huge weight had been lifted from her shoulders. Now, she had to figure out how to tell the rest of the family. She lay in bed trying to picture what she should say. Finally, she prayed in the Spirit and said, "Lord, I don't know how to do this. I need your help." In no time at all, she knew that the conversation was supposed to take place after dinner. Her mother was supposed to take Nathan out for ice cream and then she would talk to her brothers and sister. She would have to run it by her mother, but it sounded like, at least, a beginning of a plan.

Deborah decided to get up and start cleaning up the house. Her mom had left a note saying she had gone to pick up groceries. Deborah turned on her praise and worship music extra loud and went to work cleaning. She was surprised at the amount of energy she had considering everything that had transpired. She hoped that after sharing with her siblings about the abuse she would feel the same. When she thought of Mary Rachel, though, she felt sick to her stomach. She hoped that her sister had not experienced the same thing she had at the hands of their father.

———————————

Paul and Tim spent the morning driving around Deerfield reminiscing together. They were both excited to have seen Deborah the night before. Paul decided he wanted to drive by the old homestead. When they pulled up to the driveway, they were both surprised to see that the new owners had painted it a different color; it had always been white with a deep green trim. Now the house was a sunny yellow with off white trim. It was bright and cheery and there were children's toys scattered on the front porch.

As the memories of his father's voice and beatings flooded back into his consciousness, Paul gripped the steering wheel. He knew everything the Bible said about forgiveness, but he never had been able to forgive his father. Many nights he had been tormented by dreams of turning on his father and beating him to death in a fit of rage. He was feeling sick to his stomach now. "Come on, Tim, let's get going. It doesn't even look like the same place," he said brusquely.

Tim saw the change in his brother's countenance and agreed, "You're right, the place sure looks different. I think there's a couple of tree missing, too. Remember that big oak we had the tire swing on? I hope they didn't just cut it down."

"I'm sure there was probably a storm or something. That tree was just too big and beautiful just to take it out for no reason." Paul slowly eased the car away from the curb. "He sure was a son of a bitch," he said out of nowhere.

Tim knew exactly who he was talking about, "Yeah and you probably knew that better than all of us. All I know was I was scared to death of him. I wouldn't have even gone to the funeral except for Mom."

"Me, too," Paul said in agreement. For a while they drove in silence. Then they pulled up to the front of their old high school. The conversation became light-hearted again as they talked about some of their past school adventures and sports victories.

Elizabeth arrived home to find Deborah cleaning and in a very light hearted mood. She had been a little apprehensive about seeing Deborah, but it was obvious that Deborah had worked through a lot of the pain of the abuse before last night. Now, it would be Elizabeth's turn. As they were putting away groceries, she said to her daughter, "I was praying this morning on the way to the store, and I thought that it would probably be best for me to take Nathan out for a while this evening after dinner. That would give you an opportunity to talk to the boys and Mary Rachel."

Deborah nodded, "I saw the same thing. You can take him out for some ice cream and then afterwards, maybe his dad can spend some more time with him, and we can talk as a family." It made Elizabeth feel a little more peaceful knowing there was a plan in place. She and Deborah continued to work together in the little kitchen. The invisible wall that had been between them for as long as she could remember had finally been brought down.

That afternoon, Daniel was the first to arrive. He could see a change in Deborah's countenance; telling her mother after all these years had been the right thing to do. "You look beautiful," he said as he gave her a quick hug in the kitchen.

"Even though I've been a kitchen slave all day long?" she asked with a grin.

Elizabeth who was just freshly showered came into the kitchen, "Deborah, hurry up and get ready before everyone arrives. I'll take it from here."

Deborah took off her apron and handed it to Daniel. "I'll be back in ten minutes," she said.

After she left, Daniel's attention turned towards Elizabeth, "How are you doing?" he asked.

"Better this afternoon, but I have to admit last night was hard. I just knew I couldn't fall apart. Deborah's going to need me tonight. I'm so sorry, Daniel. Do you think she's going to be okay?"

Daniel said, "She's going to be fine. This was a big hurdle, but she had a lot of ministry when she went to Florida. It was hard for her to tell me too, but when she did, so many things finally made sense. I can't tell you how many times I've asked the Lord what had happened that summer she turned thirteen. I always knew something in her had changed. I just never knew what or why."

Tears flooded Elizabeth's eyes. She blinked several times and then said, "We have a dinner to put on. Will you set the table?"

Realizing Elizabeth was trying to change the subject Daniel smiled and said, "Sure Mrs. Noble, I am at your service."

When Deborah came out of her room, she found the table set, and Daniel filling glasses with ice. Before she could say a word, the doorbell rang; Paul and Tim had arrived.

Chapter Thirty-Four

Family Dinner

ॐ ॐ

Once everyone found their seats at the dinner table, Elizabeth asked Daniel to say the blessing before the family began eating. He nodded and began, "Lord, we ask You to bless this food and those who prepared it. We thank You for gathering us together today and pray for Your peace and Your presence to be with us. Amen." Paul and Tim had uncomfortably bowed their heads; saying Grace was a practice they had abandoned since leaving home. Mealtimes had always been so uncomfortable when they were growing up. Their father's presence always guaranteeing that the whole family would be on edge.

Deborah sensing the tension said, "So what did you boys do today?"

Paul responded, "Just rode around town and spent some time reminiscing. We rode past the old place; it sure doesn't look the same."

Elizabeth joined in, "Yes, it's been painted and they lost a couple of big trees in that tornado that came through last summer. Amazing the house wasn't touched a bit."

The meal was pretty uneventful. Everyone continued to make small talk about their lives, jobs, and areas where they lived. The most excitement came when Nathan ended up knocking over his glass of milk which sent Mary Rachel and Elizabeth scurrying. As everyone got close to finishing, Elizabeth said, "I made your two favorite desserts, my double chocolate cake and Sunday pie, so you better save room."

"Mom, you didn't have to go to all that trouble," Tim said.

Paul playfully elbowed him, "Be quiet, little brother. I love my wife, but she's just not a cook like Mom. You can speak for yourself, but I plan on enjoying every bite!" Elizabeth smiled and was glad she had put forth the extra effort. This was a special day

Deborah said, "I'm going to put on some coffee, I forgot to do it earlier." As she walked into the kitchen, she began praying in the Spirit. She couldn't figure out how to bridge the subject of having a serious family talk with the mundane conversations that were going on over dinner. Seconds later, the anxiety she had started feeling began to dissipate. When she walked back into the dining room she heard her mother ask, "Mary Rachel and Jonathan, would it be okay if Nathan and I run out for some ice cream while you all have dessert? Deborah has some things that she needs to share with you?"

Well, there it was, out on the table. There was no going back now. As she returned to her seat, she could feel everyone's eyes on her. Mary Rachel blurted out, "You're not pregnant are you?"

Daniel reached out and lightly patted Deborah's arm. It reassured her and she responded gently, "No, not at all. Daniel and I haven't even kissed and we don't plan to until after our wedding vows. This is just some family business that needs to be taken care of and with everyone here. Mom and I thought it would be best to do it today. It's just something that's grown-up talk."

"Okay, no problem," Mary Rachel responded, "Nathan would you like to go get ice cream with Grandma?"

"Yeaah, ice cream! Can I get sprinkles, too?"

"Absolutely!" Elizabeth answered her grandson quickly. At least one of the parties was being cooperative with the plan.

Elizabeth and Nathan gave kisses all the way around the table as they were readying to leave. Paul and Tim still had quizzical looks on their faces as they both tried to figure out what kind of family business Deborah wanted to discuss. As the door closed behind Elizabeth and Nathan, who had begun to contemplate all the combinations of ice-cream and sprinkles he could make, the room suddenly became very quiet. Deborah could feel the tension mounting and became keenly aware that moment of just how glad she was that Daniel was there with her. "How about going into the living room to finish your dessert?" she asked no one in particular.

"That's fine. I'm finished already," Mary Rachel replied as she got up to bring her plate into the kitchen. "Does anyone want more coffee while I'm up?"

Tim lifted his cup, "I just need a warm up." Mary Rachel grabbed it as she passed by walking into the kitchen.

Paul said, "I'm stuffed. I just can't resist Mom's cooking."

Daniel reached for Deborah's dessert plate, which she had barely touched and headed for the kitchen after Mary Rachel. Deborah picked up her coffee cup and went and sat in her mother's rocker. One by one the rest of the family followed her into the living room. Before she knew it, all eyes were trained on her.

Deborah took a deep breath then began, "I talked to Mom last night. I really hate to bring this up right now because I don't want to spoil our time together. But mom and I both felt all of you had the right to know." She took the plunge and blurted out, "Dad, sexually abused me for years. That's why I left home and never came back." For a moment, the room was silent as everyone processed the news. Mary Rachel started to weep. Deborah immediately asked, "Did he touch you, too?"

Mary Rachel cried louder. Jonathan put his arm protectively around her shoulder. She shook her head, "no."

Paul said, "That bastard! If he weren't dead, I would kill him! I knew he was evil, but that's disgusting. Mr. Church Elder, know it all-"

Tim interrupted tersely, "Not now Paul. We're all angry but that's not what the girls need right now." Paul quieted down but his body was tense with anger.

Deborah said, "Mary Rachel, why are you crying? What did he do to you?"

She cried harder saying, "I knew. I knew and I didn't do anything to help you. I was too scared." She began to cry hysterically.

Deborah said, "You knew? How did you know? You've never said anything."

Jonathan started gently rocking his wife, trying to calm her down. He said quietly, "One morning, she forgot her lunch and came back home. She heard a noise upstairs. She listened by your door and heard your father. She was too scared to open the door and ran out of the house. She always hoped that what she thought she heard wasn't really happening."

As he finished, Mary Rachel sobbed louder, "I didn't stop him. I could have stopped him. I left you there by yourself."

Deborah made her way across the room and hugged her sister. "It's okay. You were so young. I'm just so glad he didn't do it to you, too. I was so afraid if I left, he would start using you. I begged him not to and threatened to kill him if he touched you. I've been so scared to ask you."

Daniel, handed Deborah and her sister tissues as they held each other and cried together. Paul and Tim both sat with tears in their eyes, not knowing what to do next. As the girls began to dry their eyes Tim got up and knelt down next to them, "I'm so sorry. I'm so sorry," he repeated several times.

Paul sat paralyzed, still stunned by the news. He had spent his whole life thinking he was the family victim because of the physical abuse he had received; this new information changed everything. A beating was one thing, but being sexually abused by your father was another.

Deborah told them how it had happened. "It started the summer I turned thirteen and didn't end until I was sixteen. I bought a hunting knife and finally told him that if he did it again, I would kill him. He stopped. I wish I had stood up for myself sooner. But, I want you all to know, I have forgiven him and I want you to forgive him, too."

At her words Paul stood up and cursed, "There's no way! How can you do that? He ruined our lives!" With that, he got up and stomped outside.

Chapter Thirty-Five

Forgiveness

As Nathan finished his ice cream, Elizabeth wondered how much longer they should stay out. She would love to know what was happening right now. Part of her was glad she didn't have to be there, but on the other hand, she didn't want Deborah to feel abandoned. She was also afraid that she would come home and learn that Mary Rachel had been abused. Her grandson was trying to get her attention, "What honey?" she asked.

"Grandma are you sad?" he asked.

She didn't want to lie to him, "A little bit."

"Why are you sad?"

"Because someone hurt your Aunt Deborah a long time ago," she replied. She was thankful that the answer satisfied him and he went back to cleaning up the rest of his ice cream. Elizabeth checked her cell phone again. Deborah had promised to call her after it was done. There was still no message. She decided to take Nathan for a drive but wasn't quite sure where to go.

Daniel had gone outside and helped calm Paul down.

When they both returned, Deborah explained about the ministry she had received last April. "I know it might be hard to believe, but I really was finally able to forgive him. I know it was just the grace of God. I don't know how I would have handled it if Mom had known, but I really believe she honestly didn't know. I think she was so busy surviving herself; she didn't have time to pay attention to much else. I also have something else I need to share. I just found this out last month. It's about Dad. I had already forgiven him, but still part of me kept asking 'why?' and then Aunt Liberty helped fill in the missing pieces."

Once again, Deborah had everyone's attention. She began to reveal the Noble family secret. "Aunt Liberty told me that Dad was actually the love child of the Judge and his secretary. Grandma Regina agreed to accept the child as hers because the Judge threatened to divorce her if she didn't. His secretary, Louise, left town and had the baby. Then, Aunt Liberty helped exchange the baby; she was still very torn up about her part in it and begged for forgiveness when she told me. The story was that Regina had gone abroad but came home early, supposedly with a premature baby. That's why Regina was always so cruel to Dad. But it gets worse, when Dad was only fourteen, Regina got him drunk and seduced him, then she told the Judge. That's why he was sent off to military school." She was a little breathless as she finished pouring out the whole story complete with the details Liberty had given her. She felt exhausted but it felt good to get it all out. Daniel patted her hand reassuringly.

Everyone but Daniel looked a little dumbfounded. Mary Rachel spoke up first, "No wonder he was so messed up."

Paul said, "I still don't think it's any excuse for what he did to all of us."

Deborah explained, "I didn't say it excused him. It just made it understandable. Even though I'd forgiven him, what Aunt Liberty shared with me helped take away some of the confusion."

Tim asked, "Did Mom know any of this?"

"Not until last night," Deborah said. "It's like she lived all of those years with a stranger. Is it okay if I call her now? We'll still have a little bit of time to talk while she drives home. Mary Rachel, I bought a new Veggie Tale video for Nathan. Would it be alright if he went in my room and watched it while we talked a little more? I just think Mom needs to be here some, too." They all agreed and Deborah made the call.

Elizabeth was relieved to hear Deborah's voice. Wondering what her children would think of her now, she found her hands shaking on the wheel as she drove home. How could so much have gone on right under her nose without her knowledge? It had taken almost all she had last night, but at least she had made the decision to forgive Theodore. Because of the Biblical command to forgive, Elizabeth knew that she had to do it, but it was tough. There were still no real feelings of forgiveness, but those would have to come later. She hoped her children could forgive her and their father; especially Paul, he was so hard and bitter.

She had driven Jonathan and Mary Rachel's SUV and pulled it carefully into the driveway. Nathan was already getting out of his seat belt as she went around and opened the car door. With mixed emotions, she followed him as he went skipping up the walk. When she opened the front door and walked into the living room, the first thing she noticed was that Mary Rachel's face was swollen and her eyes were red. Her heart dropped, thinking the worst. She looked at Deborah questioningly.

Deborah shook her head, "no.'

After Deborah settled Nathan in her room with his Veggie Tale video, she and her mother walked back into the living room. Elizabeth felt everyone's eyes on her. She sat down in the chair that Daniel had brought in from the dining room. Hesitantly, she started talking, "I don't really know what to say. I just want all of you to know that I am so sorry for your suffering and for not being more aware. I was so intimidated by your father; I couldn't trust my own judgment or discernment. Last night, everything that Deborah told me was a total shock; but as painful as it was, it's brought a sense of peace and understanding. Now, I know why so many things happened. It's taken me quite a while to forgive your father for how he treated me and all you children when you were young. I think I finally got there this past year. It especially helped when Deborah came home. But after last night, I know I will have to start all over again." She paused for a minute her eyes filling with tears.

Deborah interjected, "Actually, that's where we were when you came home. I was explaining to Paul, how free I have felt since I've forgiven him. And that I didn't forgive him just because of what Aunt Liberty had shared. Knowing his truth and secret helped me understand how something so perverted could have happened. I always knew Dad was a tormented soul, but now I know why."

Mary Rachel started sniffing again and then poured out her secret to her mother. Elizabeth went over and hugged her daughter and prayed that she would be free from any sense of guilt or false responsibility.

Tim finally spoke up, "I know the Bible says we're supposed to forgive, but to be honest, it's something I'm going to have to work on…"

Paul interrupted, "Well, you can work on it if you want little brother. As for me, God will just have to do a miracle. Because right now, I hope he's rotting in hell!" They all knew the beatings that Paul had endured as a child had hardened his heart over the years. Time and time again, as a small child, he had forgiven his father and had prayed that the beatings would stop. But, over and over again, he had felt the ferociousness of his father's anger and the sting of the belt cutting his flesh.

Quietly, Deborah said, "I agree that it'll take a miracle, and I want you to know, Paul, I am praying that one day, you will have that miracle. All I can tell you is what God did for me while I was in Florida. Somehow I was able to see that hanging on to the pain and anger was stopping me from reaching out for God's love and freedom. I had to let go of one to be able to grasp the other. His grace was there to help me and I did it. It was a choice first, an act of my will, but eventually the feelings began to follow." As Deborah finished, she got up and walked over to where Paul was sitting and put her arms around him. His jaw was clenched, and she could feel the tension in his body. She said, "I love you, Paul, and I'm so sorry for your pain." She began to pray softly in the Spirit, just as Lydia and Joyce had prayed over her in her spirit/soul hurt session.

From where Daniel was watching and praying, he saw Paul's shoulders begin to shake and pretty soon he was crying in Deborah's arms. It was the first time Paul had cried since he had turned thirteen. Even though he did not confess forgiveness toward his father that night, everyone knew the softening of his heart had begun.

As the last good-byes were said, Daniel turned towards Deborah, "I am so proud of you. I know how hard this was for you, but you did it!"

Suddenly, all the poise and grace she had walked in that day left. She fell into his arms weeping in intercession, "Oh, God, heal them. Please heal them. Heal us all. Help us, Jesus, help us! Oh God, it hurts so bad!" She sobbed in his arms for several minutes as she prayed for her family.

Daniel thought of the scripture that said when we sow in tears, we will one day reap in joy. He remembered sowing his own tears for Deborah as a teenager. "Some harvests just take longer than others," he thought as she finished crying.

Chapter Thirty-Six

The Diagnosis

వ్ ∞

A couple of weeks after the engagement party Daniel received a call from Pastor Mark. After a brief hello, the pastor asked, "Daniel, do you think it would be possible for you and Deborah to meet with me Tuesday evening. I'd like to do it at the house if that's okay? The kids are spending the night at their grandparent's and Christina and I would like to have the two of you over for dinner. There's something we need to talk about. I'm sorry; I know this is real short notice. I hope it works out."

Daniel replied, "Well, I need to check with Deborah, but I'm sure she would love to if she's available. I'll give her a call and get back to you."

"Sounds good. You can reach me directly on my cell phone. I'll be waiting for your call."

When Daniel hung up the phone, he was a little puzzled about what else they needed to discuss, but, with Pastor Harrison you never knew. He called Deborah and left a message. They hadn't had a private time to let Pastor Mark know about everything that had transpired with Deborah's family; times before and after church services, did not lend itself to much privacy. A nice intimate dinner would be a good time for that. He knew Pastor Mark would be happy to hear that Deborah had been able to open up to her mother and the rest of the family. It was just one more step in her healing.

During her morning break, Deborah checked her messages. Like Daniel, she was excited about having dinner with Pastor Mark and Christina, but curious about what he wanted to share with them. She called Daniel's office. Irene answered and informed her that he was on an important call. "Just tell him I called, and dinner tomorrow evening would be fine with me."

After his phone call, Daniel received Deborah's message and returned Pastor Mark's call letting him know that Tuesday evening would be fine. He then turned his attention to the afternoon's work. He had a new client stopping by and had to finish storyboarding the commercial they would be shooting next week. He made a quick note to himself to call Missy and see if she would be available tomorrow night. If not, Deborah's mom had volunteered her services if they ever needed them. It might **be** a good idea to have her come over and watch them he thought. She seemed genuine about wanting to get to know them better. He added "call Deborah first" to the note and then went back to the computer.

———————————

Christina was looking forward to having dinner with Daniel and Deborah. She had fixed lasagna, a garden salad and garlic bread. It was a simple meal, but everyone loved her lasagna. She was putting the finishing touches on the table when Mark arrived home. He kissed her as he drew a bouquet of fresh cut flowers from behind his back. "For you," he said with a grin.

"They're perfect! I was just thinking that it was too bad I didn't have flowers for the table," she said, taking the mixed bouquet from his hand. Are you nervous about tonight?" she asked.

"No, not really, I just hope I can explain everything in a way that makes sense to Daniel and Deborah. That reminds me,

I need to get the DVD out of the office."

Heading toward the kitchen with the flowers Christina said, "I already have it in the DVD player, just take your shoes off and relax for a few minutes while I finish up. You have about fifteen minutes before they get here."

———————————

Deborah and her mother rode to Daniel's house together. Elizabeth was looking forward to watching David and Aimee and getting to know them better. She was excited about gaining two more grandchildren and she had mixed up a batch of special brownies. Holding the warm pan on her lap, she hoped Daniel would let the children have an evening snack.

When they arrived, Aimee greeted them with unreserved enthusiasm, but David seemed a little uncomfortable. Elizabeth wondered if the reality of the upcoming marriage was starting to affect him. It was one thing when Deborah and Daniel were just friends, but engagement made everything much more official. She determined in her heart to find a way of connecting with him that evening. Her work at hospice had taught her how to find common ground with people, even though it might be just a small plot.

As Daniel and Deborah left the house together, Elizabeth thought about what a handsome couple they made together. Daniel had agreed to let the children have some brownies and even volunteered the vanilla ice cream that was in the freezer. She went into the kitchen with Aimee following. "Now, where do you keep your bowls?" she asked the little girl. Aimee pointed to the cupboard and within a few minutes they were chatting like old friends. David was finishing up his homework when they arrived in the family room with brownies and ice cream in hand.

———————————

Deborah and Daniel arrived at the Harrison's a couple of

minutes early. When Christina greeted them at the front door, she seemed genuinely glad to see them. Deborah hadn't had much direct contact with her since the night she had left their home and everything had transpired with Tommie Lee and Sanchez; but tonight, Christina's demeanor put her at ease immediately.

Dinner was delicious, and the two couples conversed about what was happening in their lives. Daniel finally shared, "Deborah has some news that I think you'll be happy to hear."

"What's that, Deborah?" Pastor Mark asked.

"I finally told my mother and the rest of my family about the abuse. She didn't know. It's like the big invisible wall between us has been removed." She went on to explain what had happened the weekend of the engagement party and the family dinner. Daniel interjected with details as the story unfolded.

After they had finished eating Christina suggested, "Why don't you all go into the living room? I'll clean up and then bring in dessert and coffee. I know Mark has something he needs to share with you." Deborah and Daniel looked at each other, hoping that this wasn't about their upcoming marriage. The date was already set, but they had agreed to submit everything to Pastor Mark. Daniel was surprised to find his heart beating a little rapidly as they moved into the next room.

Pastor Mark started, "I'm sure you two are wondering what this is all about. I didn't want to talk to you until I had more information. I needed to get confirmation on what I had been sensing."

Deborah's palms began to sweat. What if Pastor Mark said they needed to delay the wedding, or what if it was something worse? Maybe God had spoken to him and there wasn't going to be any marriage. The thought made her sick to her stomach.

Pastor Mark, noticing Deborah's anxiety, instantly knew what she was thinking. "Now, this isn't about the two of you or your relationship. I'm sorry. I hadn't even thought that you might think this meeting was about your marriage. I'm so sorry."

The two of them were visibly relieved. Daniel reached for Deborah's hand and patted it. "Well, I was a little nervous riding over here, and you're opening statement shook me up a little," he admitted.

Deborah nodded, "Me, too. But I guess it was good; it made me realize that I am looking forward to this marriage more than I even realized. The prospect of it being delayed or worse yet canceled had me shaking inside."

Pastor Mark feeling terrible for not realizing what he had unintentionally put them through apologized, "I'm so sorry I didn't give you more information. I guess I didn't want you to prejudge the situation before we could all talk in person. This isn't about the two of you, it's about Andrea."

"Andrea? Isn't she still in jail? What does she have to do with us?" Daniel asked.

Pastor Mark replied, "Yes, she's still in jail. But there have been some unusual developments. I have been waiting for the court appointed psychologist to finish his report. I've got it right here."

Deborah said, "They've already taken my statement and I'm willing to testify if I have to. I don't quite understand what more we can do."

"Let me clarify. I've been working with her attorney and the state's attorney. What I have to tell you all started when Andrea requested to see me when she first went to jail. On the first visit, something very unusual happened." He explained the entirety of what he had experienced on both his visits to the jail. He ended saying, "This report confirms what I suspected. Andrea has been diagnosed with Dissociative Identity Disorder. Some of her child alters have been sharing what she lived through as a young girl. It was pretty bad."

Daniel was the first to speak up, "Is that like multiple personalities?"

"Not like it, it is. Several years ago, they changed the diagnostic term. Since my first meeting with Andrea I've actually learned a great deal about the topic. Deborah, your friend, Lydia, has helped me by suggesting some books to read and relaying some of her own personal experience," Pastor Mark informed them.

"So Andrea really is crazy?" Deborah asked.

"Actually, she's very sane. When you understand D.I.D, you find that it is a very complex coping mechanism that allows young children to survive trauma and abuse. When they become adults, their behavior can appear very erratic and crazy, but it makes perfect sense to the personalities within—each has their own identity, responsibilities, and reality. It's really been quite fascinating to study. Is it alright if I explain what actually happened related to Daniel?"

The pastor went on to share how several of Andrea's child parts had decided that Daniel would make a good father and how they liked David and Aimee. They had been scared when her husband had left and wanted someone to take care of them. He explained how Big John had played God within her mind. "I know you probably have a bunch of questions but before we continue there's a DVD I'd like you to watch. Andrea agreed to this interview and also gave me permission to show it to you. This is one of her interviews with the psychologist."

They were all focused on the television when Christina entered the room. She sat down quietly beside her husband and decided to wait a few more minutes before serving dessert. She had already seen the DVD once, but as she watched it again, it was still fascinating to see the physical changes Andrea went through as several of her different identities emerged.

Chapter Thirty-Seven

The Interview

ॐ ॐ

The room was very quiet as the TV faded to black and Andrea's interview came to a close. Daniel was the first to speak up, "That was amazing. I've never seen anything like that before. I wouldn't have believed it if I hadn't seen it myself." Deborah just sat there with tears in her eyes unable to say anything at first.

Christina said quietly, ""Deborah, what's going on inside?"

Reaching for a tissue, Deborah said, "I just feel awful for how I treated Andrea. I just hated her at times and to find out that her abuse was so much worse than what I went through—I guess I just feel like such a terrible person."

Pastor Mark said, "I understand how you're feeling, Deborah, I was her pastor and didn't have a clue. From what I've learned, many of those suffering from D.I.D. create systems that allow them to function quite normally in different settings. Sometimes, their system breaks down and other alters get involved under unusual circumstances or great stress. In this case, the unusual circumstance was Daniel. As you could see from the interview, Andrea was attracted to Daniel but it went beyond that when some of the child alters decided he would be a good daddy for them. Big John and some of the others simply wanted to help the children get what they needed and that's why they called and left you those threatening messages. Just don't feel bad, there was no way for you to know what was really going on with Andrea.

Daniel confessed, "I have to be honest, when you first started telling me about this I thought she had pulled one over on you. But after seeing the DVD I know it wasn't just an act. No one is that good."

"I just can't get over the physical changes. It was amazing to hear the different voices at times and to actually see her face change. I got chills all over just watching it," Deborah said.

Christina agreed, "So did I. Mark and I have also talked about the spirit realm related to all of this. Some Christians think that it's completely demonic and even try to cast alters out of the people, which can be very damaging. Lydia's been a big help. She's lead us to understand that just like a person can be oppressed by the demonic, so can the different alters. For example, Baby Girl who was so afraid of everything, might need some deliverance related to the stronghold of fear. Some people experiencing D.I.D have secular counselors who don't take into account the spirit realm at all. Lydia's opinion is that to really get someone free from this, they need both counseling and deliverance, especially if there was satanic ritual abuse involved."

Daniel interrupted, "That's what I was going to ask next. What are the chances of recovery? I mean, how do you help someone get over this? Is she going to be okay? She looked so confused and frightened in the interview."

Pastor Mark answered, "Actually, they are learning more and more about helping people who suffer from D.I.D. With ongoing treatment many people make full recovery, some call it integration or association. Others come to a place where their systems are manageable and constructive and decide that they want to stay the way they are. I've learned that there are a number of different degrees of disassociation and also several different ways of looking at recovery. It's something that can take time but it is treatable. Dr. McGuire, Andrea's psychologist, helped me to understand the difference between amnesic and co-conscious disassociation and how each affects the treatment process."

"What does that mean? Deborah asked quizzically.

"From what I can gather some people who suffer from this disorder are more aware than others of the thoughts, attitudes, feelings and actions of their parts or alters. Others have very distinct walls of separation between the various personalities or alters, thus, the term amnesic. So one part can go out shopping and then come home, and the following day a different part can't figure out where the new dress came from that's now hanging in the closet. They are amnesic because one part has no memory of what another part does. Part of the healing process is being able to move from amnesic to more co-conscious. For example, until recently Andrea had no awareness of any of her alters, yet several of them related to one another. You saw this when Big John was sharing how he helped protect and take care of some of the younger parts. Of course, those who are amnesic have a little more work to do and may battle even more denial. It helps to record sessions so people are able to see the reality externally, even when they're still not in touch with it internally.

"You didn't get a chance to hear about it in the interview, but on one of my meetings with Andrea, her alter, Big John, shared how he was created. He's not only a man, but what you couldn't see in the interview is that he's also black."

Christina said, "I didn't know that. Isn't that unusual?"

"From what I understand," her husband responded, "it's really not. You know how creative children are—some even have alters that are super heroes. From what I could gather, Andrea's grandfather owned a farm and while her grandparents were still alive she was able to spend time there occasionally. The farm was a respite from her life of abuse at home; an oasis. Her grandfather had hired a black farmhand named, Big John, who helped oversee the operations on the farm. He was always very loving and kind to Andrea. One time when a neighbor's dog tried to attack her, Big John stepped in and rescued her. She was only four or five years old. Her grandparents died in a car accident before her sixth birthday. She never saw Big John again but when she started school some children started bullying and teasing her. That's when Big John was created; she needed someone to protect her on the playground."

Christina interjected, "Would anyone like some more coffee? I have a feeling we might be here a little while longer."

Pastor Mark said, "I'd love some, honey. How about you two?"

Deborah and Daniel nodded in agreement. As she left the room Christina said, "Now, don't talk about anything too interesting while I'm gone. This fascinates me and I want to learn all I can about it."

————————————

While Deborah and Daniel were trying to process the complexities of D.I.D., Elizabeth had gotten the children to bed and then sat down with the book she had brought with her. She had really enjoyed the evening. Aimee had been an absolute delight, but, as much as she had tried, David had still been a little standoffish. She needed to remember to ask Deborah how he was doing with her. It wasn't anything she could put her finger on-he had been polite and respectful, but very guarded. She prayed that the Lord would soften his heart and help him to receive Deborah. Because he was the oldest, it was understandable that he had a great deal more memory and connection with his mother. Maybe she was just being a worry wart and he had just had a tough day at school. Maybe she had just expected too much, really, he hardly knew her. She decided not to even mention it to Deborah. Thanksgiving was coming up and she would see how he did then before she said anything.

Elizabeth pulled the afghan over her legs and decided to enjoy her cup of tea and quiet time. Before she knew it, she had dozed off with the book still in her lap.

Daniel and Deborah didn't leave the Harrison's until after eleven. Everyone had come to the consensus that Andrea needed serious help, but that jail was really no place for her. Deborah and Daniel had agreed to do their part, and Pastor Harrison said that he would try to find out from Andrea's attorney what the next move should be.

As they drove home Deborah admitted, "I can't believe I've gone from wanting to hurt the woman to wishing I could somehow comfort her and tell her everything is going to be okay. I'm going to write a letter to her telling her I forgive her and hope that we can be friends one day."

Daniel agreed, "I'll write a note too and drop it in your letter, but I'm leaving out the friend part if that's okay with you" he chuckled. Continuing, but on a more serious note, he added, "You know it all makes sense now, especially her confusion the night I went by and got the pictures from her. I bet that was the part called Adrian. She looked like a tough cookie during the interview."

"I can only imagine what she went through as a child," Deborah Wondered. "At least my abuse happened when I was older and it had never been physical. Did you see the look of terror in the eyes of Andrea's Little Girl alter when she talked about what would happen when the mother got mad?"

Daniel shuttered, "The thought of holding a child under water as discipline is beyond me. And then when she shared about how the mother would make her hold her hands under the scalding hot water if she touched anything that she wasn't supposed to you could see her quivering with pain. Child abuse is so hard to understand. What could make a mother treat her own flesh and blood like that?"

Deborah responded shaking her head, "All I know from dealing with my own stuff is that Lydia and Joyce say, 'Everyone has a story.' What they mean is that Andrea's mother probably suffered from her own abuse of some fashion. Look at my Dad—I know that what he went through as a child affected him. Without his being abused, he may have never laid a hand on me."

Daniel replied, "I know from what I've learned from you and now this, I'm just not going to be so quick to judge. You just never know what has happened to cause a person to be the way they are. I don't know, but I would have never dreamt that anything like this was going on with Andrea even though I knew her behavior didn't seem quite normal."

Deborah sighed, "I know, Daniel. This hit me real hard tonight. I know how I felt about Andrea in my heart. To think I could have gone to my grave with hatred and jealousy towards her is very sad. I know I have some repenting to do and then I'm going to do some more research. I really would like to learn more about D.I.D. I bet there are a whole lot more people dealing with this than we really realize." They continued discussing the subject and before they knew it they had pulled into Daniel's driveway. "I hope Mom won't be upset that it's so late."

"Me too," Daniel agreed. "I don't want to make the mother of the bride mad at me now," he joked as they walked up to the door. They went in to find Elizabeth dozing in Daniel's recliner.

Chapter Thirty-Eight

Thanksgiving Plans

Anne was looking forward to Thanksgiving dinner. The last several years after Susan's death had been hard, but this year was going to be different: the entire family was getting together. Deborah and Daniel's engagement had everybody excited and looking forward to the spring wedding. The women had decided to set time aside after Thanksgiving dinner to do some of the initial wedding planning. April would get here before they knew it, and Anne and Daniel had taken it upon themselves to convince Deborah to have a special wedding ceremony. Originally, desiring to honor Susan's memory, Deborah had wanted to simply slip off and get married. However, the Worthington family, and especially Daniel, convinced her that this was a special time in her life and that God wanted her to seek Him for the vision of her wedding. Anne had been praying since the engagement party; she knew she was supposed to host a bridal shower in March and had set a tentative date. Even though Deborah still wrestled at times because she had rejected so many traditions for so much of her life, Anne could tell she was starting to get excited about the wedding plans.

Because they had just had a big family dinner at Deborah's mother's house several weeks ago, Deborah,

Elizabeth and Aunt Liberty were all going to Anne and Robert's for Thanksgiving. Anne was looking forward to actually meeting Deborah's Aunt Liberty-she had heard so much about her. It would be the first time Aunt Liberty would actually be meeting Daniel face to face as well, and Anne knew Deborah's aunt's approval was very important to her soon to be sister-in-law.

With the children already at school, Anne decided to get the rest of her shopping done. It was already Monday and she knew that the stores would be getting busier the closer it got to Thanksgiving. Her mother had offered to make the pies, and Elizabeth and Deborah had agreed to make some vegetable dishes. Anne prayed softly in the Spirit as she walked the aisles of the grocery store. As she prayed, Andrea's face came to her mind, which surprised her. She had such mixed emotions about the woman and didn't know why the Lord would be using her to pray for her. She had been so angry at how Andrea had harassed Daniel and Deborah; but she also felt bad knowing Andrea was in jail, especially now during the holidays. Anne prayed for her and found herself asking the Lord to have mercy on Andrea and to bring healing to her. She wondered if Daniel had heard anything new. As far as she knew, there hadn't been a trial date set as of yet.

Anne finished up her shopping and headed home. She wanted to spend the afternoon getting some of her deeper cleaning done. Robert had agreed to help her move some of the living room furniture around that evening and she hoped her ideas would work. With everyone coming over Thursday, rearranging the furniture would give them more space on Thursday. Change was in the air and it would feel good to do some changing at home as well.

The last time Joyce had seen Bill was in the parking lot of the Chinese restaurant. Since then, however, they had developed an e-mail correspondence. They hadn't talked on the phone, but at least a couple of times a week she would find a message in her inbox from Bill and eventually found herself looking forward to them. There wasn't any pressure, both she and Bill found themselves sharing with each other like friends. It was nothing close to what their relationship had been before, and Joyce was beginning to realize that she had never really known her ex-husband.

Bill had also contacted their daughter, Rebecca, as he had promised. The two of them had had several phone calls. During the first call, Bill repented to Rebecca and had been very honest about his sexual addiction and the problems it created in the marriage. What really amazed Joyce was that he had actually given his daughter permission to contact his group leader, Leon, for a progress report. Out of curiosity, Rebecca had **taken** Bill up on his offer and called Leon. She shared with her mother all that had been exchanged between Leon and herself and told Joyce how she was impressed with what the group leader had told her during their conversation. Leon had been very open and honest about her Dad's progress and invited her to call again with any other questions. This was so foreign to both Rebecca and Joyce-Bill had always lived such a secretive, isolated life before the divorce. Now, mother and daughter were not always quite sure how to respond. At first they had both been very guarded, concerned that he was just looking for a way back into their lives. But they were beginning to realize that Bill just wanted to repent, connect with them and that he really didn't have any ulterior motives. He was going to be flying in from California to spend the weekend holiday with Rebecca. It was going to be the first time she would see her father since he had left home. Bill and Rebecca had a lot planned and Joyce noticed that she was actually battling feeling a little left out. Her Thanksgiving was going to consist of helping feed the homeless at noon, and then going to Lydia's daughter's home for dinner later that day. Part of her had just wanted to stay home alone but

Lydia had insisted that she join their family for Thanksgiving dinner. One thing she knew for sure: she would definitely be in prayer; Rebecca wouldn't be able to handle having her heart broken again by her father. Joyce prayed against any spirit of disappointment or hindrances to their plans.

In the county jail that week Sanchez had been doing a Bible study on thankfulness. Even though he was locked up he was still thankful for his new found freedom in Jesus Christ. Several of the other men he was in jail with had already given their lives to the Lord because of his witness-his zeal for the Lord was infectious and genuine; men found themselves attracted and drawn to the light within him.

Pastor Sam hadn't told Sanchez yet, but the church had helped prepare a Thanksgiving surprise for him. They had taken up a special offering and purchased a plane ticket for Mrs. Torres, Sanchez's mother. She would be flying in Wednesday evening and would be given special visiting privileges for that Thursday. It had been a long time since she had seen her son. When Pastor Sam had called her with the news, she had broken down weeping and praising God in Spanish. Pastor Sam had agreed to pick her up at the Columbus airport and drive her to Deerfield. The church had also arranged and paid for a hotel room for her near the county jail. Pastor Sam wished he could be there for the reunion, but he and his wife had a large number of people already coming to their house; they often opened their Thanksgiving meal to those in the church who didn't have family or any place else to go for dinner.

On the Tuesday before Thanksgiving, Daniel, Deborah and Pastor Mark had a meeting scheduled with Mr. Vespia, the D.A. who was handling Andrea's case. Pastor Mark had set up a meeting with the District Attorney, Andrea's attorney, and

Deborah and Daniel after they had agreed to do whatever they could to help. Ms. Talbot, the lawyer representing Andrea, had felt that if Daniel and Deborah dropped their charges and they could present the psychologists report along with recommendations for treatment, there might be a good chance of a plea bargain.

After the meeting, Deborah was the first to speak as the three of them left the courthouse, "Well, I felt it went well. I think Mr. Vespia was a little surprised but over-all I think it was a good meeting, don't you?"

Pastor Mark agreed, "Ms. Talbot told me in the hall that it went even better than she expected. She hopes to have Andrea out by Christmas and in a treatment program. I was glad to hear her that she's already found a special program in Boston. It's a six-month residential treatment program which specializes in Dissociative Identity Disorder. Andrea would be court-ordered there. I'm visiting Andrea tomorrow and I'll be sure to let her know what you two have done for her. She's still a bit confused by everything, but the reality of what is going one is starting to set in more every day. She told me how much your letters forgiving her meant."

Daniel replied, "Well, it's the least we can do. I pray they can get her out as quickly as possible. Her staying in jail can't be helping her. I hope the D.A. can see that what she really needs is treatment."

Pastor Mark agreed, "Hopefully the D.A. will take that into consideration, also. From all the research Ms. Talbot has done, the program she recommended is one of the very few in the country that offers residential treatment. It's not like she's just going to be doing whatever she pleases and then seeing a therapist once a week. It sounds like a great program. At their maximum they only have twelve women in the facility at a time. Andrea has excellent insurance with the bank and it will cover the majority of the cost. She owns her house free and clear and will be able to rent it out while she's in treatment. So I guess the next step will be for Mr. Vespia to contact Ms. Talbot and see if they can negotiate an agreement. I think at this point we've done all we can do. Now it's time to leave it in God's hands." As and Daniel and Deborah got into their cars Pastor Mark noted, "In case I don't see you before then, have a Happy Thanksgiving. Give Anne and Robert my love, and please keep Andrea in your prayers."

Chapter Thirty-Nine

A Family Affair

ॐ ॐ

Thanksgiving Day dawned with a light dusting of snow from the night before but it had completely melted by the time everyone started arriving at Anne's and Robert's for dinner. Anne had scheduled the meal for a little later in the afternoon to give everyone time to sleep in and prepare the dishes that they were bringing. Daniel, Deborah and the kids were the first to arrive. David and Aimee ran in ahead and were already in the family room where the other children were being entertained with a movie when Daniel and Deborah were greeted by the smell of turkey roasting. The kitchen was already warm and cozy. Daniel carried in the beverages, his contribution to dinner, while Deborah brought in her homemade sweet potato pie.

It was the first time Deborah had attempted to recreate one of her mother's specialties. The night before she had even taken out and used the same stained, dog-eared recipe card that her mother had used when she was a child. Anne took the pie from Deborah, "Here, let me have that—I'll put it on this warming tray. It looks delicious." She knew that Deborah had been secretly nervous about preparing a dish for everyone to eat. Deborah had confided in her that she had never really developed her cooking skills but was determined to work on them between now and the time she and Daniel were married.

Before they could get talking there was a knock on the front door and in came the Worthington's. All the grandchildren ran to greet them. Aimee, pulling on her grandmother's hand trying to induce her to come and watch the rest of the movie with them, was only appeased by the promise that after dinner and clean-up, Grandma Betty would definitely watch a movie with her. Grandpa made his way to the living room where Robert and Daniel had already settled in to watch some college football. Even though Ohio State wasn't playing, Florida State and LSU were and it promised to be a very close competitive game.

Betty greeted Deborah warmly as she came into the kitchen, "Well, hello dear. It's so good to see you again. People haven't stopped talking about the engagement party; everyone had such a good time."

Deborah loved Daniel's mother, who had always treated her kindly even when she was a child, but sometimes she felt a little awkward around her. Now especially, because she wasn't sure what to call her. To be safe, she said, "Hi Mrs. Worthington, the party was…"

At that Betty interrupted her, "You can call me Betty or Grandma Betty or Mom like Daniel and Anne do, but Mrs. Worthington will just not do." Seeing Deborah's reaction, she decided to help her out, "Why don't you start by calling me Betty and then we'll see what develops from there."

Relieved at not having to make a choice, Deborah smiled, "That sounds fine to me." She appreciated Betty's sensitivity. Then, to test it out, she said, "Happy Thanksgiving Betty."

Daniel's mom reached out to hug her and said "Now that sounds much better." Then she turned and hugged her daughter, "Okay, Anne, what's left to do? Give me a job or I'll feel useless."

Anne pointed to the salad she had been preparing, "How about if you finish that up for me? I'll get the turkey out so it has time to sit a bit before Robert carves it." Betty reached for one of the extra aprons Anne had hanging behind the door and went to work slicing tomatoes. At that point, Deborah's cell phone rang; her mother was calling to let her know that she and Aunt Liberty were almost there. They were running a few minutes late because of the snowy condition of the roads earlier that morning.

The women were already putting the food on the table when Elizabeth and Aunt Liberty finally arrived. Both made their apologies for running late. Filling the dining room table and buffet, the family observed the feast before them; there was enough food to feed an army. But before everyone began eating, Robert said a blessing and then asked each one to share one thing they were thankful for this year. Daniel was thankful that the Lord had reunited he and Deborah; Elizabeth was thankful that her daughter, Daniel and Pastor Mark had been protected; Anne was thankful that Daniel had asked Deborah to marry him; and little Aimee was even thankful that she was going to have a mommy again. Deborah was a little embarrassed that they focused on her and by how many people were thankful for her. It brought tears to Deborah's eyes, but also along with it, a bit of a panicky feeling which was beginning to sink in-she didn't want to let all of these people down. Understanding responsibility and being in relationships was starting to penetrate Deborah in a deeper way. In her old life, no one had really mattered to her and she hadn't really mattered to any one except for Tommie Lee, who had only really wanted to possess her. Now she was surrounded by people she loved and who loved her back; she was overwhelmed by this new feeling.

At another Thanksgiving dinner on a windy Montana day, Tommie Lee sat uncomfortably at the Heglemen's dining room table; there was no way he could turn down Ed's offer to come to dinner, not after everything he and his parents had done for him. When he had run from Deerfield he knew he couldn't face the Renegade's—not after botching the job like he had. He remembered that he had put Ed's address and phone number in his wallet the day he had walked out of prison as a free man.

Ed Heglemen had been Tommie Lee's cell-mate for about six months; he was in his late twenties and had spent seven years in prison for DUI vehicular manslaughter. Ed's family had always been in the cattle ranching business, but in rebellion, Ed had left the family ranch in Montana to get as far away as he could. He went to work on the Louisiana coast on an off-shore oil rig. During a shore leave he had gotten drunk and had passed out while driving back to the docks. He didn't remember the accident, but a little six year-old boy had been killed by his vehicle. It had really tore Ed up and he was sentenced for ten years; he only did seven with gain time.

While they were cell-mates Tommie Lee and Ed had gotten to know each other pretty well. Right before he got out, Ed gave Tommie Lee the slip of paper with his address and phone number on it, "If you ever need anything, call me. There's always work to do on the ranch so if you need a job or just want to come for a visit, I know my folks will be glad to have you." Tommie Lee had actually met Ed's parents, Ed Sr. and Delores, when they had driven down to the state penitentiary to visit their son. Ed Sr. was a tall, stern, no nonsense sort of a man, and Delores was sweet and bubbly and obviously loved her son. When Ed shared stories with his parents about the times Tommie Lee had stood up and protected him, they both opened their hearts up to Tommie Lee. He knew they were good people and that they shouldn't even get involved with the likes of him; but with nowhere else to go, he had decided to give Ed a call. The invitation to come to the ranch still stood so he ditched the old, green Chevy in a ravine in northern Kentucky, started it on fire, and walked to the nearest town in the dark of night. Early the next morning, he bought a bus ticket to Great Falls, Montana. The trip seemed like it took forever but he finally arrived at the station. Just like they had promised, Ed and his Dad were there waiting for him.

Tommie Lee hadn't minded the work on the ranch; mostly he turned wrenches, which was something he was used to doing. It seemed like there was always something or a piece of equipment breaking down. He kept to himself as much as possible but Ed was always trying to include him in everything as part of the Heglemen family. Not that he didn't appreciate the generosity, family just made him uncomfortable; like sitting down to Thanksgiving dinner at the dining room table surrounded by Ed's brothers, sisters, and nieces and nephews; he just didn't know how to act.

After Tommie Lee finished his meal at the Heglemen's he politely made his way out the door as soon as he could. Since the night he and Sanchez had found Deborah and tried to kidnap and kill her, he hadn't drunk any alcohol or used drugs at all. He knew Ed Sr. wasn't the kind of man to put up with much, but tonight he had decided to drive the fifty miles into town and tie one on. He had saved up some money and was going to get a room and a woman in town and not come back to the ranch until Sunday evening, if he came back at all.

———————————

By the time the last person left Anne and Robert's late that evening, Anne was tired but very happy with how well everything had gone. By all appearances, Aunt Liberty had taken to Daniel-they had been deep in conversation several times-and Elizabeth and Betty seemed to have hit it off pretty good as well. Even though the mothers had known each other years before, they had never been close friends. All of the women had had gotten especially excited when, after dinner, they began discussing plans for the wedding shower and the wedding itself.

Robert said to his wife, "It was a wonderful meal, honey; I'm actually looking forward to the leftovers for lunch tomorrow."

Smiling at him she noted, "And the next day, and the

next. I tried to send some food home with everybody but it just seemed to multiply like the fishes and the loaves. I can't get another thing in the fridge."

Robert said, "I know I'm a glutton for punishment, but I think I'll have just a tiny slice of your mom's pecan pie. I know it's going to take you a little time to unwind, would you like a piece, too?"

"I'm just too full, but I would love a cold glass of water. The kids are awful quiet, I'm going to go check on them and get them off to bed. Then how about spending some time in front of the fire?"

"It's a deal. Meet you there in ten minutes. I have to get the trash out to the curb before I forget.

On the drive to Deborah's, Daniel realized that his fiancé was unusually still. Trying to make conversation, he started off, "I thought it went very well didn't you? You're awful quiet."

"Just thinking the same thing. Daniel, you have to understand some of this is very foreign to me. It just takes a little time to digest. I'm always so amazed with how your family accepts me and how nice they are to me. It's overwhelming at times."

Daniel was glad to hear her response; he had hoped that nothing negative had happened to hurt her. "I just love your aunt; we had the best time talking. She was telling me stories of revivals and camp meetings from years ago and how the Spirit of God would move. Had she ever told you about the time she shook for three days under the power of God?"

"No, I'll have to ask her about that one. Just when I think I've heard everything, Aunt Liberty has another story to tell."

"Are you looking forward to tomorrow?" Daniel asked.

"Yes and no," Deborah replied. "I'm excited about shopping with you for the kids, but to be honest, I've never done anything like that before."

Daniel reassured her, "We'll have a great time in Columbus. Remember, I'm picking you up by eight. It'll feel good to get most of the Christmas shopping out of the way."

"It was so nice of Anne and Robert to volunteer to keep David and Aimee."

"Just remember, we will be reciprocating. Ever since Susan died, Anne and I have had this agreement: I get my shopping done on the day after Thanksgiving, and then one Saturday I keep her kids so her and Robert can spend some time shopping together."

Chapter Forty

The Holidays

ॐ ॐ

Two days before the New Year, Andrea finally got the news of her release date. She had spent both Thanksgiving and Christmas in jail and had never felt lonelier in her life. She thanked God for Pastor Mark-he had been her life-line. She thought about all the times she had been so critical of him and the ministry; now, she didn't know what she would have done without him. Besides helping to uncover her disorder, Pastor Mark had been the one who initiated, orchestrated, fought for and informed her when the D.A. had accepted her lawyer's plea deal. She would be released from the county jail at the beginning of January and enter *A Safe Place*, a residential program known for their work with and help for those suffering from D.I.D. The name made Andrea feel a little better, but fear of the unknown still gripped her.

Recently, Andrea had been having bad dreams of herself as a little girl. In these dreams things were happening to her and she would wake to the feeling of objects being put in her body. She wondered if these terrifying dreams were just dreams, or if they were something that had really happened to her. Both her psychologist and Pastor Mark had told her that Dissociative Identity Disorder was always the result of being severely abused as a very young child. Andrea remembered her Mama yelling at her a lot, but not much else. It did feel as if she were living in a dream world at times. How she had ended up in jail was still beyond her. It was hard to believe she had done the things everyone was saying she did. She remembered thinking that Daniel was her husband, but she didn't remember meeting with Tommie Lee or making the threatening phone calls to Deborah. Sometimes she still wondered if it was all a plot; Deborah's permanent way of getting rid of her. But that didn't make sense anymore because she and Daniel had dropped the charges. She just wasn't sure what or who to believe. Right now she didn't even feel like she could trust herself.

For Pastor Mark the holidays were always such a busy time. His calendar was always full. On one hand there were festivities, Christmas programs and parties; and on the other, many people dealt with a great deal of emotional stress and family problems this time of year.

That morning he had been to the county jail to visit Andrea and inform her that the plea bargaining agreement had been accepted and that *A Safe Place* would have an availability for her the second week of January. He knew it had been hard for her being in jail over the holidays. He had genuinely hoped everything could have been handled before Christmas, but there had been more obstacles than he realized. At least she wasn't going to have to stand trial and she could begin to get the intensive help she desperately needed. At times it was hard seeing the confused look on Andrea's face. During the past few months he had really grown to love Andrea and had a whole new compassion for her.

Pastor Mark and Pastor Sam had also been keeping in contact concerning Sanchez. Pastor Sam called frequently to report Sanchez's progress, and had shared with Mark the precious details of the reunion between Sanchez and his mother at Thanksgiving. The church had received thank you notes from both Sanchez and his mother, and Pastor Mark had been delighted with his progress in the Lord. Pastor Mark was in his office preparing for his New Year's message when he received a call from the jail. The corrections department informed him that he had been given special permission to visit with Sanchez. The pastor's visit would be a short one, taped and monitored, the following afternoon at three o'clock. Pastor Mark was looking forward to the meeting-he hadn't seen Sanchez since the night he had led him to the Lord. Pastor Mark was also informed that Sanchez's trial date had finally been set: it was March third. He made a note of both appointments on his calendar.

Pastor Mark was especially interested to see what would become of Sanchez's trial. There had been some talk of extraditing him back to Louisiana for some of his previous crimes, but since Sanchez's time in jail had been spent maintaining good behavior and he had been faithful in his quest to convert cons into Christians, those charges had been dropped. It had to have been the hand of God. From Pastor Sam's perspective, Sanchez knew he was going to do some time and was not fighting the fact. He believed God wanted to use him within the prison system and this was his way of making restitution. For a moment, Pastor Mark reflected on what could have happened that night. Thank God for prayer and His protection. He knew that it still really bothered Christina that Tommie Lee had yet to be apprehended. He had to be honest, thinking about having to deal with the man again left him a little unnerved as well.

He went back to his New Year's message: *A New Beginning*. Before he knew it, it was time to go home. As he walked to his car a man, looking very down and out, approached him. "Are you the pastor of that church?" he asked.

"Yes, I am," Pastor Mark said.

"Can you spare some change? I haven't eaten and I just want to get a cup of coffee." Pastor Mark prayed quickly, trying to get discernment.

Sometimes people just wanted a hand-out so they could buy some more alcohol and drugs. This time he heard the Lord say, "Help him."

Pastor Mark said, "How about if I do one better than that? Let me buy your dinner."

The man was totally taken back. "I don't smell so good pastor."

"You're fine. Get in, and I'll drive you down to the diner."

Hesitantly the man got into the car. Pastor Mark asked him his name and slowly they began to strike up a conversation. By the time he had dropped the man off at the diner he had learned that his name was Ray. At one time, Ray had owned his own painting business but he was an alcoholic and had lost his business, his family and his dignity. Pastor Mark had invited him to church on Sunday and gave him several vouchers for the local Salvation Army. He would find a bed there and a warm shower. "The title of my message is 'A New Beginning.' Sounds like you need one, Ray. I hope to see you there."

After Ray watched the pastor pay for his meal and walk out of the diner he felt a little hope return to his heart. Maybe this year things could be different. Rather than grating on him, the Christmas music playing in the background was somehow uplifting. He found himself humming to "Joy to the World" as he ate his roast beef and mashed potatoes.

———————————

Closing up the travel office, Deborah realized she was looking forward to a quiet evening at home. She had been extremely busy ever since the engagement party. Last year, she and her mother had just spent a quiet holiday at home. This year had been quite a contrast. Between church, Daniel's family and her own, it had been a busy time; but she wasn't complaining, it felt so good to feel like part of a family.

Tonight Daniel was taking the kids to dinner and a movie. They would be back to school soon and tomorrow night she and Daniel were spending New Year's Eve together. They were invited to Anne and Robert's for a couple's evening that would begin with dinner. She didn't know how Anne kept up with her family and all the entertaining, but she sure seemed to love doing all of it. Deborah would be getting off work at noon the following day to help Anne prepare dinner; she was trying to get all the cooking lessons she could from her soon to be sister-in-law.

As she reached for her long, off-white cashmere coat, the one that Daniel had bought her for Christmas, she was glanced at it slowly once again. It was the most beautiful thing she had ever owned. Every time she put it on she felt like a princess. She could only imagine what it cost. When she had opened the gift she had started to say, "Daniel, I just can't accept..." and then she saw his face. She had quickly corrected herself, "I'm sorry, that was the old me talking. It's beautiful and I definitely needed a new winter coat." Thankful that she had caught herself, it was still hard to understand or accept that Daniel found pleasure in blessing her. Deborah had never known a man quite like him before. She slipped on her coat and gloves and headed to the car, wondering what the New Year held in store. As she pulled out of her parking lot, she heard the Lord whisper to her heart, "It's a new beginning, a new life, a new day." Little did she realize that it was the same message Pastor Mark had been getting that afternoon. God always confirmed his Word out of the mouths of two or more witnesses.

Chapter Forty-One

A Safe Place

֍ ֍

Pastor Mark received special permission to take Andrea to the airport so she could catch her flight to Boston. He had decided it would be best to have Christina ride along with them. He had been building a relationship with Andrea, but would have still felt uncomfortable riding to Columbus in the car alone with her.

When they pulled up to the entrance of the county jail, Christina was shocked when the young woman walked out. Gone was Andrea's perfectly coiffed hair, make-up and clothes. Standing in front of her was a woman whose face was pale and frightened looking, her hair needed trimming and color on it's dark roots that were showing and her clothes needed a good ironing. Christina wouldn't have recognized Andrea if it hadn't been for her husband pointing her out. Trying to hide her surprise Christina embraced her warmly, "Hi, Andrea, it's so good to see you."

With a faint smile Andrea said, "Thank you so much for doing this for me and for all the times you let Pastor Mark visit. I can't tell you what it's meant to me."

Christina hesitated and then said, "Andrea, we want you to know that we're very proud of your decision to go for treatment. We want you to know that we'll be here for you even while you're gone."

Pastor Mark gave Andrea a fatherly squeeze around the shoulders, "We sure are proud of you. Right now, however, you have a flight to catch. Let's get you in the car." He opened up the door to the back seat and Andrea slid in. He and Christina got in the front seat of the car and they began to make their way to the airport.

After they had driven a bit Andrea said, "Christina, I can't begin to tell you how much I appreciate your packing my things. I had direct orders that I had to proceed straight from the jail to the airport. I really am surprised they let the two of you bring me."

Christina responded, "It was no problem. The list and directions you gave me helped immensely. I hope I got everything. Your suitcases are full; I hope they're not overweight."

The three of them continued to make small talk on the way to the airport. Then a very interesting thing happened which amazed Christina, but Mark seemed to take it all in stride. When they arrived at the terminal, Andrea all of a sudden stuck out her hand and said in a deep voice, "Thanks Pastor Mark, I don't know what we would have done without you. Don't you worry, I'll take care of the girls from here. You were a big help."

Mark replied, knowing that he was now talking to Big John, "No problem, it was the least I could do. Now you make sure she catches her flight and gets to Logan International Airport in Boston. I'll be waiting for a call when you arrive." Christina could barely keep her mouth from hanging open; it was one thing to see Andrea switch on the video, but quite another to watch her switch personalities right in front of her. Then someone else hugged Mark's neck like she was afraid to let him go, it was Little Girl. Andrea's voice now switched to a much younger child who said, "I'm scared but Brave Girl and Big John keep telling me it's going to be okay. Is that right Pastor Mark?"

Patiently Mark replied, "That's right, I want everyone to hear me. You're going to be fine. This is the best thing for everyone. You're going to a very special place where people will understand you and love you. Remember Andrea and Big John have my phone number so if you any of you need me, you can call. Adrian if you can hear me, no getting into trouble; you don't want to land back in jail. Remember, Andrea has been court-ordered to this program. You need to cooperate and help her out."

Suddenly, just as quickly as the alters had come, the Andrea that Christina had always known was back and saying goodbye. Christina was amazed at how well her husband had handled the whole conversation without blinking an eye. They stood and waved as Andrea made her way to her departure gate. As she disappeared from sight Mark said in a soft, concerned voice, "I sure hope she's going to be okay."

"She'll be fine. She doesn't have to change planes, and they've promised to have a staff member on the other side. I want you to know, you amazed me back there. You just took that whole conversation in stride. I wouldn't have known what to say," Christina complimented her husband.

Mark seemed pleased with her encouragement, "Well, I have had some practice and I've done a whole lot of studying on the subject since this was uncovered. I've just learned to treat each personality with respect and understanding. I've come to see that each part has a purpose and a redemptive quality; they just have to understand how to help Andrea in a positive way. Like Big John, he's kind of like her internal Father God. If she can begin to connect with her heavenly Father, she won't have the same need to have him taking care of her.

The Harrison's continued to talk and share their observations as they headed to the mall; they had decided to do some after the holiday's shopping. They had received several gift certificates from some of the members of their congregation and all the stores were offering huge discounts. They both decided that just spending time together after the past few months would be a nice way to end the day.

———————————————

The staff at *A Safe Place* was preparing for their new arrival. Janette had been assigned as Andrea's roommate and would be helping her acclimate to her new surroundings. Janette was a forty-four year-old, mother of three. She was on the last phase of the program and had made remarkable progress.

Corrine shared and reminded her, "Just remember what your first week felt like. Make her feel welcome, but don't smother her. Be available to answer any questions and show her around, but be sensitive. Sometimes, people just need their space, especially when they first come here. Janette nodded, remembering the condition she had arrived in. She had been depressed for months and had actually tried committing suicide. Thank God an observant therapist was able to help diagnose the condition and referred her to the residential program.

When her youngest child turned six, things had begun to unravel for Janette. Her two older sons had not triggered any problems, but when her daughter became the same age she had been when her grandfather had started molesting her, all of a sudden she had begun having panic attacks and deep depression. Now she understood everything that had happened and why, but then everything had seemed so out of control. Her husband and family thought she was losing her mind-he had come home at times to find her rocking herself in the closet, scared to come out. She now understood that those were some of the child parts that had been awakened by seeing themselves in her daughter, Samantha.

Once she arrived at *A Safe Place,* more memories of physical abuse and molestation that had occurred at even a younger age began to surface. It had been hard the last nine months being away from her family and children. They lived in New York and had visited several times, but they had all made the decision that they would all sacrifice so that she could get better. Her daughter had just turned nine two months earlier. Yes, she knew what it felt like to be dropped off at a strange place, with strange people, with so much confusion in your head; she determined in her heart to do everything she could to welcome her new roommate.

Mercifully, Andrea had fallen asleep right after takeoff and had slept most of the way to Boston. The flight had been pretty uneventful. As she made her way to the baggage claim area, she saw the sign with her name on it. There were two women waiting for her. She heard one say, "Hi, are you Andrea?"

"Yes, I am."

"Well, it's so good to see you. I'm Corrine and this is Janette. She's going to be your roommate and decided she'd like to come and meet you. Let's go find your bags." Andrea didn't know what she had expected, but these women seemed to look and act pretty normal. She followed them to the carousel and before she knew it, they had her and her luggage loaded into a silver mini-van. She had half expected to see the name of the program written on the side of the vehicle and was relieved to see there was nothing there. Within twenty minutes, they were walking into the entrance of the facility. There were several other women in the large front room; two were playing scrabble and another one was curled up in front of a gas fireplace reading. They barely noticed her as she walked in and began to check out her surroundings.

Andrea was glad to see that the place was clean and homey. It appeared to be a very large older house- something that would have been built by a wealthy family in the early nineteen hundreds and recently restored. Later she would learn that it had been given to the foundation by a wealthy family from the Boston area. One of their sons had married a woman who was D.I.D. He hadn't known it at the time, but she was eventually diagnosed. When they learned how little help and treatment was available for people suffering from the disorder, they made a commitment by funding programs specifically designed to help in this arena. The family donated the house and money towards the monthly budget and the foundation raised money for the renovations. Between continued fundraising and what people and insurance paid for the program, someway, somehow *A Safe Place* continued to stay afloat.

For the moment, all Andrea knew was that she was glad to be out of jail and into such pleasant surroundings. As they were about to show her to her room, she was approached by another woman who came in behind them. "Hi, you must be Andrea. I'm Dr. Lisa, I'll be working with you. Are they taking good care of you?"

Andrea nodded, and the doctor continued, "Tomorrow is going to be orientation. We won't actually meet until the following day. It's good to have you with us. I'm looking forward to getting to know you better." With that, she disappeared through one of the other doors.

Janette looked at Andrea, "You must be exhausted, let's get your things to your room so you can get some rest before supper." A little overwhelmed, Andrea followed her quietly to the room they would be sharing. Sensing that she needed to let Andrea catch her bearings, Janette showed her around the room and then left saying she would be back to check on her before it was time to go to supper.

REDEEMED

Chapter Forty-Two

Daniel's Turn

જ્જ ન્જી

It was March and most of the snow had melted and the weather was getting warmer each day. Daniel was preparing for the trip he had promised to Deborah. As his wedding gift to her before they were to be married, he had promised to go through the *Restore Your Soul* ministry in Florida. He had turned in his paperwork several months before and had been assigned to Mr. and Mrs. Thorton, a couple from England, who had flown in for training. Lydia would also be in on his sessions overseeing the trainees. That had really excited Deborah-she thought so highly of her. Daniel was also excited because he was looking forward to finally meeting the woman he had heard so much about. Because of the time factor, Daniel would be doing his counseling a bit differently than Deborah had. He would be flying in Wednesday morning and would start his ministry that afternoon. Then he would have a session each morning and afternoon until Saturday, and then fly out Saturday morning. He wasn't exactly sure what the Lord wanted to do in him, but he knew it couldn't hurt. He was actually excited; he remembered the difference it had made in Deborah when she had gone to the ministry the previous April.

Deborah drove Daniel to the airport in Columbus. She

reminded him as he got out of the car, "Don't forget to give Lydia and Joyce their gifts and my love. I wish I was going with you, Daniel."

"I'm not so sure it's me you want to be with. I think you just miss Lydia and Joyce," he said with a grin.

"Well, to be honest it's both. I just loved Florida the last time I was there. I checked the internet and the weather is in the mid-seventies; with your schedule, though, you probably won't get to enjoy it much. I wish you could have taken more time off."

Daniel replied, "I've just got too much going on right now and remember, Lydia said they do it this way all the time." As he was getting ready to walk into the terminal Deborah gave him a quick hug which surprised him. Even during their engagement they had had very little physical contact and Deborah was rarely the initiator. It was probably for the best. He had been celibate for over three years now and it was best to keep his desires under control-it was hard enough just being around Deborah at times. When it came to her he still felt like a fifteen year old boy: intimidated by her beauty and strength, yet captivated by her at the same time.

Taking in his surroundings, **it** was interesting for Daniel to be sitting in the very room Deborah had been in almost a year ago. It looked very much as she had described it. He remembered praying for her that week as she went through the ministry never thinking that they would be together, or that one day he would be going through the same process.

Arriving a little breathless, Lydia welcomed him like an old friend, "Daniel, it's so good to finally meet you," she said as he stood and extended his hand.

"I've heard a lot about you, too. I think Deborah is your number one fan!"

Lydia chuckled, "Well, thank you, but we all know the

only one who deserves a fan club is Him," she pointed towards the ceiling. "All I do is show up. He does all the work."

Daniel had already met the Thorton's. Even though it was a little intimidating for him to be in the room with three people who he thought were ready to scrutinize everything he said, they put him at ease right from the start. After he had completed the generational interview, Daniel figured he ought to come clean and share his prejudice during his break. He quickly admitted to the Thorton's that he had a stereotyped mindset related to the British: a little stuffy and unemotional. Carole and Douglas were nothing of the sort; they were both very warm and open. They all had a good laugh and Carole said, "You should have seen us before the ministry. We would have probably fit your expectations perfectly. It's amazing what getting rid of generational and cultural sin can do for a person!"

Douglas added, "And don't forget all of those ungodly beliefs. But we'll still take the compliment."

After the full interview was completed, Lydia met with the Thorton's. This was their third training opportunity. During the first training they had observed the counseling session, they then had participated in the second one, to a degree. During Daniel's ministry, Lydia was having them lead-she would be available to add input when needed or to model something for them. "Douglas, you did a good job in the interview," Lydia complimented. "It had a good rhythm and you kept Daniel relaxed. I hope you understand that this one is pretty unusual. Most times you don't find generations as spiritually clean on both sides of the family. It's rare in this day and hour to minister to someone who has never used drugs, alcohol or been involved in the occult. I don't think this will be hard, but I also know God wants to minister to everyone and Daniel will be no exception.

It was nearly time for bed by the time Daniel had gone out for a bite to eat and returned to his room. He decided to give

Deborah a quick call but only reached her voicemail so he left a message letting her know he had survived the interview but was going to turn in early. It had been a long day. Giving an account of his entire life had left him drained; he could have only imagined how Deborah must have felt. Compared to her, his life had been pretty uneventful. He decided to listen to his audio tape assignment on generational curses the next morning. His session would start at nine and he was used to getting up early to get the kids off to school.

Getting ready for counseling that morning, Lydia couldn't say enough about Daniel. "Stephen, he's even better than I had hoped. He's going to be perfect for Deborah. I really like him."

Stephen called from his closet, "That's great, dear, but now do you know where my gray sport jacket is?"

"Did you hear a word I said?" she asked. "That jacket is still at the cleaners. Why don't you wear your blue one?"

"Will it go with this shirt and tie?" Stephen asked holding them up for her approval.

"They're fine. What's all the fuss about?" she asked.

"Did you forget? I'm speaking at the Rotary Club today."

"To be honest, I did. I'm sorry I can't be there to cheer you on. You know how it is when I'm training-I have to use my lunch break to review paperwork. Even though the Thornton's are doing a great job, I still need to do mine."

"I understand. I know how you hate stuff like that anyhow. I just couldn't turn down Charlie; he's one of my best patients and is always referring more people to me. And I did hear you telling me about Daniel. He sounds like a great guy. Now, give me a kiss, and I'll see you tonight." He bent down, kissed his wife and said, "Have a good day. I'll be praying for you."

Lydia returned his kiss, grabbed her briefcase and headed to the car. She didn't want to be late, especially on training days-it set such a poor example.

As Lydia expected, Daniel's generational sin session was pretty uneventful. He went through the process faithfully but his generations were pretty clean on both sides. It was one of the reasons that Daniel hadn't fallen in to sexual sin or addictions as a young man. Even though he had experimented some as a teenager, alcohol and drugs had no right to ensnare him. There were, however, still a few areas of generational sin that had impacted him. Anxiety, worry and fear were things that his mother and maternal grandmother had dealt with, and an area that he always battled even though he was usually able to keep it under control.

During their lunch break, Lydia and the Thorton's sat around the table in the office eating while they worked on Daniel's list of ungodly beliefs for the next session. Daniel was next door fixing himself a sandwich. He had decided to eat and then take a little walk.

When it was time for the afternoon session, everyone returned to the ministry room. Carole laid the scriptural foundation for the session and drew graph of the ungodly belief cycle on the board. Daniel and Deborah had talked about this area of the ministry quite a bit so he was interested to discover what ungodly beliefs the ministers had uncovered in his previous sessions. The first ungodly belief on Daniel's list was, "It's my job to always take care of everyone else and not be a burden to anyone." As he went through the prayer process, Daniel realized that this had been planted in him as a child when his father had traveled quite a bit; his dad would even tell him to take care of everything while he was gone. Daniel was the oldest and always felt he needed to take responsibility for his mother and sister. It had made him responsible and self-sufficient, and he had really been quite proud of himself because of it. The Lord lovingly dealt with him and helped him see the sin in it. Lydia gently pointed out how dangerous it was, even in his relationship with Deborah, because it could make him more of a caretaker than a husband. The counselors helped Daniel to see that it was important for him to find a balance regarding his responsibilities. His new godly belief was, *"It's the Lord's job to take care of everyone. It's my job to simply be obedient and also to learn how to receive care as well as give it."* He had to admit, as he finished his list of ungodly beliefs that afternoon, he felt like the weight of the world had been lifted from his shoulders.

Chapter Forty-Three

Homecoming

৯৯ ৰৄ

On Saturday, Deborah was supposed to meet Daniel in the baggage claim area; she could hardly wait to see him. It had only been a little over three days, but she had missed him and couldn't wait to find out everything that had happened. His plane was late, but when she finally saw him coming down the escalator she immediately knew that there had been transformation. She could see a new confidence in how he carried himself. When he got to where she was waiting, the first thing he said was, "Thank you. I know this was supposed to be my present to you, but I think I got the present. Now I understand what you mean. It was an awesome experience." Daniel could now relate to how Deborah had felt when it was time to go home. God's presence was so strong at *His House*, and the unconditional love people received while they were there made it hard to want to step back into the real world again. He was glad to have his new Godly Beliefs and True Identity to hold on to and was looking forward to sharing them with Deborah.

She had only talked to Daniel twice while he was gone but, when Deborah had, Daniel had sounded surprised at the depth of the counseling he was receiving. She could tell by the sound of his voice the previous night that, even though he had been there a much shorter time than she had, he felt a connection to his counselors, just as she did. Like Deborah, Daniel had also fallen in love with Lydia and the Thorton's. He had been able to meet Joyce, but hadn't had the opportunity to spend any real time with her.

On the drive home, Daniel talked most of the way. Usually he was somewhat on the quiet side, but not today. He was as excited as Deborah was to have gained a deeper understanding of the ministry tools which would help them work through any ongoing issues. He already had a good understanding of them just by reading a book on integrated ministry, but it was nothing like experiencing it first-hand. Inwardly, Deborah thanked God for allowing this to come to pass and for his positive experience. She was so happy that he not only received but had enjoyed the ministry. Maybe someday, they would share her dream of being able to minister to others. For now, though, she just kept quiet and listened to Daniel as he poured out what the Lord had done. "Some of it is just hard to describe," he was saying, "God does things but you're not quite sure what He's done and how He did it. You just know that you're different. I really want to talk to Pastor Mark about having Lydia present a workshop at our church. I think he and Christiana would love the ministry. You know maybe someday, when the kids are older, we'll have time to get trained, too."

Deborah could hardly believe her ears! Maybe God was answering her prayers already. Trying hard to contain her excitement she said, "I think it would be a great idea to have Lydia in; she could stay with us. I'm so happy you enjoyed the ministry, Daniel." Deciding to use wisdom rather than opportunity to share her desires related to ministry, she decided not to say or do anything prematurely. In her heart, she thanked the Lord for meeting Daniel and touching him to such a degree. Not wanting just to come right out and ask, she hoped that he had even received healing for some of the damage she had done to him when they were young. She knew how deeply she had wounded him as a teenager. He always said that he had forgiven her, but after going through the ministry she also knew that forgiveness was only the doorway to healing. You still needed to be ministered to by the Jesus, the Great Physician. On the morning of the session when they normally dealt with spirit/soul hurts, she had specifically prayed for Daniel to be healed in that area.

The Holy Spirit, knowing Deborah's need to know Daniel's true feelings, prompted him. Turning toward her, he said, "I want you to know the Lord really healed the one part of my heart that still wrestled with trusting you. I didn't even know it was there, but the Lord revealed it. The Thorton's had no idea about everything that had happened between us and the prom didn't even come up in my interview. During my spirit/soul hurt session, Douglas received a word of knowledge about it from the Lord. He saw me with a group of people watching a door and a young woman with dark hair walking out of it. When the Lord showed him the picture, he said it felt like his heart was being ripped in two. I knew exactly what he was talking about and so did Lydia; it was when you walked out on me at the dance. I'll be honest with you; I broke down crying when he said it. The pain was almost overwhelming. I realized that I had never really cried or dealt with how badly you had hurt me and how disappointed I was that night. I guess I had always protected myself and you from how I really felt. The Lord showed me that a part of me was still scared to trust you. I felt the pressure of having to be perfect so that you wouldn't walk out on me again, but not anymore. It feels so good to be free! The Lord brought healing and spoke truth to my heart. The Enemy might have had a plan, but the Lord had a different and more glorious one. Even though it's been painful going through everything, He's made beauty from ashes. He wanted us to be a testimony of His Redemption." Daniel reached out and touched her chee**k gently** and felt the tears trickling down her face, "Now, I can love you with my whole heart!" Deborah could hardly drive she was so overwhelmed with the goodness of the Lord and her love for the man who sat next to her.

Daniel talked almost non-stop the entire way back to Deerfield. Both he and Deborah had a laugh when he shared about his deliverance session. Even though he had been a Christian since childhood, he had never had any one lay hand on him and pray deliverance over him. "I'll be honest; I didn't think anything was really going to happen even though Lydia prayed that the Lord would make it real to me."

Deborah interrupted with a chuckle, "Her prayers are always dangerous!"

"I couldn't believe it, I first started out burping. I sounded like a truck driver. Douglas had told me not to worry about being polite, but it was pretty embarrassing. Then when we got to the stronghold of independence and self-sufficiency I actually heard the demons say, 'Tell them I'm not here.' I was just getting ready to say it out loud when I realized if they were talking, they were there. I actually heard them say on the way out, 'You're going to be sorry.' It was amazing to me how different I felt afterwards. When I stepped outside afterwards, the grass even seemed greener and everything was so sharp and bright. It was as if a fog had lifted."

"I know Daniel. Don't you just want everyone to get to experience it? I remember how awesome it felt. I've got to confess, I was so afraid you'd come home and be just ho-hum about it. I knew what an impact it had on me, but I was still such a mess when I went. I didn't know what it was going to be like for you. Just so you know, I love you the way you've been, but I want you to know that you have freedom to change. I know anything that God has done in your heart will make life better for both of us." Deborah's words encouraged him. Both the Thortons and Lydia had really impressed on Daniel that he had to be very careful not to walk in a parental, enabling role with Deborah. Because of both of their pasts and personalities, it would be easy for them to develop a parent/child relationship, rather than the husband and wife relationship God had ordained. He knew there were areas of adjustment he was going to have to make, but it comforted him knowing that Deborah would be understanding and supportive.

Saturday morning the Thorton's and Lydia had a quick meeting to wrap up their training time. Douglas and Carole were scheduled to do some sight-seeing that afternoon. Their return flights to England left on Monday and they also wanted to attend church with Lydia on Sunday. Lydia and Carole had decided that their husbands would probably get along very well if they ever had a chance to meet so the four of them were scheduled to have lunch together after church.

The Thorton's and their pastors had invited Lydia to come to England in the summer for some further training with them and to introduce their congregation to the integrated ministry process. Lydia hadn't had time talk to Stephen about the invitation as of yet, but she hoped that he might want to join her for a combination vacation and ministry trip in July. Lydia had been very pleased with the Thortons' skills and had enjoyed working with them. Daniel had been perfect for the first counseling session they did on their own. There were enough things to work on but his issues had been minor compared to many that came for ministry. Sometimes they arrived with announcements like, "If this doesn't work I'll probably kill myself," or, "If this doesn't work we're going to get a divorce." It was never fun to have to train someone under those conditions. Lydia had really enjoyed the past few days. The Thorton's had always been prepared for their sessions and Daniel had been very cooperative.

After reviewing Daniel's file, which they had assembled, Lydia went over her evaluation with them encouraging them on their strengths. "I think you two are going to make a great team. Just don't second guess your instincts. Really, the main thing you need right now is more experience, and that is only going to come from doing. I'm going to send a letter of recommendation to your pastor to release you for congregational ministry. I think it might be good for you to do one or two more single people before you do your first couple alone. I know that some of your training was with couples, but, as you know, it requires a lot more time and can be more complex because of the additional dynamics between them.

Chapter Forty-Four

Getting Ready

❧ ❧

Wedding plans were moving along. Anne hosted the bridal shower at her home where family, friends and church members were all in attendance. They played games, oohed and aahhed over gifts and enjoyed refreshments. Deborah thought about how corny and phony she would have thought it all was before, but now she was touched by all the love and care she felt from everyone. She went home with both her and her mother's cars loaded with gifts. Everyone had been so generous and thoughtful. Daniel's mother had presented her with a family heirloom-a beautiful antique tea set which had been in the family forever. Deborah had wondered how Anne felt about the family treasure being given to them as a gift, but the look on her soon-to-be sister-in-law's face was one of excitement and joy. There was absolutely no sense of jealousy which relieved Deborah. However, the one thing she hadn't planned on was how uncomfortable she was when she opened Anne's present. Anne had given Deborah a lovely negligee for her trousseau. Deborah had blushed with embarrassment when she unwrapped the gift, and could barely hold it up for the others to see. It was a reminder that her relationship with Daniel was going to be moving from something other than friendship, which was all she had ever known with him. On the drive home Deborah prayed that her reaction hadn't upset Anne or been too obvious to the other guests. She would have to give Anne a call tomorrow. The negligee was beautiful and she really wanted and needed to thank Anne for the shower and the gift.

Anne's gift had shown Deborah that she still had some work to do concerning areas related to intimacy. She was probably going to have to call Lydia and talk out some of her feelings related to all of this. Deborah knew she loved Daniel, but the thought of having sex with him stone-cold sober was a frightening idea; using drugs and alcohol to numb herself started as a teenager when the abuse from her father took place. In fact, during almost all of her subsequent sexual encounters, she had been under the influence of some kind of substance. Deborah loved being with Daniel and knew that the Lord had ordained him to be her husband. The scary part was that there was no test driving this area of their relationship. They had both made a commitment to remain pure and had worked hard not to even show too much physical affection toward one another. She had felt nauseated after opening the gift from Anne. She prayed that the bulimia she had fought so hard to overcome wouldn't return.

Her mother, Elizabeth, was already in the driveway and Daniel was there waiting for them. He had agreed to come over after the bridal shower to help them unload the gifts. Soon, every available corner was stacked with items. The couple had fun looking through some of the presents, but Deborah had made sure the gift from Anne was kept out of sight.

Tommie Lee had made it through the winter and early spring working at the Heglemen's ranch. Life at the ranch had been pretty uneventful. It was very different than anything he had ever experienced before. Adjusting to the cold winter days, with the winds blowing across the prairie, hadn't been easy. But for right now, he didn't have anything better to do. One day, after Christmas, Ed Sr. had come home with an old Ford Ranger one Saturday afternoon; a dealer friend had picked it up for him at a car auction. He had tossed the keys to Tommie Lee and gruffly said, "It needs some work, but if you want it it's yours." Gratefully Tommie Lee had caught the keys in his hands. He hated borrowing Ed Jr.'s truck when he went into town. He still wasn't able to make it sober for any length of time. His weekend binges were the only thing that kept him going and he didn't like the idea of driving someone else's vehicle when he was drinking.

Another thing Tommie Lee didn't like was that he was still tormented by thoughts of Debbie. Even though he tried to get over her, none of the women in town helped wipe her out of his mind; one in particular had actually reminded him of her every time he saw her. She was part Indian, just like Debbie. Her name was Elana. She tended bar in one of the places he frequented in Great Falls. There were times he wished he could just settle down and build himself a new life, but there was still a nagging restlessness on the inside of him. He missed his motorcycle, life on the Gulf Coast, and still fought a burning desire to even the score with Debbie. Her new boyfriend's face as he stumbled out of the garage that night was still etched in his mind. There were even nights when Tommie Lee was tormented by dreams of the two of them together.

One afternoon as he was driving to the church, Daniel's cell phone rang, looking down, he didn't recognize the number. It was an out of town area code. He figured he better answer it. It was Dr. Lisa, Andrea's therapist from *A Safe Place*. He was surprised but glad to hear from her. They had agreed to keep in touch concerning Andrea's progress, but until now, he always initiated the contact.

After beginning with the normal pleasantries, Dr. Lisa got to the main purpose for the call, "Andrea was very surprised to get an invitation to Daniel and Deborah's wedding. And I didn't know what to think myself. I wasn't sure if it the couple getting married did it because it was the social thing to do or if it was an honest invitation."

Pastor Mark replied, "To be honest with you we hadn't discussed it. Is Andrea actually considering attending?"

"Right now, we are just in the discussion stage. She's really made a lot of progress and I wouldn't want to see her jeopardize that. On the other hand, it may actually be beneficial for her to be able to reestablish relationships with and have a chance to face everyone. Andrea also has some personal financial business to take care of. We've been weighing her options, and I wanted your opinion. I would release her to go only if she was in your care."

Pastor Mark replied by asking, "Can I pray about it and give you a call in the morning?" He wanted to talk to Daniel and Deborah to see if they had only sent the invitation to be gracious, or if they really wanted Andrea there. "The life of a pastor," he thought to himself as he reached for the phone to call Daniel.

The Enemy had been lying low. He wanted everyone's guard down so he had allowed Daniel's and Deborah's wedding plans to move along without much hindrance. But, if Deborah thought that he was just going to just lay down and let one of his own off the hook that easy, she had another thing coming. He had a plan-which was one thing he had learned well from The Master. One always had to have a Plan B when working with humans. He had already begun working on his plan and was eagerly awaiting the time for everything to unfold. He thought it was a masterpiece. He relished pulling something off just when the humans thought they were going to live happily-ever-after. He hadn't forgotten how they had humiliated and defeated him last fall with their prayers. And just the thought of Sanchez had going over to the other side infuriated him. Yes, he was ready. Everything was right on schedule. He just had to be careful not to alert heaven. He didn't want to sound an alarm that would begin to awaken the prayer warriors. They had been his downfall last time and Deborah's protection. No, this was perfect; all everyone could think of was that stupid wedding.

"Well, good morning Pastor Harrison. Thanks for getting back to me. What did you decide?"

"Good morning, Dr. Lisa. I talked to Daniel this morning and he assured me that he and Deborah were sincere in sending their invitation to Andrea. I just wanted to make sure, for all the parties involved, that this invitation was a mutually agreed upon thing. I know it's a little unorthodox, but their hearts went out to Andrea after seeing one of her interviews with the psychologist who worked with her at the jail."

Dr. Lisa responded, "Andrea and I spent some time yesterday afternoon discussing what it would mean if she did go. She really has been doing well and is learning to manage her disassociation, rather than it managing her. She's much more aware of what's happening on the inside. I agree with you that it's a little unorthodox, but you all seem to be the only people she has and it may be helpful for her to see everyone. She left so abruptly and under such a cloud of shame from being in jail. This could be an opportunity for her to redeem herself. I do want to add, though, that the visit will not happen if her probation officer rejects the idea. I didn't even want to begin recommending the home visit unless I talked to you first."

"Well, we appreciate the consideration. My wife has gone one step further and wants to invite Andrea to stay with us while she's home. We both agree that would help make some of the child alters feel safe since they know me."

"That's wonderful! That makes me feel even better. I was concerned about her being in a hotel room alone." It was obvious she had made up her mind to allow Andrea to come home for the wedding. She continued, "I'll need your home address. The fact that you've been Andrea's pastor and were involved with her placement here should help the probation officer's decision. I am very impressed with your level of involvement, Pastor Harrison. I will let you know what the probation officer decides as soon as possible. If her visit is approved, we can make travel arrangements from there."

Chapter Forty-Five

The Week Before the Wedding

કેર્ટ ન્કે

At her appointment on Friday morning, Andrea and Dr. Lisa rehearsed again what Andrea needed to do if any of her child alters started acting up when she went back to Deerfield. Pastor Mark and Christina had agreed to let her stay with them and, since they had a good understanding of her condition, Dr. Lisa and her probation officer had agreed to the visit. The consensus had been for Andrea to try and make the trip back home and see how she did. Daniel and Deborah had genuinely extended the invitation and were happy to know that Andrea wanted to come. Dr. Lisa thought it might be helpful to put to rest any fantasy or shame that Andrea—of any of her alters— might still have related to them. It really was a miracle that the couple had been willing to invite her after everything she had put them through. It was unusual, but Dr. Lisa felt it was just a testimony of the mercy and grace the Lord extended to His broken ones.

Dr. Lisa was also quite pleased with Andrea's progress. Additionally, it was pretty normal for those with D.I.D. to experience a home visit during this time of treatment. It was always a good test of how much progress really had been made. With regular, individual and group therapy, and a therapeutic environment, what might take years in a normal counseling venue was able to happen quite quickly in their program. Since Andrea had arrived at *A Safe Place*, she had made consistent progress. Together, she and Dr. Lisa had been able to uncover and diagram her system. So far there had been no new parts or memories surfacing since the end of February. Andrea was becoming more and more co-conscious and had learned to dialogue and work with her other parts. Janette had also been a big help to her.

Janette had finished the program and left in the middle of March; that had been a little hard on Andrea but the two had begun to e-mail each other regularly. So far, Janette was doing very well on the outside and had found a counselor with some training in D.I.D. She also had a very supportive husband. Having a good support system to go home to was always one major concern. Many of the women made great progress at *A Safe Place*, but what they went home to, always made a huge difference in their journey towards wholeness. Dr. Lisa was smart enough to realize that in Andrea's case, her pastors and their congregation would play a major role in her returning to normal life. The wedding would give her an opportunity to keep relationships established. The ceremony was on Saturday, and Andrea would be flying in on the Tuesday prior; it would give her time to take care of some of her personal business and get rested up before the wedding. She had volunteered to help Christina decorate the church.

Over the past couple of months, Dr. Lisa had been impressed with the Harrison's faithfulness in keeping in touch with Andrea. Andrea had absolutely no other family support and the encouragement of others was always an important part of the treatment and recovery process. Dr. Lisa hoped that the Harrison's attempts to find Andrea's sister would pay off. There were still some holes in Andrea's life history, but they hoped she might be able to fill in some of the blanks one day. For now, they had to work with what they had.

———————————————

Tommie Lee left the Heglemen ranch and headed in to town Friday night for another weekend of drinking. Elana had Saturday off and the two had planned to spend that night and the next day together. Earlier in the evening Tommie Lee had started drinking tequila at the bar where Elana was working. Normally, he tried to stay away from it because tequila always made him mean. He didn't know what had gotten into him, but Tommie Lee started doing shots at the bar with one of the other locals. The next thing he knew, a brawl erupted and he was in the middle of it. As he picked up a bar stool to start swinging he heard the sirens in the distance. There was no way he was going to take the chance of getting arrested so he quickly fought his way out of the bar. Tommie Lee made it to his truck right as the police car was turning the corner. He made his way out of town cussing himself and the police as he went.

Knowing that he had broken up one of the guys pretty bad in the fight, Tommie Lee figured it was probably time to get out of town.

Still half drunk and not knowing where he was going to go, he began the drive south. He knew he couldn't go back to the ranch and he hated that things always had to end this way. Ed Sr. and Delores had been good to him, but there was no way he was going to take the chance of ending up in jail. There was probably still and open warrant for his arrest in Ohio, and he knew it wouldn't help his cause if he got another one. He was glad for the overnight bag that he had packed for the weekend, and for the rest of his pay that was still in his wallet.

Bright and early Saturday morning, there were two sheriffs at the Diamond H Ranch asking about Tommie Lee; one of the guys who had been involved in the fight last night was beaten so badly that he had been admitted to the hospital and charges of assault and battery had been filed against Tommie Lee. They gave the officers what little information they had.

Before dozing off Monday evening, figuring it was because of the wedding on Saturday, Liberty had Deborah on her heart. Elizabeth was coming to pick her up on Thursday evening and she would be staying at the same hotel that Paul and Timothy would be staying at with their families. She was looking forward to seeing everyone; what a great day it was going to be! She thanked the Lord that she was going to live to see it: Deborah married, and to such a nice young man!

Thursday was going to arrive before she knew it and Liberty needed to get her rest. She still had to get her hair done and find a pair of shoes to match her dress. One of her neighbor's daughters was coming over the following morning to take her shopping. Talking to the Lord as if she knew Him like a friend she said, "Lord, I'm really tired. If there's anything else you want me to pray for Deborah or the wedding, can we talk about it tomorrow?" The Holy Spirit gave her a peace that anything more could wait until morning. She closed her eyes and in minutes was sound asleep.

Andrea arrived safely in Columbus Tuesday morning and Christina was at the airport to pick her up. Before they knew it, the women were making their way back to Deerfield. Andrea looked a lot different from the last time Christina had last seen her; she wasn't back to the same picture perfect Andrea, but her hair was nicely styled and she had lost some weight. She actually looked healthier and more natural than Christina had ever seen her.

On the way to the Harrison's from the airport, Andrea was very open and talkative and shared what it was like at *A Safe Place.* From what Christina could tell, Andrea seemed very relaxed; obviously, the treatment program was working. With everything going on related to the wedding, Christina was relieved. She didn't need to have any major problems and she had been second-guessing her decision; but after seeing Andrea, she knew they had made the right one by inviting her to stay with them.

———————————

Friday had Deborah's last day at the travel agency and she found she was exhausted. Both she and the Mitchells knew it was time for her to quit, but she also knew she was going to miss her work. It had been sad saying goodbye to the employers that had been so good to her, and her friends, but she knew that she needed the week before the wedding to take care of all her last minute preparations. She had discovered that it was one thing to talk about getting married, but another thing to do it.

Deborah and Daniel had both been so busy that they had hardly had time to talk. There was so much that needed to be done that they had to schedule time to be together. Tomorrow was Wednesday and they had agreed to have lunch. Deborah was looking forward to it; she had a list of questions to ask him. With her mind swirling with wedding plans, she finally fell asleep.

At two in the morning, Deborah awoke to her mother pounding on her door, "Deborah, Deborah, are you alright? What's the matter?"

Half-asleep Deborah said, "I'm sorry Mom, I was having a bad dream. Did I wake you? I didn't know I was yelling out loud."

"You were screaming, 'Help me! Help me!' I'm still shaking. It scared me half to death, Deborah. I'm glad you're okay. Do you need anything?"

Tried to sound calm, but shaking all over, Deborah told her mother she'd be all right. She had been in the middle of a nightmare when her mother had knocked on her door. Tommie Lee and some of the other Renegades had been in the dream. Just like the night when she had been gang raped by Hootch and the other Renegades, they had been exacting their due once again. She couldn't believe that she had had such a perverted dream-especially now, right before her wedding. A demon of fear that had been sent on special assignment gripped Deborah tightly. Just the thought of Tommie Lee made her blood run cold. She tried to pray in the Spirit but it felt like her prayers were going nowhere.

Deborah had never bothered Daniel so late at night before, but this time she felt like she had to call him. He answered his phone groggily to the sound of Deborah sobbing on the other end. He quickly came to his senses as she explained what had just happened. Daniel immediately responded, "Thank you for calling me. It means so much that you would share that with me. Listen to me, Deborah. It's just warfare. The enemy is angry and he's just trying to stir up the past. Don't let him get to you. Let me pray for you, ok?"

As they prayed together the demon of fear had to loose his grasp on Deborah; she began to feel more of a peace. "I'm feeling better now. I'm really sorry to wake you but I didn't know what else to do. I think I'll be able to sleep now. Daniel," she hesitated for a moment, "thank you."

As Daniel hung up the phone he knew that it was a major breakthrough for Deborah to call and reach out for help tonight. It was a good sign. He was angry that the enemy had tormented her and was determined to cover her with more prayer, which was not what the enemy wanted to tonight. Satan hated the power of agreement that had overcome the demon he had sent to terrorize Deborah! He knew that when people started getting scared and tired, it affected their decision making abilities. He needed Deborah as distracted as possible.

On Sunday evening Tommie Lee still hadn't arrived back at the ranch, as was his usual practice. Ed Jr. wasn't surprised; Tommie Lee had lasted at the ranch longer than he thought he would have and he knew potential trouble with the law would send the man on the run. He hoped his parents wouldn't be too hurt with Tommie Lee's sudden departure after all of the hospitality they had extended to him. He decided to wait until Monday morning and if he still wasn't back, he would box up his things. He was glad, his dad had insisted that Tommie Lee put the truck in his own name; at least, they didn't have to worry about that.

As much as he had hoped that the ranch and his family could bring some healing to Tommie Lee and give him another chance, deep inside, he knew it was like corralling a wild stallion, eventually they would find a way out. He hoped that the guy in the hospital didn't die; all Tommie Lee needed was another manslaughter charge. Even though they had promised to call the sheriff's office at the first sight of Tommie Lee, he figured there would be another visit from them tomorrow morning. He walked out to the barn to check on one of the mare's that was ready to deliver at any moment.

Chapter Forty-Six

The Sighting

෨ ෬

After the drunken brawl in Great Falls, the Enemy had filled Tommie Lee with rage and murderous thoughts. He made up his mind: it was time for revenge—he had nothing left to lose. He began to make his way back to Ohio. Arriving in Columbus on Monday night, Tommie Lee found a cheap hotel on the outskirts of the city and slept late the next morning. After breakfast he drove to Deerfield looking for Debbie. He found the travel agency, but not her.

Like the last time he had hunted down Debbie with Sanchez, Tommie Lee was prepared this time as well. He had two rifles from the ranch under the seat and had decided to take them both out, Debbie and her boyfriend. He was tired of his face haunting him. All of that target practice at the ranch would finally come in handy. Not only would it redeem him with the Renegades, but he would finally be able to return home to the club, his friends and his normal way of life. The club would hide him and take care of him. He missed the safety and company of the gang members. Who knows, they might even send him down to do business in South America for a while until the heat was over. But those were thoughts for later. Right now all that mattered was finding Debbie and her boyfriend.

Cruising the streets of Deerfield, Tommie Lee pulled his cowboy hat down low. Today he was going to keep an eye on the travel agency. He was surprised at how easily he had remembered where it was located. He watched both the back and front entrances for Debbie at different times, but, to no avail. Finally, tired and hungry, he decided to head back to his motel room and come back on Wednesday.

Tommie Lee wasn't in any rush now that he was in the area. Driving back to Columbus, he decided that he would stake out the house that he and Sanchez had found her at the last time on the following day. He knew the name of the subdivision started with an "L." From his last experience there, he knew he had to be careful in that neighborhood-bunch of nosey, old people! At least no one would recognize the truck, and the Montana license tag helped, too. He hoped that he would be able to find it again; he had been pretty messed up on drugs and alcohol that night. The one thing he had remembered from that night was Debbie screaming, "Daniel!" He couldn't wait to find and kill the two of them. He thought about how he get to both of them at the same time. Then it occurred to him: from the house, all he had to do was follow her. She would lead him right to her pretty boy, Daniel!

———————————————

Daniel was busy Wednesday morning trying to wrap up business before the wedding and honeymoon. Since the previous night, he had been looking forward to lunch with Deborah later that afternoon. They had decided to meet at the deli next to the travel agency so Deborah could stop in and check on the Mitchells and the new girl they had hired. He had to remember to finalize the details concerning their wedding night. He couldn't believe that there were just three days left until the wedding. So far the plans all seemed to be coming together. He was so thankful for the help his mother and Anne had been to Deborah. Her brothers and their families would be arriving on

Friday afternoon. He was getting excited to see them, but with everything that was going on he thanked the Lord that they had rented their own vehicles and were driving themselves from the airport in Columbus to Deerfield.

He picked up the phone and pressed the intercom button, "Irene? Where is that e-mail from the Sergio's? I need you to go online and get the directions to that address for me. I sure don't want to get lost on my wedding night!"

Irene responded, "Already done, boss. It's in the file marked 'Honeymoon' along with all of your other reservation information."

"Thanks, Irene. You're always one step ahead of me."

"That's what I get paid to do," she replied with a chuckle. Irene smiled at the thought of seeing her boss happy again. It had been difficult for him since his wife had gotten sick and passed away. Although she didn't know Deborah all that well, she could definitely tell by the affect she had on Daniel that she made him happy. That was enough for her. She was looking forward to the wedding. "Don't forget, you're meeting Deborah for lunch," she reminded Daniel.

"I remember, but just in case, can you page me at about ten till twelve? I don't want to get busy and lose track of time."

"No problem, boss," she said as she set the alarm on her cell phone.

Daniel went back to work reviewing account information, thankful that God had blessed him with a secretary like Irene. It hadn't been easy starting a business from nothing, but things had started to pick up. He was glad that Irene had stuck it out during the hard times and he hoped to make it up to her as his business prospered.

Wednesday afternoon Christina pulled her husband into his office at the church. She and Andrea had started doing some of the decorating for the wedding earlier that day and, even though things were coming together regarding the decorating, something didn't seem right to Christina as far as Andrea was concerned. Her first words to her husband were, "I'm very concerned about Andrea—you've got to come and talk to her!"

Mark said, "What's going on? Has she disassociated?"

"I'm not sure. I sent her to the party store earlier to pick up a few items that we needed. She seemed fine before she left but when she returned she was shaken. She said that she had seen the bad man, the man with the pictures, drive past her in a dark blue pick-up truck. She keeps saying 'I know it was him. I know it was him.'"

Pastor Mark groaned, "Oh no. All we need is Andrea disassociating! Sounds like one of her child parts saw someone that reminded her of Tommie Lee. Let me try and talk to her and see if I can make any sense out of it."

When Pastor Mark walked into the sanctuary, Andrea began to tell him excitedly, "I know it was him. He had a cowboy hat on but I saw him. We've got to warn Daniel and Deborah! We need to call the police right away!" Andrea was nearly hysterical.

Pastor Mark tried to discern if it was an adult or child alter speaking to him. It didn't seem like a child, but he wasn't quite sure what was going on. "Hold on Andrea, let's just calm down a minute. If it wasn't really him, we don't want to frighten them. I don't want to call the police because then we might have to get your probation officer involved. I think what you and Christina need to do right now is to go home and let you take a little nap. When I come home, we'll talk some more."

Andrea started to protest but Christina was firm, "Now, you heard Pastor Mark. I think that's a good idea. I need to get dinner started anyway." She started to gather up her things. Pastor Mark could tell that Andrea was not a happy camper, but he also knew that sometimes if she fell asleep it would help her switch back to normal. He wondered what had triggered this response. That's all Daniel and Deborah needed was for everyone to start thinking about Tommie Lee and looking over their shoulders every minute. No, he was not going to have them robbed of this joyous occasion. He hoped it hadn't been a mistake bringing Andrea in for the wedding. Maybe by the time he got home she would have forgotten all about what she thought she saw.

———————————

Brazenly, Tommie Lee drove through the streets of Deerfield hunting his prey. He still had not found Debbie's subdivision, but he was feeling confident, almost cocky, that today was his day. He decided to cruise past the travel agency one more time.

Suddenly, the car in front of him stopped. He almost rear-ended it as he saw Deborah walking out of the front door of the Worldwide Travel Agency. He pulled his cowboy hat down low. With only one car in between him and Debbie he sat at the stop-light watching her cross the street right in front of him. Not wanting to make a scene, he had to proceed when the light changed. He watched her out of his rearview mirror and saw her enter a little restaurant just up the street. Not sure what to do next, he drove around the block. As he circled back around, a parking place opened up almost directly across from the restaurant Debbie had just entered. He parked slowly, doing whatever he could not to draw any attention to himself. Tommie Lee had bought a newspaper just for this purpose. He picked it up from the front seat and pretended to read as he watched the front door of the restaurant out of the corner of his eye.

———————————

Daniel had arrived just minutes after Deborah. Tommie Lee had missed his entrance while driving around the block. It took a few minutes for Deborah to calm down once she saw Daniel; she quickly realized that she had been more uptight than she had thought. Maybe there was something about those "wedding jitters" everyone talked about; but, by the time the waitress had taken their order, Deborah was in a different state of mind. She wasn't sure if it was just the stress of the wedding plans or the dream she had had the other night. Whatever it was, she hadn't slept well the last couple of nights. Just seeing Daniel put her at ease.

In no time their salads and sandwiches arrived. As they ate they went over their "To Do" lists adding a few items and crossing off others. It seemed like the meal was over before they knew it. Though she would have loved to have spent more time with him, Deborah knew Daniel had to get back to the office; this was his last full day at work until they returned from their honeymoon. He was going to go in for a couple hours tomorrow morning, and tonight he had planned special time with David and Aimee.

As Deborah and Daniel stepped out from beneath the deli's awning, Tommie Lee spotted them immediately. They stopped for a minute; Debbie was smiling and looking up at Daniel. It made him sick to his stomach. He thought for a minute that they were going to kiss, but Daniel just gave her a quick hug and started to walk away. Tommie Lee didn't want to lose him, but he also didn't want to draw attention to himself.

Tommie Lee waited for a minute as Deborah turned and started walking in the opposite direction. Slowly he eased the pick-up truck out of its parking place and began to follow Daniel. He almost lost sight of him a couple of times, but finally Daniel stopped and walked into a business. The sign out front read "Worthington Advertising and Marketing, Inc." Tommie Lee parked down the street and waited awhile. Daniel didn't come out so he figured Daniel must work there. He decided to find a phone book and look up the number.

Tommie Lee's adrenaline was pumping. The Enemy had surrounded his truck with hoards of demons; he wasn't taking any chances this time. So far the prayers of the saints were limited but he had to work fast. This one was going to be glorious. No one was expecting it. Not only would it rock the faith of the church, but it would shake and shock the entire town.

REDEEMED

Chapter Forty-Seven

The Delivery

ॐ ॐ

Andrea woke up from her nap frustrated knowing the Harrisons did not believe her. She didn't know why she was so sure, but she felt positive that the guy who drove by her in the dark blue truck that morning was the same one who had been in the car with her and Sanchez the day she bought the pictures of Deborah. They had even shown her mug shots for identification purposes when she was in jail. It had taken awhile for the full memory to come back, but during counseling she had been able to retrieve everything that had happened the day she had met the man called Juan and his friend. She tried to call Dr. Lisa to see what she thought she should do. All she could do was leave a message for her. Running out of options and not knowing what to do, she called her friend, Janette.

"What do I do next? No one believes me. They probably think I'm trying to stop the wedding. Janette, I'm sure it was him. I could just feel evil when he drove by. He looked like he was looking for someone."

"Do you think you're supposed to call the police?" her friend asked.

"Not after what happened the last time. I'm sure they'll just think I'm trying to stir up trouble again. Actually, I feel like

I'm supposed to call Deborah, but Pastor Mark said he didn't want them worrying about this. Please pray for me, I just don't know what to do."

When Tommie Lee found a pay phone and flipped through the yellow pages, he realized Daniel didn't just work at the agency, he was the owner. His grinning picture peered out at Tommie Lee from the yellow page ad. He had hit the jackpot. Barely able to contain the elation he was now feeling, he ripped the page out of the phone book and walked back to his truck. Suddenly, he had a plan.

The Yellow Page ad gave five o'clock as the closing time for the advertising agency. Tommie Lee had made his decision: he was going to wait until closing time and then he would take Daniel as his first hostage. From there, he would either have Deborah come to them or they would meet her somewhere. Once he had Daniel the rest would be easy!

Tommie Lee knew he couldn't sit in his truck the whole time without looking obvious, but he needed to make sure Daniel was going to be there at closing time. He fired up the ignition and drove down the road stopping at a little burger joint; there was a pay phone in the parking lot. He dialed the number in the ad, "Worthington Advertising and Marketing, this is Irene speaking, how may I help you?"

"Ma'am, this is Air Express, I have a delivery I need to make and I'm running a little late today. How late will you be there today?"

The woman hesitated on the other end of the line, "Daniel, how late will you be at the office today? I have to leave right at five. There's a delivery man who's running late. It must be another wedding present."

In the background, Tommie Lee heard a man's voice say, "I have to finish this proposal before I leave so I'll probably be here until about six o'clock. Just leave the front door open when you go and tell him to leave it on the front desk."

Irene came back on the line and relayed the information he had just overheard. As he hung up the phone, Tommie Lee wondered if Debbie and her boyfriend were the ones getting married. They looked awful cozy together this afternoon, but he would find out soon enough. At about quarter after five, he would be meeting face to face with Daniel. It would give the secretary the opportunity to leave-he didn't want anyone else involved who could mess things up for him. Tommie Lee hoped there would be no one else at the office, but he would have to take his chances. He went inside and ordered a double cheeseburger, fries and a large, chocolate malt. His order came quickly, and he found himself a booth in the corner where he ate his lunch and planned what he was going to do next.

Christina called her husband, "You were right, Andrea seems much calmer after her nap. She hasn't said another thing to me. What time do you think you'll be home?"

"Probably around five-thirty. That's good to hear dear." Christina hung up the phone knowing her husband was preoccupied with something.

After talking to Janette, Andrea had decided that she didn't care what happened, she was going to call and alert Deborah. She called a couple of times and received her voicemail. Not wanting to leave a message, she went down to help Christina with dinner. She had decided her best bet was to just keep quiet about it. After about thirty minutes she excused herself, pretending she needed to use the bathroom. She went back up to her room and redialed Deborah. This time she answered her phone.

"Hi, Deborah, I hate to do this and Pastor Mark told me not to, but my friend, Janette, and I prayed and I have to do this."

It took Deborah a minute to recognize Andrea's voice as she rattled on, "Hi, Andrea. Okay, what is it?"

"I saw him today. I saw the bad man, the one with the pictures of you." Inwardly, Deborah groaned. What had they been thinking when they had invited Andrea home for the wedding? She decided that it was best just to humor Andrea and let her talk, then she would notify Pastor Mark and he could get in touch with Andrea's counselor. It was obvious she wouldn't be able to attend the wedding. "He was driving an older, dark blue pick-up truck. He was wearing a cowboy hat." Now, Deborah knew Andrea had lost it. The thought of Tommie Lee in a cowboy hat and pick-up truck was ludicrous! She covered her mouth to keep herself from giggling.

At about ten till five, Tommie Lee pulled into a parking place in front of the agency. He had already walked around the back of the building and found the back exit which had no parking. It was perfect. He would be able to see the secretary leave. Sure enough, a few minutes to five the door opened and an older lady with slightly graying hair walked out. She headed towards the public parking lot that was right down the street. Tommie Lee watched her until she was finally out of sight. Once he was ready to go in, he would tuck the rifle up under his jacket and be in the door before anyone knew it.

Deborah had decided that it would be best to stop by the agency and talk to Daniel about the strange phone call she had with Andrea. They could pray together and decide how to gracefully handle the situation before she called Pastor Mark. She knew he was working a little late but figured this was too important not to deal with right away.

As she drove down the street looking for a parking spot near the agency Deborah gasped. In front of the building sat a dark blue truck with a man in the driver's seat. He also had on a cowboy hat. She couldn't really see his face because of the newspaper he was reading. She felt herself shaking all over as she drove by. She didn't dare stop. What if Andrea had been right? Nothing was making any sense! She drove two blocks down the street and pulled over. Her hands were shaking as she reached for her cell phone to call Daniel.

Daniel heard the front door open. "Just put it on the desk," he called from out of his office. There was no reply. Before he knew it, there was a figure standing in his door pointing a riffle at his chest.

"Okay," Tommie Lee said, "I'll put it in on the desk. Remember me?"

"Yes," Daniel replied, "I don't think I could forget you." Daniel's cell phone rang. He looked down and then back at Tommie Lee, "Its Deborah."

"Answer it," the man said gruffly, "Get her over here."

Not taking his eyes off of the man standing in front of him, Daniel slowly picked up his phone, "Hi, honey what's up?" he tried to sound calm. Deborah started rattling off about the phone call from Andrea and seeing the truck parked outside of his office. Daniel knew he had to try to talk in such a way Deborah that would know Tommie Lee was already in the office. Not responding to a word she said about Andrea he answered her, "That's right, I'm working late. We had a special wedding present delivered. It just got here. If you're still in town, I'd love for you to come by and see it."

Confused, Deborah replied, "Daniel, I'm telling you Andrea has resorted back to her alters and...wait. Is Tommie Lee there? Daniel, he's already there isn't he?"

"That's right, dear. I'll be here until six," he responded.

She said, "Daniel, are you okay? Is he trying to hurt you? He has a gun doesn't he?"

"Yes, I'd love something to eat. Surprise me. I'll see you in a little bit." As he hung up with Deborah, Daniel hoped he had bought a little time for Deborah to notify the authorities. He said calmly and politely to Tommie Lee, "Would you like to sit down? She'll be here in about fifteen minutes."

"So when's the big day?" Tommie Lee sneered.

"This Saturday," Daniel replied.

"So sorry to mess up the wedding plans," Tommie Lee said sarcastically. He motioned with the rifle, "Get comfortable, you might be sitting in that chair for a while."

Daniel shifted in his office chair wondering what he should do next. After the last incident with Tommie Lee he had decided to keep a gun in his desk, but he knew it wasn't loaded. He hoped the police were on the way.

Deborah quickly called the police and tried to explain everything. Not sure if she was overreacting or if the story she was telling could be true, the Deerfield police department dispatched two officers to the address she gave them. Next she called Pastor Mark. "I know she wasn't supposed to call, but Andrea was right about Tommie Lee being here. I don't have time to explain just pray for Daniel and me. Tommie Lee's in Daniel's office and he's got a gun. I've got to go."

Before he could respond Deborah had hung up. He quickly called Christina and told her about the strange phone call. "Ask Andrea if she called Deborah. Call me back and let me know." Not sure about what else to do, he simply did what Deborah had asked, he prayed earnestly.

Chapter Forty-Eight

The Crash

જી ન્જ

With Tommie Lee sitting across the desk from him, Daniel was amazed at how calm he felt. He had only read about situations like these but now he found himself right in the middle of a story that was made for *Guideposts*. He decided to listen to the prompting of the Holy Spirit as he spoke to Tommie Lee, "I know that you're angry and hurt, but there is nothing you've done that cannot be forgiven. Just like Jesus has given Deborah a new life, He has one for you, too." Tommie Lee's eyes just got blacker and more demonized as Daniel talked. At the mention of Deborah's name, Daniel heard an almost animal-like growl come out of the man.

Tommie Lee yelled, "Shut up! Shut the hell up or I'll blow your brains out before she gets here." His hands were shaking on the rifle he had trained on Daniel's chest.

As if he didn't even hear him, Daniel continued, "Lord, please give Tommie Lee a revelation of Your love."

It seemed like hours before Daniel finally heard the front door of the office open. He prayed that it wasn't Deborah. He hoped she had understood his code and that she knew Tommie Lee was in the office. Then he heard her voice, "Hi honey, I brought us some dinner. Where do you want to eat? The conference room?" She sounded so calm. What Daniel didn't know was that two police officers had met her outside the agency and were behind her with their guns drawn. Tommie Lee glared at him and pointed at the floor adamantly with his finger. He wanted her in the room.

"Let's just eat in here." Daniel prayed she wouldn't be foolish enough to enter the room.

"I'm going to get some plates out of the break room. I'll be right there."

As quickly as the words were out of her mouth, Daniel's office door burst open. He dropped to the floor as Tommie Lee's rifle went off. The next he knew the two officers were attempting to wrestle with Tommie Lee. Tommie Lee struck one of them in the head with the butt of the rifle and shot the other in the shoulder. With that, he ran out of the Daniel's office looking for Deborah; she had locked herself in the bathroom. He began to beat and kick the door when he heard police sirens in the distance. Cursing, he ran out the front door, jumped into his truck, and tore out of the parking place.

When Deborah heard the shot, she was so stunned that she had fallen into an almost catatonic state. The thought of not knowing if Daniel was dead or alive was more than she could bear. She had hardly heard Tommie Lee screaming at her before he left the building. When she finally heard Daniel's voice on the other side of the bathroom door, it took a little convincing that it was really him and that he was okay. When she finally opened the door, Deborah fell into Daniel's arms sobbing.

Pastor Harrison arrived at the office right as the ambulance arrived. He feared the worst as he walked into Daniel's office. When he saw Daniel holding Deborah, he said, "Thank God, you two are okay! Was Tommie Lee really here in town?"

They both shook their heads in affirmation. Daniel said, "But, I'm afraid he's gotten away again."

Pastor Harrison said, "Andrea had said that she had seen

him earlier today, but, I confess, I didn't believe her."

"When she had called me earlier I didn't believe her either," Deborah replied, "but if it wasn't for her, I don't know what would have happened. When I drove by Daniel's office and saw the dark blue truck with a man with a cowboy hat sitting inside I knew she had been telling the truth. When I called Daniel, Tommie Lee was already inside of the office. Without Andrea's phone call, I would have just blindly walked inside."

Pastor Harrison recognized, "You both know the Enemy just wants to ruin your wedding plans. I know this has been quite a shaking but you need to trust the Lord. He's bigger than Tommie Lee and all the evil that's within him."

Deborah nodded, "I just pray that he's apprehended before the wedding. I don't want to have to move out of town but I can't imagine having the children involved in anything like what went on here today."

Daniel nodded, "I did witness to him, but to be honest, I don't know how much good it did. Every time I mentioned the name Jesus, it infuriated him.

Panting with anger and frustration, Tommie Lee raced towards the city limits. So far he hadn't seen any police cars in his rearview mirror but he needed to get out of town fast. Maybe he had lost those local yokels already. He careened around the corner and found a country road off to the right. Tires screeching, he made the quick turn and hit the accelerator; he was doing ninety miles an hour down the dirt road. Tommie Lee was totally unaware that his master had come for him and that his time was finished. Satan wasn't going to take the chance of him going over to the other side, especially after Daniel had sat in the office actually witnessing to him. No, Tommie Lee had messed up again and had used up his usefulness—that meant it was time for disposal. He wasn't going to take any chances. A demon of malfunction was dispatched to interfere with his brakes. As he drove, Tommie Lee heard a gentle voice in his mind saying, "Are you ready to give your life to Me?" Without knowing how he knew, he knew it was the Lord.

"I'd rather rot in hell," he responded in anger. God had sent angels to stand by ready to help him if his heart had turned; but with his response, they were left helpless. Another soul was on its way to eternal damnation.

At the next curve, Tommie Lee's brakes failed and he had no ability to slow down. Losing control, the pick-up truck went airborne as it left the road and began to flip over and over again. As the truck landed on its roof, gas began to spill out everywhere. Tommie Lee's neck was broken immediately and the still-burning cigarette, he had had in his mouth when the car began flipping, fell to the ground. Once the gas found its way there, everything exploded.

Angels stood by watching helplessly. It was the one thing they couldn't understand: how could their adversary be so cruel to his own? Once he was done with a life he would dispose of them so easily and in such torturous ways. There were no rewards for serving Satan, just death and damnation. It was a mystery to them why humans kept serving a master so full of hate, when their Lord wanted to do nothing but overwhelm them with love and blessings. But what did they know? They were just angels and the earthly realm carried its own mysteries. They were just here to serve these created beings. Their Master loved them, and that was enough for them. The heavenly beings left the scene and went to report what they had just observed to Michael.

Meanwhile, the farmer, whose field the charred remains of the truck ended up resting in, called the police after hearing the explosion. Soon a highway patrol car was at the scene of the crime. The officers had heard over on their radios that the Deerfield Police Department was looking for a suspect who had been driving a pick-up and that there had been an officer down. This had to be the vehicle, but until the fire was brought under control they wouldn't know for sure. Soon the sound of sirens filled the air as the fire department arrived on the scene.

The emergency crew pulled out the charred remains of Tommie Lee once the fire was out. The smell of burning flesh filled their nostrils as the body continued to smolder. The fire had blistered the license plate, but the number matched the one they had been given. It would take days to get all the forensic evidence back to prove they had the right man but they were sure it was him. What the emergency crew couldn't see with their natural eyes was that Tommie Lee's soul was still burning in the torments of hell.

The fire in hell was hotter than any they had ever experienced and the worms of death crawled through Tommie Lee's tortured body. This was hell. He was in hell. He hadn't really believed it but hell was real, and it was for eternity. He screamed in anguish over and over again. He knew God had tried to give him one last chance. He had been such a stubborn fool and now it was too late-he was buried under the hopelessness of eternal judgment. His screams fell on deaf ears; there was no one to hear him. He was out of fellowship with God and man, and Satan could care less. The Enemy wasn't concerned for the souls he had won, and he had no desire for fellowship. He just wanted to punish God for throwing him out of heaven and sentencing him to eternal damnation by destroying His sons and daughters. He was unredeemable and enjoyed it when others suffered the same fate. He heard Tommie Lee's screams from afar. "What a fool. They're all fools," he laughed heinously. The only way they could escape his grasp on earth was if the Lord helped them. Fortunately for him, most were either too ignorant or too proud to ask for help. This one had been both. The population of hell had just increased by one-it would make up for having lost Sanchez to the other side.

Chapter Forty-Nine

The Wedding Morning

❧ ❦

The morning haze was lifting as Deborah went out for a walk. Even though it was early, she was too restlessness to go back to sleep. The weather had been unseasonably warm, and today appeared to be no different. She was so glad it wasn't going to rain. Even though they had opted for an indoor wedding at the church, bad weather would still be inconvenient. It was hard to believe that this was her wedding day. Tomorrow morning she would wake up as Mrs. Daniel Worthington. Her heart pounded faster at the thought. As much as she loved Daniel and his children, it was her own inadequacies that she feared.

Having a ready-made family was a little different—most people had the opportunity to grow into theirs. As she prayed against her fears of incompetence, Deborah was reminded of the vision she had seen driving home from Florida. It was almost exactly a year ago. She would have never believed it even if someone had told her everything that had transpired this past year. She tried again to picture the man standing at the front of the church as she walked towards him. Whenever she thought of the vision, it brought her peace. As long as she was in the Lord's will, she knew things would be okay.

The rehearsal and dinner had gone well the night before and she didn't have many worries. Even the underlying fear that Tommie Lee could show up at any moment had been put to rest with the crash. She had felt guilty at how relieved she was when they had received the word that his remains had been identified. It was amazing how the Lord worked, but even though that all of that had transpired just a couple of days ago, the trauma from the whole event had already faded. Pastor Harrison had prayed for both of them that day as they had once again forgiven Tommie Lee. When they had heard of Tommie Lee's death, she knew Daniel was thankful that he had been obedient to witness to him before he died. She wondered if it had made a difference or not. All she knew was that as the psalmist promised, "The Lord had delivered her from the violent man."

Now her main concern was David; the closer it had gotten to the day of the wedding, the more he had withdrawn from her and Daniel. Deborah prayed that David would open his heart and accept her. She had felt bad that there wasn't a place in the wedding party for him, but now she realized it was probably better. It seemed that he was having much more difficulty with everything than his sister. Aimee was a different story; she had been younger when her mother had passed away. Aimee was all excited about the wedding and her part as the flower girl. Nathan, Deborah's nephew, was the ring bearer. She had asked Anne to be her matron of honor and Robert was Daniel's best man.

Deborah and Daniel had decided to keep the wedding party small. But, with all their family, friends and members of the congregation in attendance, there would be over two hundred guests. Even Lydia and Joyce were coming! Deborah knew how busy they both were but had sent them each an invitation to the wedding because of the impact they had had on her life, and recently, on Daniel's life. There was no doubt in her mind that without their help and prayers, this day would have never come. She was both overjoyed and amazed when they had both responded that they planned to attend. She hoped to steal some time with them at the reception.

On the plane ride into Columbus that morning Joyce had finally decided to share everything with Lydia. Bill was moving to Florida; he had received a transfer to a company branch in Orlando which would take effect that month. Joyce also shared how the two of them had continued regular e-mail correspondence throughout the winter and spring, and had spoken several times on the phone. It was like she had met a new man, and she found she liked him.

Bill was a little concerned about leaving his support group and had said he would turn down the raise and promotion if Joyce had any problem with him moving to the area. They had seen each other once the month before when he was in town doing consultation work for the branch that had requested him for the new position. This time, she actually had found him physically attractive even though things were still a bit awkward at times. E-mail and the telephone had allowed for an intimacy that wasn't as intimidating as seeing each other eye-to-eye. On the ride home after their evening together, Joyce had felt an overwhelming sense of loneliness. She was a little confused by their relationship-Bill hadn't made any physical advances towards her and was very polite and respectful. She remembered when they had dated before—it seemed like every time they had gone out, there had been a wrestling match. At that point, sexual contact was the only way Bill felt loved and received. They had never really gotten to know each other like they had in the last six months. Now, they even prayed for each other and Rebecca.

As she told Lydia that Bill was being transferred to Florida, Lydia could barely contain her excitement. "I know you thought I was crazy all along, but I God had me praying for him. I think He's doing something here, Joyce." She looked at her friend to see her reaction.

Six months ago, the comments she had just made might have enraged her friend. Now, Joyce smiled and said, "Could be. I know he's really changed. But its easy long distance, I guess this will be the test. It's funny though, I don't even know if he's interested in me in that way anymore. The last time he was in town, he didn't even kiss me good-bye!"

Lydia laughed, "He's just a smart man, Joyce. I know Stephen and I really liked him. Can't you believe that the God we serve in Florida, who sets people free, might just be working in California, too?"

She finally got a chuckle out of Joyce, "All right, all right, maybe God has done a work in him. Are you going to take all the credit? I did pray for him a bunch before I ever met you!"

Lydia responded, "I won't take all the credit, just my due! What does Rebecca think about all of this?"

"Actually, I think she's more excited than both of us. She's going to spend some of her summer vacation with me and is already planning things we can all do together. Needless to say, it all makes me a bit nervous. Even though I have to admit that if he really has gotten free I might be tempted to consider remarriage." Joyce continued on listing some of the qualities she admired in Bill while Lydia listened, amazed that they were even having the conversation at all.

———————————

Daniel went to wake the kids up for breakfast. Because of the week-long honeymoon he had planned for Deborah, this would be the only time they would have together as a family before he left. Anne and Robert had agreed to take them for the week, with his parents helping out over the weekend.

He went into David's room first. His son was already awake, but Daniel noticed the tear streaks on his face. "Son, are you okay? Have you been crying?" David rubbed his face with the arm of his pajamas.

Embarrassed, but not able to lie to his father, he said,

"I'm just a little sad. I was thinking about mom." His father nodded understandingly. "I'm afraid she's sad today, Dad. If she's really watching us like you've said, isn't she going to feel sad if we all just start loving Deborah and forget about her?"

Daniel was grateful that what had been on his son's heart was finally in the open. He knew exactly what to tell him. "Can I tell you a story, son?" David nodded and Daniel sat down next to him on the bed. He proceeded to share the story of when Susan had made him promise, before she died, to remarry, to find a wife for himself and a mother for the children. Daniel continued, "Your mother was one of the most unselfish people I've ever met and I know she's been praying for this day. I know Deborah can never take your mother's place and she doesn't want to. She just wants her own little place in your heart. All you have to do is be willing to give it to her-that's what your mom would have wanted." By the time, he was done, tears were streaming down both of their faces, and they were hugging each other. They spent another twenty minutes talking, and by the time he left David's room, his son's countenance had totally changed.

Before he woke up Aimee, Daniel stepped out on the back porch to call Deborah; they had both been concerned about David for some time. After he shared with her concerning the discussion he and David had just had, Deborah was elated. "When I went for my walk earlier I had been praying about David. I know this has to be hard on him. Oh Daniel, I am so glad he finally opened up to you. We just need to give him time to adjust. I can only imagine how hard this all is for him. Maybe now he and I can have that talk I've wanted to have with him. Even though, he's always polite and respectful, up until now he's just been so closed. That's the best news I could have had this morning." After a few more minutes of conversation, Deborah finally said, "I don't know about you Mr. Worthington, but I have a wedding to attend this afternoon so I can't spend all day on the phone with you!"

Daniel laughed and said, "Well, I just might see you there Miss Noble. By the way what are you wearing to the occasion?"

Teasingly Deborah said, "I guess you're just going to have to show up and see for yourself."

Chapter Fifty

A Radiant Bride

༄ ༅

Deborah had asked her brother, Paul, to walk her down the aisle and he had agreed. Due to the striking resemblance between their father and him, she knew it was another sign of her freedom. Today she was glad she had spoken to him and shared what had happened because right now, her knees were trembling and it felt good to have his arm to hold on to. Arm in arm, they stood in the foyer watching the bridal party proceed to the altar.

Deborah had chosen a violin instrumental for the first part of the procession, but now she heard the first strains of *Here Comes the Bride*. Her heart began to beat rapidly as she and Paul stepped from the foyer into the church. Then she saw Daniel waiting for her at the altar. Deborah decided to focus only on him as she made her way down the center of the church. His gaze was steady and unwavering as he watched her, smiling, slowly making her way towards him.

The guests were all on their feet, carefully watching the bride as she glided down the aisle. As Deborah moved past Lydia, Lydia thought she had never seen a more beautiful bride. Deborah's dress was white with a silvery sheen; elegant was the best word to describe it. Classically cut and simple, unlike some brides who were overpowered by their wedding gowns,

Deborah's bridal gown showed off her beauty like precious jewelry. It was the setting, and she was the jewel. Lydia turned to Joyce, "She's radiant, isn't she? You can see the glory of God all over her. She looked good when we finished ministering to her last year, but this is a whole other level!" Joyce nodded her agreement.

Lydia had been watching Daniel carefully. It was strange to know both of them as intimately as she did without ever having seen them together. But just the look on his face as he saw his bride enter the church, was enough for her. The man was definitely in love. His whole face lit up when he saw his bride and he never took his eyes off of her as she proceeded down the aisle.

When Deborah arrived at the front of the church, Pastor Harrison asked, "Who gives this bride to be married?"

Paul answered, "I do," presented her to Daniel, and then found his seat on the front row next to his wife. Daniel stepped into his place at Deborah's side and escorted her up the three steps of the altar. They were greeted by a warm smile from Pastor Mark and the ceremony began.

Pastor Mark welcomed family and friends and gave a short exhortation on the meaning of covenant. Deborah and Daniel had decided to say their vows under the chuppah. Several of Daniel's friends and the women from Deborah's Bible study had made the canopy especially for the occasion. The canopy cloth was white satin with wide ribbons of blue and silver decorating its outer edges. The poles that lifted it above their heads were gold and tassels made of blue, gold, and crimson were attached to each of the four corners. The men holding each of the four poles were dressed in white shirts with black pants and a crimson cumber bun. On the front of the canopy, the Scripture verse, Isaiah 62:4, *"You shall no longer be termed Forsaken, nor shall your land any more be termed Desolate; but you shall be call Hephzibah and your land Beulah; for the Lord delights in you and your land shall be married."* was written in gold.

With Deborah and Daniel standing before him, Pastor Mark began their vows, "Daniel, do you take Deborah to be your wife, for as long as you both shall live?"

"I do," Daniel said in a clear strong voice.

"Deborah, do you take Daniel to be your husband, for as long as you both shall live?"

"I do."

Daniel then began to read the covenant he had written for Deborah, "Deborah, I covenant to stay faithful to God and to you and to pray for you, care for you, and love you in the good times and the bad. I promise to provide for you and protect you to my best ability. All that I have is yours and all that I am I give to you."

Pastor Mark asked, "Deborah do you accept this covenant?"

"Daniel, I accept your covenant."

Now it was Deborah's turn, "Daniel, I covenant to be your help-mate, your friend and a Godly woman. I promise to always pray for you, to respect you, and always believe the best. I will love your children as my own, and I choose to lay down my life and become one with you."

"Daniel, do you accept this covenant?"

"Yes, I do."

After exchanging rings as a symbol of their covenant, communion was served to the bride and groom while the song *"Amazing Love"* played in the background. Before they knew it, Pastor Mark was pronouncing them man and wife and telling Daniel that he could now kiss the bride. It was the first time that they had ever kissed. Tenderly, Daniel cupped Deborah's face in his hands and then gently kissed her. Noting the tenderness in which Daniel handled the moment, Lydia thought to herself, "Daniel's definitely the right man for the job, a true horse whisperer; every other man had tried to break Deborah and possess her. It was obvious that this man was going to love her into submission. Lord, thank you for sending Deborah a man after your own heart."

Just like the day they had been reunited in the front of the church, everyone was in tears as the newly married couple walked down the aisle as Mr. and Mrs. Daniel Worthington. Even Andrea, who had received a special invitation and was on a home-visit, let genuine tears of happiness flow along with the others'. Seeing Daniel and Deborah, Andrea knew in her heart they were meant to be.

Elizabeth and the Worthington family followed the wedding party out of the sanctuary and then everyone else began to file out of the church. After receiving their guests outside the fellowship hall, the bride and groom went back into the sanctuary for pictures.

All of the women were jostling into position as Deborah got ready to toss her bouquet. Lydia and Joyce were at the edge of the crowd saying their goodbyes to Pastor Mark and Christina. The next thing Joyce knew, the bridal bouquet landed at her feet. Without even thinking she picked it up. Everyone started cheering and she realized what had just happened. As Deborah turned around, she saw the bouquet in Joyce's hands and began to clap. Lydia said, "It looks like someone's getting married," and started to laugh with joy.

After she got over her astonishment, Joyce joined in the merriment. She went over to say goodbye to Daniel and Deborah, "Now, did you do that on purpose?" she asked.

Deborah said, "I promise, I wasn't even looking. But Lydia told me earlier that Bill is moving to Florida!"

Joyce blushed, "Well, he hasn't asked me to marry him yet, and I don't know that he will."

Deborah smiled knowingly, "Oh, he will, he will," she said.

"Alright, little prophetess, that's enough. Joyce is

already scared to death," Lydia had overheard the conversation. Then she whispered in Deborah's ear, "I will be praying for you tonight. If God can do all of this, He surely can take care of that portion."

Deborah squeezed Lydia's hand tightly, "Thank you, I keep telling myself that, but the closer it gets the more nervous I am."

Lydia smiled and said, "Some of that's normal. It's just part of being a bride, you'll do fine. That man is so in love with you, as long as he's with you. You'll be happy!"

Deborah smiled. Lydia always had a way of normalizing what Deborah was going through and putting her at ease. If some of this was normal, then maybe Daniel was just as nervous as she was. She hadn't thought about that before, and she was thankful for a different perspective.

REDEEMED

Chapter Fifty-One

A Night to Remember

৵ ৵

Deborah felt her stomach knotting. Up to this point she had been focused on the wedding, but now, as the reception was drawing to a close, it meant their wedding night was also drawing closer. She knew that she loved Daniel with all of her heart, but the thought of being intimate still scared her. As much as Deborah had been promiscuous, most of it had been under the influence of drugs and alcohol; the thought of a sexual encounter, cold sober, was enough to make her feel sick to her stomach. After the bridal shower, she had experienced some terrible dreams about her honeymoon night. She couldn't really talk to Anne or Daniel about it, so she had finally called Lydia.

Lydia had helped her to understand that it was fear and quite normal because of the severe damage she had experienced sexually. It wasn't surprising. Lydia had reassured her, "You just need to be very honest with Daniel, and don't do anything you're not ready to do. If he's the man you say he is, he'll understand. I know you've already told him about the abuse."

Deborah still wasn't sure exactly where they were going to after the reception; Daniel had kept it a surprise. He had made all of the honeymoon arrangements. They had both decided that she would take care of the wedding, but the honeymoon was up to him. He had shared the itinerary with Anne, and she had helped Deborah pack.

The negligee, that made her so uncomfortable at the bridal shower, was packed in the suitcase. Deborah had only tried it on once. It was one of the most beautiful things she had ever seen. It looked like something an Indian maiden might have worn on her wedding night. The bodice was cut low and embroidered with turquoise and silver. The white fabric wasn't a sleazy sheer, but revealed just enough so that she could see her form in the mirror. It had a long slit up the front and as she moved, it revealed her legs. The embroidery continued around the very bottom and outlined the front opening. She had only seen herself in it for a moment, and then had gotten so uncomfortable she had taken it off.

She prayed that her honeymoon night would not be a disappointment to Daniel. "God you've got to help me. I don't know if I can do this. I'm so afraid; please don't let me hurt him." A part of her wished the reception would never end so she didn't have to face her wedding night.

———————

The marble bathroom floor was cool to her feet as Deborah surveyed herself in the bathroom mirror. She had let her hair down and washed her make-up off. She re-added some light touches; nothing that would smear, but enough so that she didn't feel totally naked. Then she misted the air lightly with perfume and walked into it. It was a scent that Daniel loved called, *Heaven Scent*. She wasn't sure if it was the name he liked so much or the actual smell. He would always smile and say, "You are heaven sent, sent just to me."

Daniel was in the next room waiting for her to come out. They had driven to Columbus and were set to fly out the next afternoon-that much Daniel had told her when they arrived. For the night, however, they were staying in a luxurious condominium; it was an eighteenth floor penthouse with a

KATHLEEN STEELE TOLLESON

spectacular view of the city. Owned by the Sergio family, Deborah and Daniel had been offered their honeymoon night's stay as their wedding gift. Not only that, the Sergios filled it with fresh cut flowers and had stocked the refrigerator. Daniel enjoyed seeing the look on her face as she peered around the room after they had first arrived.

But as beautiful as the penthouse was, Deborah didn't know if she had the courage to open the bathroom door and come out. She knelt down beside the Jacuzzi tub and prayed, "Lord, I need your help. I know that I've had prayer to restore my sexuality, and I really do feel like a virgin tonight, but please help me not to be a disappointment to Daniel. I don't know if I can do this."

When she finally was able to leave the sanctuary of the bathroom, she discovered that Daniel had turned the lights down and the room was softly lit by candlelight. She was thankful for his thoughtfulness. He also had one of her favorite instrumentals playing. It was "Peace Like A River" and she could feel the anointing filling the room.

When he saw her, Daniel's tears filled his eyes. "You are so beautiful," he said. The Lord had already prepared him and, looking at her face, he knew what he had to do next. Taking her hand in his he assured her, "Deborah, I want you to know that tonight, and every other night, you are free to set boundaries with me. You can say 'no' to anything and I will respect you. I only want from you what you're able to freely give. I don't care how long I have to wait."

Tears streamed down her face, and she said, "I'm not going to tell you I'm not scared. But I want you to know, I give myself to you," and knelt at his feet. Daniel took her hand and helped her to her feet. Suddenly she was in his arms and the passion that she felt was overwhelming and took her by surprise. It was as if a dam within her had broken and she was flooded with desire.

Daniel was the first one pull away, "Before we go any

307

further, I want to prayer over our marriage bed and anoint it," he said. Together they knelt down and prayed. Daniel anointed the bed posts and lightly touched her forehead and his while they both prayed in the Spirit; this was completely different from anything she had experienced. Sex had always been so shameful; for the first time she could understand what it meant for Adam and Eve to be naked in the garden before each other and God and not be ashamed. It was strange to feel the Holy Spirit's approval on something that had always just felt dirty to her.

Suddenly Daniel's arms were around her, lifting her up and placing her on the bed. As he kissed her, she was once again flooded with waves of desire. For one moment, she thought to herself, "So this is what it's supposed to be like." Then, she wasn't able to think any more; she had totally surrendered herself to him.

Chapter Fifty-Two

Two Years Later

ॐ ॐ

As Daniel finished dressing he caught himself smiling as he looked at his beautiful and very pregnant wife still buried beneath a small mountain of covers. It was hard to believe everything that had happened in the past two years.

Daniel heard Aimee and David bickering as they came out of their rooms. He quickly and quietly said a simple prayer over Deborah as he slipped out of their bedroom. "Aimee and David, that's enough!" Daniel said firmly as he walked down the hallway. "Deborah needs her rest. She had trouble falling asleep last night, and I'm trying to let her sleep in this morning."

They walked down the steps without a word but as soon as the kitchen door closed behind them Aimee said, "Dad, tell David to stop calling me 'oogly.' He says it doesn't mean anything, but it sounds like ugly to me."

Daniel said, "Alright you two, that's enough. David, you apologize to your sister. Remember there's no name calling in this house. You know what I've taught you about word curses, and how, even in fun, they can pierce a person's heart."

By this time, David was gulping down his cereal and looking a bit sheepish. In between spoonful's he replied, "I'm sorry, but what she didn't tell you is that her and her friends have been following me around at school. I just wanted her to leave me alone."

Daniel now turned his attention to Aimee, "Okay little one, why are you giving your brother a hard time at school?" He reached for the box of cereal as he waited for her reply.

Now it was Aimee's turn to squirm. "We were just playing spies, Dad. They were the bad guys and we've had them under surveillance."

"That's a pretty big word for such a little girl," Daniel smiled at his daughter. It was hard to be mad with her when she looked so cute. "Tell your brother that you're sorry, and let your friends know they probably need to find a neighborhood dog to put under surveillance."

"I'm sorry for making you mad, David, will you forgive me?" Aimee asked wide-eyed.

David nodded a "yes" as he rinsed out his bowl and stuck it in the dishwasher. He started to grab his book bag and head for the door.

"Before we leave, let's take a minute to pray over our day," Daniel said. They all joined hands as he began to pray, "Lord, we ask you for your protection today. We pray for all of our family including Auntie Anne, Uncle Robert, Joanna, Joshua, Jacob and Grandma Elizabeth. I pray that you will help David and Aimee learn today. Give them the mind of Christ and help them make right decisions. I bind all evil influence from affecting any of us. We pray for Deborah and little Mercy and that you refresh and bless them today. Amen."

David and Aimee responded in unison, "Amen."

Daniel reached for his briefcase and said, "Let's get going. Does everyone have everything?"

Aimee nodded struggling into her jacket and reaching for her fluorescent pink book bag. "I just need you to sign my permission slip for the field trip, Friday."

"Okay, remind me when I drop you off," he replied as they both started for the door.

After dropping the kids off at school Daniel began to reflect on the fact that he was going to be a father again in two short months. Deborah's due date was on February fourth. The whole family was excited but the pregnancy had been touch and go. She had started spotting at three months and there had been concerns that she might even lose the baby. The whole church had rallied behind them in prayer and now Deborah and the baby were doing quite well.

They had decided on an ultrasound test and discovered that Deborah was carrying a girl. After praying over the name for several months, one morning, Deborah rolled over in bed and said, "Mercy."

Daniel was just waking up and said, "What's that, honey?"

She replied, "Mercy, let's call her Mercy. The Lord gave me a dream last night and I was holding a baby and telling someone about God's mercy in my life, Daniel, what do you think?"

"It's perfect," David replied. "I felt the anointing all over me when said you it. Mercy, it is." He patted Deborah's stomach.

She had responded by turning towards him, and, as they embraced, tears began to flow between them. They were both overwhelmed by the presence of God that filled their bedroom, and His mercy which had brought them together.

Before he knew it, David was pulling up to his office after having dropped the children off at school. Accounts had multiplied since the success of the Sergio campaign, causing several other restaurant chains in the region to contact Worthington Advertising Agency. Trying to meet the increasing demand, Daniel had hired a new associate, Jimmy Penelli, six months ago.

Jimmy had been referred to Daniel by Sergio Sr.; he had known Jimmy's father for years. Jimmy's dad had actually owned the accounting firm the company had used for years. Daniel and Jimmy had met over dinner and clicked immediately. Daniel had seen a younger version of himself in him and hoped that he would be able to groom the young man for management.

As he walked into the office he smiled at his devoted secretary. "Morning, Irene, what's our day look like?" Daniel asked as he entered the reception area.

"Well, Boss, it's pretty busy so let's pray that there aren't any fires to put out today," Irene replied with a grin. She handed Daniel several files as he walked past her desk. Daniel walked into his office thanking the Lord again for sending Irene to him. With all the transitions he had experienced in his personal life in the last five years, he had desperately needed and relied on the peace, stability and good, old common sense Irene had brought to both him and the business. He needed her as much as he appreciated her and everything she had done and helped him through.

Chapter Fifty-Three

Looking Back

ন্ত ন্ত্

Deborah awoke with a start. She hadn't even heard Daniel and the kids getting ready. Rolled over she looked at the clock. It was 9:30 already and the baby was putting pressure on her bladder. She got out of bed and headed for the bathroom. When she was finished, Deborah brushed her teeth and was getting ready to turn on the shower when she decided to savor the moment and the quiet. Daniel had been preaching to her about getting her rest now because it wouldn't be the same once the baby came. She decided to savor the moment, climbed back in bed and reached for her devotional. As she did, she caught sight of their wedding picture and wondered if she would ever be that size again.

Today's devotion was all about thankfulness. She decided to take a moment and thank the Lord for all He had done in her life. She began with Daniel and the children, including Mercy, and patted her stomach as she gave thanks for the baby growing within her. As she looked around the room she was also thankful for the home the Lord had provided. They had decided, for the sake of the children, to start out their marriage in Daniel's home. It had been difficult at first because there had been many reminders of Susan and the life they had lived before she had arrived on the scene. She remembered the first night when she had gone in to say goodnight to David on her own. It had been a big step for her. As she had knelt down beside the bed she had come face to face with the picture of David and his mother playing in the front yard. Somehow she had made it through the goodnight part, but had broken down in the privacy of their bedroom. That was another thing she was thankful for, Daniel's patience as she learned to be both wife and mother at the same time.

She was thankful for how well Aimee had received her and all the help Anne had given her in understanding the two children. They were as different as night and day. David was thoughtful and more serious, a deep thinker even at his young age. Aimee was like a ray of sunshine, and everything with her was pretty much on the surface, whether it was her smile, anger, or pain. Deborah had to learn that even though Aimee was a cheerful child, she was still very sensitive. She remembered the first time she had made Aimee cry; it had crushed both of them and Daniel had come home to find them crying in their rooms. Now, she couldn't even remember what had been said or done. They had somehow survived and now Aimee was looking forward to being a big sister to Mercy. Deborah prayed that the baby would not bring any separation between herself and Aimee.

She continued on her list of things to be thankful for and then decided it was time to get up and get a few of her household chores completed. Most of the time, Deborah enjoyed being able to stay home and take care of the children. It had been a major adjustment, taking care of a home, two children and a husband. At times she regretted the undisciplined years of her life. Thank God for her mother and Anne-they had given her a lot of good advice and now, most of the time, she had things under pretty much under control. As she showered, Deborah wondered what a new baby would to bring to equation. They would all just have to cross that bridge when they came to it she decided.

The morning had put Deborah in a reflective mood all

day. As she tidied up the house she remembered the day they had found out she would be having a baby. The kids had been at Daniel's parents for a sleepover and she and Daniel had been out driving around. They had already been married for a year and had recently started talking about selling the house they were in and buying one together. Deep down, Deborah could hardly wait; even though Daniel and the kids had made her welcome, she somehow still felt like she was living in another woman's home.

That day they happened on a new development. It was closer to the Harrison's home and in a semi-rural area. Each home had a one-acre lot; it was a subdivision, without a subdivision feel. As they had driven into the subdivision, the thought of building a home and picking everything out had felt a little overwhelming. But Daniel had wanted to investigate so she had agreed. They stopped into the model-home office and talked to the agent. When they told her what they were looking for she replied, "You know, we just recently had a home go up for sale that we thought was sold. Right before the closing the couple who was supposed to purchase the home ended up divorcing, would you like to see it?"

Daniel responded quickly, "Yes." When they reached the house at 331 Jasper Lane, Deborah instantly fell in love. It was a simple, clean, two-story home that was white with black accents, shutters and a bright red door. It also had an inviting wrap-around porch, a circular drive, and even though the landscaping was new, you could tell some real thought had gone into it. The lot was wooded and there was plenty of privacy. She could just picture it decorated at Christmas time. Now she was glad she had stopped that morning. As they walked up to the front door, she prayed that this home was everything on the inside that it was outside. As soon as they walked in the door and saw the gleaming hardwood floors, Deborah felt the witness of the Holy Spirit all over her. She looked at Daniel to see if he was feeling the same thing. He caught her look and nodded. The home had four bedrooms and a study that would be a perfect office for Daniel. Within ninety days, they had closed on the new home and moved.

It was the first time in her whole life that Deborah really had a home of her own. As she decorated it, her confidence increased and the day of their housewarming party everyone was impressed with the job she had done.

As she got ready to make herself some lunch, Deborah decided to send Lydia and Joyce a quick note. Just as she had prophesied at her own wedding, Joyce and Bill did remarry about a year later. Bill had been trained in the *Restore Your Soul* integrated ministry and now the two of them ministered together; Lydia and Joyce still worked together occasionally.

Even though in her heart Deborah knew this wasn't the time for her and Daniel to receive training in the *Restore Your Soul* ministry process, everything in her longed to be trained to do the same thing she had witnessed and gone through a few years earlier. She prayed that one day, she would have the opportunity to go to Florida and be trained. If only somehow, someday, God could use her to help set others free! She had shared her longing with Lydia and confided in her that her only concern in marrying Daniel was that she would not have the opportunity to minister to others and fulfill the plan of God for her life in that way.

As always it helped Deborah to talk to Lydia because she always brought her back into balance, "Deborah, you're still young. Daniel and the children are your ministry right now. Be faithful with them and serve in your church, and I promise God will reward you and use you. This is all part of your foundation. Just enjoy this stage of your life." God had taught her a great deal this past couple of years. She finished the note and walked it out to the mailbox.

The phone was ringing when she got back inside the house; it was Daniel. "Hi honey, how are you feeling? Did you sleep in this morning?"

"I sure did. I didn't even hear you and the kids get up. I'm feeling pretty good today. I guess you're right, the extra rest does help." Then she added, "Daniel, I've been thinking a lot today about the past couple of years. Sometimes I might forget to tell you how thankful I am that God put you in my life. I can't imagine it without you."

"I was just thinking the same thing as I watched you sleeping this morning. I know it all hasn't been easy for you but I thank God that he brought you back to me. I went to the bank this morning and Andrea was working. I hadn't thought about it in a long time, but I was reminded of the night I almost lost you for the second time. It seems like another life, but it was just three years ago."

"I know," Deborah said. "I was just thinking today about how God's Word says that we become new creations in Christ, but that also means we'll have a new life to go with our new selves. It's taken me awhile to grow into the new me, but I think I like her!" Deborah laughed as she made the last statement.

"Well, I know I do," Daniel said. "Now tell me, are you up to cooking dinner tonight or should I pick something up on the way home."

"Actually, supper is already in the crock pot and will be awaiting you. What time do you think you'll be home?"

"Probably around five-thirty. I want to get those curtains hung in the nursery. I wouldn't want Miss Mercy to show up with her room undone."

"All right, I'll see you then," as she hung up the phone she thought that she didn't know what she had done to deserve such a special man. "It was grace," she thought to herself, "simply grace. Nothing she had earned, nothing she had worked for, and nothing she even deserved. Simply grace!" It reminded her of the Scripture that talked about the Israelites receiving homes that they did not build and harvests that they had not planted. Most of her life she had spent running from everything that God had now handed to her on a silver platter.

Chapter Fifty-Four

The Baby

༭ ༜

It was six days before her due date and Deborah was having mild contractions; they had been coming and going over the last couple of days. The doctor had said the baby was just positioning herself, but it could be any day now. Her due date was April fourth. Ever since she had been saved, April had become a significant month for her; she had went through the integrated ministry which had changed everything for her in April, married Daniel in April and now she would be having a baby in April. The last few days she had been pretty tired, but today she had some energy so she decided to cook a couple of meals that the family could eat while she was in the hospital. The phone rang as she walked into the kitchen. It was Anne, "Hi, just checking on you. Are we going to have a baby today?"

"No, just some minor contractions, Braxton Hicks, the doctor called them. Actually, I decided to do a little cooking today. I have a little more energy than I've had the last few days."

Anne was happy, "Well, that's a good sign; I was always cleaning or cooking something right before I had all three of mine. It's that adrenaline surge. I think you're getting ready, are you nervous?"

"At this point, I'm so uncomfortable I don't even care anymore. I'm sure once the labor starts it might be a whole other story." The two chatted for a few more minutes and then hung up.

———————————

After the women had hung up Anne immediately called Daniel, "I think she's getting ready to have the baby, but there's something I need to tell you."

"What's that sis?" Daniel asked a little preoccupied.

"Daniel, I know you too well, are you on your computer while I'm trying to talk to you. This is important."

Caught in the act, Daniel said, "Okay, you have my attention. Now, what's so important?"

"I had a dream last night. It was about the baby."

Now, Daniel was all ears, he could hear the concern in his sister's voice. He asked, "What happened?"

"The cord was wrapped around the baby's neck. It wasn't good. I woke up not knowing what happened. I hated to call you, but I think it's a warning. We need to pray. I don't feel like we're supposed to scare Deborah. I just called her to see if she's dealing with any apprehension but she seemed fine."

For a moment, Daniel was gripped with panic; the thought of losing the baby or anything happening at this point was unbearable. He could only imagine what it would do to Deborah. "I'm calling Pastor Harrison for prayer," he said. "You did the right thing. Call Mom and Dad for me will you?" He tried to sound calm but his voice was trembling. He knew Anne's prophetic gift well enough. He didn't want to take any chances; if this was a warning, then God had given it to them for a reason.

———————————

Daniel came home from the office early that day and surprised Deborah. "Thought you might need your feet rubbed," he said. "If you'll sit down for a minute, I'll get the lotion and then I'll help you clean up this kitchen. It looks like you've been cooking for an army."

Deborah said, "Sounds like a deal. What are you doing home so early?"

"I just kept thinking of those beautiful feet of yours and wanted them all to myself for a few minutes before the kids got home."

Deborah laughed, "Are you saying that's the only part of me that's still desirable?"

"Now, that's not what I meant at all. If you don't behave, you could miss out on a good foot rub!" he said teasingly. He went upstairs to get the lotion and soon, her feet were in his lap. As he rubbed them, he prayed to himself for the baby and Deborah. She had her eyes closed and dozed off for a few minutes. Suddenly, she jumped as a much harder contraction gripped her.

Daniel knew in his heart that tonight was going to be the night. Around seven o'clock Deborah's pains were getting harder and more regular. Deborah decided to call Dr. Redding who suggested they, "See what happens over the next couple of hours." He told them to call back about nine.

God, impressing Deborah's pain onto Anne's heart, called Deborah to see how she was feeling. As they talked Anne told her that if she thought this was it, to start walking. So, in between contractions, Deborah paced around the house. When Daniel called the doctor at nine o'clock, the pains were a regular three minutes apart. "Okay, bring her in and let's check her out. This may be it." At that point, Daniel was more nervous than Deborah; he tripped on the steps running upstairs to get her bag. "Daniel," Deborah called after him, "slow down. I'm fine, don't hurt yourself." She had never seen him so nervous.

———————————————

After being examined, Deborah was admitted into one of

the birthing rooms. Her water broke almost immediately. She had decided to have the baby as naturally as possible. Everything was moving so fast, she hardly had time to think and the pains kept increasing. The nurse informed her that she had dilated to six centimeters; four more to go. They had called the doctor, and he was on the way.

Daniel helped her with her breathing, and Anne was in the room praying and wiping her forehead with a cool cloth. She was glad Anne was there. Her sister-in-law always brought such strength to her. The pain gripped her once again. Soon she would be in transition, she prayed for the Lord to help her.

Daniel stepped outside for a moment to try and catch Dr. Redding. He had just approached the nurse's station. "Dr. Redding, may I talk to you one moment. I'm Daniel Worthington, Deborah's husband." The doctor nodded in recognition. Daniel began, "You might think I'm crazy, but my sister had a dream last night that the cord was wrapped around the baby's neck. I know you know what you're doing, but I felt I needed to tell you. Deborah doesn't know."

The doctor was a little surprised, "Well, I don't know about that, but I'll check her carefully. If the cord is wrapped around the baby's neck, she may need a C-section."

As the baby moved down the birth canal, Daniel and Anne prayed fervently. At seven centimeters, Dr. Redding checked Deborah himself. "She's doing fine, but the baby is showing some signs of distress. You may be right; we might have to do a C-section."

"Daniel, what's going on? Is the baby okay?" Deborah asked alarmed with what she had just overheard.

"Everything is fine; the baby might have the cord wrapped around its neck. Just pray, Deborah."

Deborah immediately began to take authority over the spirit of death. No longer was she in touch with the pain she was feeling. This was war-the Enemy was after her baby. Not caring who was in the room, Deborah began to war in tongues. Daniel and Anne prayed with her. Suddenly the baby began to shift; Mercy had turned herself and her heart rate was slowly returning to normal. The nurse, bewildered, said, "I've never seen anything like this. I'm going to get the doctor."

When he re-examined Deborah she was between eight and nine centimeters, "Everything looks fine now. We're going to have a baby."

At twelve-fifty-five a.m. on April fifth, Mercy Danielle was born. She was seven pounds, two ounces; and twenty-one inches long with a head full of thick dark hair. As Daniel placed the newborn baby in Deborah's arms he said, "I'm so proud of you, honey. You did awesome. She's beautiful. And, we thank you, young lady, for being obedient and turning yourself." Daniel and Deborah had been totally unaware of the two angels who had been sent to overpower the spirit of death and turn the child in the womb. Mercy was a child of destiny. God had warned Anne in her dream, and the angels had been on call-ready to respond to the prayers of the saints. One of the angels had been given a permanent assignment with the newborn child; he watched curiously as the parents and grandparents admired the new baby, wondering what God had in store for this earth creature.

Chapter Fifty-Five

But a Vapor

❧ ☙

Even if it had been only once, Deborah was so thankful that, Aunt Liberty had actually been able to hold Mercy. Over ninety-years-old, Aunt Liberty had been quite frail at that point; but, as soon as the baby was in her arms, she had immediately started praying in the Spirit. The anointing of God had been so strong in the nursing home room that afternoon and it had been a touching sight: the newborn baby-just beginning life-held in the arms of a woman preparing to leave the earth. It was the last time Deborah had seen her aunt conscious. Several weeks later, she had lapsed into a coma.

At her aunt's request, Deborah did the eulogy at the funeral. As she walked to the podium she felt a bit shaky. The room was filled with people; it was obvious that her aunt's life had touched so many others besides her own. She realized that she had not stood before a group of people and spoke since her high school speech class. Somehow, when she had agreed to do this for her aunt, the reality of what she would have to do had not really hit her. Gripping both sides of the podium, Deborah began to speak, thankful for the three by five cards that Daniel had helped her with the night before. Her aunt had requested a verse from 2 Corinthians 5: 6-8, "*So we are always confident, knowing that while we are at home in the body we are absent from the Lord. For we walk by faith, not by sight. We are confident, yes, well pleased rather to be absent from the body and to be present with the Lord.* As she shared the joy that Aunt Liberty was now experiencing in the presence of the Lord, it became something tangible inside of Deborah. She began to realize that, as she was speaking, she was being delivered from a fear of death which she hadn't even known she possessed until that moment. Leave it to Aunt Liberty to continue ministering from her grave! Deborah began to relax and moved to the next text her Aunt Liberty had asked her to share, James 4:14: "*Whereas you do not know what will happen tomorrow. For what is your life? It is even a vapor that appears for a little time and then vanishes away."* Deborah began to feel the anointing in a different way-it was as if the Lord was speaking through her, taking this opportunity to beseech the funeral attendees with an urgency of not waiting to appropriate salvation because of the shortness and unexpectedness of this life.

After Deborah shared the scriptures her aunt had asked of her, Aunt Liberty's pastor came forward and invited anyone who did not know the Lord to open up their hearts and receive His forgiveness and everlasting life. Deborah wished her brothers had been there. Neither of them had ever had as close of a relationship with their Aunt as Deborah had in the last few years. They had decided not to come in for the funeral, but both of them had sent beautiful flower arrangements.

Later that afternoon as they left Liberty's graveside, Daniel and Deborah hurried to Anne's home where five-week old Mercy had stayed behind with David and Aimee. "She slept most of the time," Anne said smiling down at her niece as she handed Mercy to Deborah. "She was just starting to get a little fussy. I'm glad you called because I was just getting ready to feed her the milk you had pumped."

"I'm glad you didn't. I really need her to eat right now," Deborah said taking her daughter from Anne. She went into the den where her daughter began to nurse hungrily. Holding the tiny infant brought comfort to her. As she looked down at Mercy, Deborah felt an overwhelming desire to pass down her aunt's legacy to her-a legacy of being sold-out to the Lord; a watchman on the wall. She laid her hand on her nursing daughter's forehead and prayed, "Lord, I know Mercy is going to be dedicated by Pastor Harrison in a couple of weeks, but today I dedicate her to you. I pray that you anoint her and I share with her today the prophetic prayer mantle that was imparted to me by Aunt Liberty." The baby looked at her intently as if she knew what was transpiring in the spirit realm. Deborah smiled down at her—she was amazed at what motherhood had already done to her. Bits of hardness or rough edges in her heart were being softened by the overwhelming love she felt for her daughter. Daniel cracked opened the door to check on them. He felt the anointing of the Lord flowing from the room and quietly pulled the door shut; obviously something very intimate was taking place.

Several weeks after the funeral, Deborah was shocked when she received a phone call from Aunt Liberty's attorney in charge of her estate; he informed her that she had been her aunt's sole beneficiary. He wanted to go over the will with her. The following afternoon, with Daniel accompanying her, Deborah was surprised to discover that Aunt Liberty had left them nearly seventy-five thousand dollars in a mutual fund, another thirty thousand dollars in cash, and everything else she owned. Her estate was well over a hundred and fifty thousand dollars. Deborah was almost speechless as they walked out of the attorney's office. She knew her aunt had been comfortable, but Liberty had always been so frugal. Deborah would have never believed that she had had that kind of money, and the fact that she had made her the sole beneficiary was overwhelming. For a second, she hoped her aunt had never thought that she had pressed into the relationship because of the possibility of an inheritance. The thought passed as quickly as it came; Deborah knew her aunt's discernment was too keen for that to have happened.

As Deborah and Daniel drove home early that evening they discussed what they should do with the money. The one thing they both agreed upon was that the first thing they would do would be to tithe. They were excited about what a blessing it would be to their church. There were several projects that Pastor Harrison had on his heart, but there just hadn't been the money to do them. As they continued to talk, Deborah realized her only other desire was to put some money aside for a time when they would could both go to Florida and receive training in the *Restore Your Soul Ministry.* She knew it would be awhile because Mercy was still just a baby, but just knowing the provision was already there made her feel more confident. She and Daniel also talked about her enrolling in an on-line Bible School so she could begin working towards her degree. After talking with Lydia, Deborah had decided to get a Master's degree in counseling, but she had no desire to do that in a secular university. Lydia had told her about a couple of ministries that had good programs where individuals could study from home. One ministry in North Carolina had particularly interested her. It was called *Worldwide Christian Outreach.* When Deborah had gone online and studied their website, she had discovered that they also ordained and provided covering for ministers. She and Daniel had already decided to go to one of their conferences to check them out. She hoped that they wouldn't have to wait too long. The thought of being able to raise her daughter and take care of the family while still being able to get her degree excited Deborah. To be honest, it had always been one of the heartbreaks of her life. As a young girl she had always wanted to go to college, but because of the events that had transpired, it had just been added to her pile of broken dreams. Daniel watched her face glow as they talked about the prospect of her taking courses and studying from home. He decided that as soon as they could they would take a trip to North Carolina and visit *Worldwide Christian Outreach.* They talked about who would call who. They decided that Daniel would call Pastor Harrison and let him know about the blessing they had just received, and Deborah would call Lydia about getting started with the on-line course. She could hardly wait! Lydia loved to see redemption in people's lives and she would be so excited about the generational blessing that Deborah had just received. The Lord knew she had lived a lot of years under generational curses, and she knew this was just another part of the redemption. She remembered the scripture in Leviticus 26:42, *"then I will remember My covenant with Jacob, and My covenant with Isaac and My covenant with Abraham I will remember; I will remember the land."*

Chapter Fifty-Six

The Ordination

෧෧ ෧

Sitting in the front row of the church were none other than Lydia and Joyce. Deborah could not believe their faithfulness. They had driven all the way to North Carolina for the ordination. The ministry, Worldwide Christian Outreach, which they were being ordained with, was headquartered out of Charlotte. She had sent an invitation, but really hadn't expected them to attend. Excitedly, she walked over to greet them, "I can't believe you came all this way to be here. You're amazing!" She tightly hugged both of her good friends.

"We wouldn't have missed it for the world!" Lydia exclaimed.

"Daniel, look who's here. Mercy, I want you to meet Miss Lydia and Miss Joyce. They're very special to me," Deborah said, her voice cracking.

Aimee and David strolled up just then. Daniel said to them, "Do you remember Miss Lydia and Miss Joyce? They were at our wedding."

"Sort of Dad, but remember that was eight years ago, David replied. He stuck out his hand and greeted the two women, a younger version of his father.

Lydia and Joyce and seen Daniel and Deborah several

times since the wedding but had only seen pictures of the children. They couldn't get over how they had all grown. It was hard to believe that the woman standing in front of them was the same one they had ministered to nearly ten years ago. Gone was the shame and pain from the past; a self-assured radiance now surrounded Deborah. Tonight she was stunning in a simply tailored, off-white suit. Around her neck hung a simple silver and gold necklace with a Hebraic inscription; translated it meant "a woman of excellence." It was the necklace Lydia had purchased for her on one of here trips to Israel.

Lydia turned her attention to Mercy. The child had the most beautiful aquamarine eyes-a combination of both her mother and father. She also had her mother's olive skin and brown hair, it was a couple shades lighter than Deborah's. She was a striking little girl and had the same vibrant quality her mother possessed; charisma, it was the only thing you could call it. The energy of the Lord vibrated out of their very beings with an irresistible drawing power; yes, Deborah had it, and so did Mercy. In Hollywood they would call it "star quality;" but Lydia knew it was more than that—their destiny required it. And, just like Queen Esther, Deborah and her daughter possessed it. More than beauty or personality, it was a sparkle deep within that only the Lord could give. She wondered what God had in store for this very special family. The next thing she knew, she was being greeted by Pastor Harrison and his wife, Christina. "It's so good to see the two of you again," he was saying.

Lydia and Joyce stood up and were warmly embraced by the pastor and his wife. A Hispanic man was standing off to Pastor Mark's left. Pastor Harrison motioned him over as he asked, "Have you all ever met Sanchez, I mean Tony?"

They replied in unison, "No," as the man stepped up to be introduced. Of course, they had heard about his testimony-Pastor Harrison and Daniel had kept in contact with Sanchez after his dramatic salvation in the driveway, and Deborah relayed updates on occasion.

Sanchez had only been out of prison for the past year. Since that fateful night his life had been transformed; not only had he turned his own life around in prison, he had won hundreds to the Lord and was known for his gift of evangelism. Another prisoner had even drawn a picture of the vision Sanchez had had that night. It was a picture of the Lion of Judah with his paw on the chest of a man lying flat on his back; it was called, "Apprehended." It was very popular throughout the prison system and one could find reprints of it in Christian bookstores. Where ever and whenever he could, Sanchez continued to give his testimony of how the Lord had apprehended him just as He had apprehended Saul on the way to Damascus. Since getting out of prison, he had started using his first name, Antonio, but most people called him Tony. It just helped remind him that he really was a new man.

After the introductions, everyone found their seats. Joyce whispered to Lydia, "It's hard to believe he was once a cold-blooded killer. Did you see the love in his eyes?"

Lydia, nodded and said, "But he's in good company. Remember the beloved Apostle Paul was a murderer before he met the Lord." No matter how long Lydia served the Lord, she never ceased to be amazed at the miraculous transformation that took place in the lives of people who truly encountered Jesus.

"Religion only has the power to conform, but God's Spirit has the power to transform," Pastor Rick always said. Sitting in church with a reformed killer who had been saved by the grace of God and who was celebrating the ordination of a man and woman that he almost killed was incomprehensible to Lydia. The power of God was almost more than she could grasp; no wonder people outside the Kingdom have such difficulty understanding us she thought to herself.

Deborah and Daniel were called up to the front of the church. As they walked up to the platform Deborah felt unsteady. The power of God was already touching her. She looked at Daniel one more time, "Are you sure?" He nodded yes and squeezed her hand. They both knew after tonight their lives would never be the same. Just as they had stood, eight years ago, over a marriage covenant with each other and the Lord, they were now entering into a ministry covenant.

Deborah couldn't believe how much her life had changed. Here she was ready to become an ordained minister of the Gospel. As she looked out at the front row tears filled her eyes as she saw her family. Mercy was sitting in between Daniel's parents and Aimee and David were on either side of them; her mother had found a place next to Lydia and Anne, Robert, Joanna, Joshua and Jacob had found seats on the second row right next to Pastor Mark and Christina. The only person missing in the church was Aunt Liberty. As Deborah's thoughts went to her, she started to think about the great cloud of witnesses. Yes, she could almost see Aunt Liberty peering over the rim of heaven at the events that were about to take place. It made Deborah smile just to think about it.

Then she saw a miracle walking down the aisle. Her two brothers, Paul and Tim, entered the church with Mary Rachel. She had no idea that they were coming. Just as she had vowed never to darken the door of a church, so had her brothers. Up to this point, Deborah knew they had kept their vows except for the day she was married. She could tell they were uncomfortable as they made their way to the seats next to Anne. But they were there! Deborah wanted to greet them but could only smile and nod. Her heart was bursting with love and excitement as she said her silent prayer, "He is a Redeemer! Lord thank you for what you've done in my family. Please touch my brothers' hearts tonight."

As she turned her attention to the presbytery gathering around them, Deborah thought to herself, "With God, nothing is impossible!" Deborah squeezed Daniel's hand wondering what the future held and wondering if he was as nervous as she was. He gave her a reassuring squeeze back.

The prophet began to prophesy, "Son and daughter, you

have been redeemed for such a time as this." The words removed all doubt from her heart; they were the same words the Lord had whispered to her the day she and Daniel were married. Only God could have known.

Recommended Materials and Ministry Sources

☙ ❧

For more information on other products and materials by Kathy Tolleson or for speaking dates and locations, please contact **info@kingdomlife.com**

An Integrated Approach to Biblical Healing Ministry,
Chester and Betsy Kylstra, Proclaiming His Word Ministry
www.rtfi.org

The Prodigal Daughter , the 1st novel in the *Prodigal Daughter* series
Kathy Tolleson, Kingdom Life Now
www.kingdomlifenow.com

Birth Assignments,
Kathy Tolleson, Kingdom Life Now
www.kingdomlifenow.com

Bitter Roots Video,
John and Paula Sanford, Elijah House

www.elijahhouse.org
Women's Guide to Freedom
Kathy Tolleson, Kingdom Life Now,
www.kingdomlifenow.com

Prophets and Personal Prophecy,
Dr. Bill Hamon, Christian International
www.christianinternational.org

Restoring Sexuality - Book, DVD or CD Series
Kathy Tolleson, Kingdom Life Now
www.kingdomlifenow.com

Restoring the Foundations Manual,
Chester and Betsy Kylstra, Proclaiming His Word Ministry
www.rtfi.org

Soul Battles,
Kathy Tolleson, Kingdom Life Now
www.kingdomlifenow.com

You are My King; CD Title-*Adoration: The Worship Album* by
Newsboys; Song written by Billy Joe Foote,
www.newsboys.com

In order to locate ministry providers near you, please go to
www.healinghouse.org.

To learn more about Restoring the Foundations training and
equipping contact Proclaiming His Word Ministry at
www.rtfi.org.

For further ministry training contact Christian International at
www.christianinternational.com.